THE LOVERS PENTACLE

Love and Madness in South Florida

Teresita Blanco

KDP

Cover design by: Art Painter
Library of Congress Control Number: 2018675309
Printed in the United States of America

CONTENTS

INTRODUCTION

The Lovers Pentacle is a romance book inspired by tarot cards. The Titular lovers are the best friends Kain and Carina. The two have been friends since High School. Overtime, their relationship degraded into toxic codependency.

Whenever Carina gets dumped, she bullies her best friend into dating her. As soon as she finds herself someone better, she leaves him. After getting dumped so many times, Carina is finally ready to settle for Kain, but unsurprisingly, Kain refused to marry her.

In order to change her destiny, Carina visits a psychic to get a tarot card reading, and a love spell that will bind the two lovers together. The spell can only be activated on the new moon. Before she uses the spell, Carina meets a new man called Bruno.

Carina immediately becomes infatuated with Bruno. Now, she must decide whether to use the love spell on Kain or on Bruno. The book is commentary on modern relationships, and a cautionary tale on the dangers of tainting one's friendship, with the expectations that it must evolve into something more.

TERESITA BLANCO

CHAPTER 1

The Lovers

◆ ◆ ◆

It was a sunny Summer afternoon in Hialeah. The year was 2003. There was a group of maidens waiting in line in the Savannah Apartment. In room 14A, there lived a famous psychic by the name of Irina. Irina was rumored to have the power to bind the fates of individuals. Waiting in line with the rest of the other poor desperate women was Carina. Carina had recently broken up with her boyfriend. Since she was afraid of ending up alone, she decided to bind herself to her best friend Kain. The pair had been together since High School. They had a typical on again, off again relationship. She was hoping that with a bit of witchcraft, their relationship could evolved into something more.

Carina Garcia was almost 24, and all her friends where married. Carina had a petit built, a well-toned body, raven hair, expressive hazel eyes, honey colored skin and curly brown hair. Carina didn't consider herself to be a prize, but she knew that she wasn't ugly either. She kept waiting and waiting for her turn to speak with Irina. She was sweating either from nervousness, or due to the overwhelming heat. After two hours that felt like an eternity, Carina was finally able to speak with Irina. This was the first time Carina had entered the home of the infamous psychic.

She was surprised by the cold, calculating blue eyes of the Cuban, Russian old maiden. Carina sat before Irina. Irina was dressed all in white. The only color came from the black and red beads necklaces, and bracelets. The centerpiece was an Elegua, covered in honey, surrounded by marbles. Carina looked about the small apartment filled a cluttered of children's toys. Only the round table had enough free space to accommodate Irina's things.

Irina said coldly, "You wish to bind your fate with that of your boyfriend?"

"Wow!" said Carina impressed, "They truly were not exaggerating when they said you were powerful."

"I am going to give you the same advice that I give all the woman who pass by my shop. If you want to force your boyfriend to marry you, just get pregnant," said Irina.

"But I don't want to have to do that," protested Carina, "I want Kain to want to form a family with me, not because he has to, but because he loves me."

"Let us consult the cards," said Irina shuffling her tarot cards. Irina threw the cards. Like all augury totems, the meaning of the cards varied from psychic to psychic. The first card that was revealed was the lovers card upside down, followed by the Hangman…, "Scars upon Kain's very soul keep him from settling down. His father is the source of all his frustrations."

"So what you are telling is that I need to force Kain to confront his father, in order for him to finally marry me?" asked Carina desiring a concrete plan of attack.

"I haven't told you to do to anything. The cards only reveal the road you have traveled, and your destination. Though, one doesn't need to be psychic to know that what you are planning to do is a bad idea. My advice is that you stop trying to force your best friend into marrying you. Instead, cherish your beautiful friendship," advice Irina, "Why don't you want to meet new people?"

"Aren't you the psychic?" asked Carina, "You should already know the answer to that question."

Irina flipped the last card. Irina saw the card, and she had a hardy laugh. She whipped a tear from her eye, before saying. Carina paid Irina for her time. She also acquired a brown paper bag, with a spell components and a set of instructions. Carina had to throw the paper bag into the Okeechobee river, on the new moon. This would give her enough time to decide whether she wanted to bind herself to Kain. Carina on impulse decided to send an anonymous letter to Kain's father. She opened the yellow pages and she looked up the address of Jack Sanson. Carina wrote and rewrote the letter till she was satisfied with the proper tone:

"Father,

I do not resent you for abandoning me. You were always so busy with your work, that often times I felt neglected. I don't hate you father. Now that I am older, I understand the importance of your calling. I do not want to spend the rest of my life being angry at you. When you are ready to be forgiven, you know where to find me.

Sign,

Your son Kain, who is still waiting patiently for his father to return home."

Carina giggled proud of her tearjerker letter. If Jack truly cared about his son, this letter would compel him to go speak with Kain. When she was satisfied with the letter, Carina drove up to Jack's apartment. She slipped the letter under the door, before fleeing the crime scene.

With this problem out of the way, Carina returned home to prepare herself for her date. There was a time when Carina fancied that she loved Kain. The Kain that she loved no longer existed. In his place, there was the cynical, apathetic, nihilist.

The metamorphosis had been slow. So, slow, that Carina didn't realize the change, until, it was too late to do anything about it.

Today, they were going to the Cheesecake Factory, in Dadeland Mall. Kain liked the interior decorating of the restaurant, as well as the desserts. Her grandma Esther was also tagging along to the date. Esther was an Irish Catholic lady, age 67. She had long, silky silver hair, a wrinkle face, and ash colored eyes.

Carina looked at her boyfriend over the top. Physically, Kain was a handsome devil. At the age of 23, he was built like Michelangelo's David. Kain had started life as a weak, skinny little twig. He beefed up quickly when his Grandpa Raphael began to mold him into his idea of a perfect man. While in school, Kain distinguished himself in both track and wrestling. These days Kain maintained his form more out of habit. His face had even features, that complimented his short raven hair. The main point of interest of his face were his almost feminine full lips. His grey eyes were lackluster, almost as if the soul had left the body years ago.

Kain arrived to his date in his police officer's uniform. This was a bit unusual. Kain wasn't the type of person to work overtime. Kain handed Carina the Trophy he was carrying. Carina studied the trophy with bored curiosity. It was a Lifesaving award.

Kain explained, "Last year, I saved a stupid brat from drowning, so, uncle gave me this plastic trophy. I would have preferred a raise, instead of this worthless piece of plastic."

"To get raises you need to be promoted, son," said Esther dryly, "And to be promoted, you need to put in a bit of effort."

"I show up to work, don't I, grandma? I do everything my uncle Gent tells me," said Kain, "And last month, I ticketed more drivers than any of my peers. Where is my trophy for that accomplishment?"

Carina said, "What happened to you Kain?"

"Life happened to me, Carina," said Kain.

"I…I…spoke to my doctor…" said Carina changing the subject.

"You mean your psychic," corrected Kain.

"You weren't always like this, Kain," protested Carina, "What happened to you?"

"Here we go again," said Kain rolling his eyes, "Can you at least wait till we eat dessert before criticism me?"

"I am not here to criticize you. I am worried about you. I think you need help Kain," said Carina, "Maybe, if you finally confront your father you wouldn't be so angry and bitter all the time."

"I agree with Carina," said Esther, "It will do you both good to finally patch things up. It isn't his fault that he wasn't able to take care of you…"

Kain tapped the table nervously with his index finger. When dessert came, Kain breathed in a sigh of relief. Carina usually forgot most things whenever a dessert was nearby. The threat of seeing his father again created a temporary change in Kain's behavior. He chatted away like a little parrot of all the things Carina liked. He pretended to be interested in Carina's psychic. At a certain point during the conversation, Carina suggested that they do yoga together. Kain agreed to it, for the sake peace.

Kain figured he could add this stupid Yoga class to his workout routine. The trio went to Kain's house. Kain sometimes shared living arrangement with his grandmother. Esther paid the utility bills, while Kain paid the mortgage. Since her husband's death, Esther spent most of her time with her grandson. Her grandson was so much liked her dead husband, that at times it was painful. When the three arrived at the house, they found a large box by the door.

"Did anyone order anything?" asked Carina.

"This box wasn't left by the mailman," said Kain flipping it about, "It doesn't have stamps or even my home address."

"Maybe it has a bomb inside," said Esther hiding behind Carina.

"Suegra, you watch too many news!" said Carina laughing.

The lovers lugged the mystery box back inside. Based on the sound of it, the box contained something solid. Carina brought a kitchen knife and she opened the box. Inside, there were two plastic guitars, and a PS2 game. Kain smiled happily. This was the first time in ages that he had gotten a present he actually liked. As of lately, the only gifts he got were clothing or decorations for his house. Esther was thoughtful about the present. Esther imagined that this present was Gent's way of encouraging his nephew to keep up the good work. Esther got changed into her pajamas and she sat down on the couch in order to watch the news.

Carina entered Kain's bedroom. There was the bookshelf littered with comics and books. There was a roll dedicated to Weekly World News. Kain had gotten into the habit of buying that spoof News magazine every time he bought groceries. In total, he had of 75 issues. The other reading material where the Harry Potter, Tokyo Babylon, Claymore, Alichino, Saikano, Laughter in the Dark, How to Draw books, and a bunch of Ozamu Tezuka mangas he had bought at the flea market. Below the print media, there was a shelf littered with CDs. Saved inside where the music, books, movies, episodes and comics Kain hadn't felt like paying for. He also had a decent collection of public domain books in digital form.

In a corner of the room, by the window, was the computer. It was still turn on, forever downloading from Limewire whatever had picked Kain's interest. There was a drawing station beside it, with the paper, the pencils, and the reference books inside the drawers. Dominating the entire room was the King sized bed. Kain had slept most of his life in a tiny uncomfortable bed. When he was finally able to afford his own bed, he spared no expense, at least in the mattress department. The Paris themed bedcovers had been a gift from Carina. She wanted to implant into Kain's head, the idea of going to Paris, as a couple.

Everything in the room was so tidy that Carina half suspected that Kain suffered from OCD. As if to confirm this suspicion, Kain noticed that his pencil wasn't properly aligned with the table. He gave it a quick fix before focusing on his girlfriend. Seeing Kain take a minute to fix that stupid pencil irritated Carina to the very core. She rubbed her temple as migraine began to manifest.

Kain saw his girlfriend rubbing her temple. He said with a look of concern, "If you have a headache, we can just call it a night. We do not need to make love at the end of all our dates."

"It is fine. It will pass," said Carina doubly irritated.

Carina pushed Kain into the bed, and she got him out of his officer uniform. The two became locked in the mating embrace. After an hour, Carina got bored of the exercise in futility. The headache was making it impossible for her to enjoy her boyfriend's familiar touch. She took her chill pill for her headache and she closed her eyes to sleep. While she tried to rest, Kain left the bed and he showered off Carina's cooties. He always did that after each play session. At the end of his libations, he went to his side of bed, and he slept as close to the edge as possible. While Kain slept peacefully, Carina turned in the bed like a spinning wheel. She turned her head to watch Kain's peaceful slumber. How she envied the fact that he could fall asleep so easily. She stretched her hand towards him. He was so far away in the bed that she actually had to roll closer in order to pet his silky, black hair.

Carina closed her eyes and instead of sleeping, she thought of High School. The former cheerleader had fond memories of her time in Barbara Goleman. She was in the best shape of her life, and she had her hot boyfriend Kain to boot. Kain was quite active in the afterschool Clubs, and he was the Trackstar. Whenever the school had a late night event, there was Kain either in the audience or as a participant. At times it felt, that Kain spent more time at school than at home. This was to avoid going home to an empty house.

His grandparents where not always home. Grandpa Raphael and Grandma Esther had other responsibilities, that also included helping Jack get rehabilitated. When they were home, they pair were busy grooming Kain. From his grandpa, Kain learned how to shoot a gun, how to fix the sink, how to change the oil in the car and other manly lessons. While he lived, Grandpa Raphael encouraged Kain to maintain a healthy lifestyle, to always exercise and to kiss girls whenever the opportunity presented itself. From his grandmother, Kain learned how to cook and clean after himself, and how to balance a checkbook.

Carina was trying to find the exact moment when Kain started changing. Before Carina realized it, she had fallen asleep. Carina awoke around the afternoon. While she slept, Kain had gotten up bright and early. Kain made breakfast for himself and his grandma. As tradition among grandmothers, Esther began her day by nitpicking Kain's relationship with Carina.

"I can't believe you allowed that alley cat back into our house," said Esther.

"I know that you don't like that grumpy old cat, but I worry about him," said Kain alluding to a tuxedo cat he would sometimes allow into his house, "Zombie looks like he might drop dead soon, and I want to make as many fond memories with him, before it is too late."

"I wasn't talking about that stupid cat," retorted Esther, "I was talking about Carina! She comes and goes like she owns the house, leaving her little presents in every corner of the room."

"If you don't like that large ornamental cherry, you can just regift it," said Kain pointing to a cherry ornament he had received as a gift from Carina.

In order to mark her territory in Kain's home, Carina was of the habit of leaving random things. Sometimes it was as benign as leaving her toothbrush. Other times, she would give Kain a

Wall Art made by a Cuban painter she particularly liked. Kain turned his head to admire the painting. It featured a Menina on bike wheels, on top of her head she had a meat grinder that was turning poultry into fishes.

"It is whimsical," commented Esther, "I must admit that it truly livens up the dining room."

"Well…you know grandma, that I have a fondness for cat. Carina is a lot like a cat," said Kain.

"But do you love her?" insisted Esther.

"People throw that word around like it means anything," said Kain, "I enjoy her company. She is amusing, and most importantly, she is predictable. She hasn't changed one bit since I met her. Nor does she need to change…she is perfect just the way she is. Well…she is almost perfect. Whenever her friends start giving her stupid ideas, she becomes a total pain in the ass."

"Does she want you to go to Paris again?" asked Esther.

"Yes…that is the newest thing she wants me to do," lied Kain. Carina wanted Kain to confront his father.

"Doesn't she care that you get air sick?" asked Esther.

"No, she does not," said Kain dryly, "As long as I do whatever she wants, she doesn't care how much I suffer."

"Did she bring the whip, again?" asked Esther worried.

"That was a onetime thing," said Kain, "It was her birthday, so my hands were tied. Heheheh. Literally, and figuratively."

"I truly do wish you would find yourself a nicer girl to settle down with," said Esther hugging and puffing.

"They don't make nice girls anymore, grandma," said Kain sadly.

With breakfast concluded, Kain went to do his morning jog around the neighborhood. In order to distract himself, he putted on his Zune and an Audiobook. The device had been a gift from Uncle Gent. After his morning job, Kain did weight training.

After an hour workout, he was finally free to continue with his life. When he entered the living room, Esther and Carina stopped talking.

"If you two are done plotting against me, I am taking Carina to her Yoga class," said Kain holding up the flier.

"Yes...yoga...yay," said Carina yawning. She had forgotten the couples activity she had suggested.

The two got inside the car, and Kain drove to FIU. The class was to be officiated by a Jainists nun. It was only for FIU Students, though the nun never bother to check for student ID. Any person could enter her classes whenever they felt like it. Kain parked and the two left the car with their carpets. The class took place in the park area facing the Library. Kain laughed when he saw that the letter I from the FIU Library was missing. Kain pointed this out to Carina and the two got a good laugh out of it.

"I was thinking why don't we take a class together?" asked Carina.

"Lest finish with the Yoga class first, and then we will see," said Kain.

The two took their place in the backrow of the group. The Jainists Nun walked into the scene all in white. She was walking with a broom before her to avoid stepping on tiny ants. She also covered her mouth to keep herself from devouring microbes. Her assistant that was dressed for the part directed the class, with the nun making corrections every so often. From time to time, the nun would ramble a bit about the Jainism philosophy. Kain removed his jacket and he stretch his elegant limbs. Carina frowned when it came for her turn to do the same. Her tight leggings had given her a muffing top.

Carina grabbed her small fat folds and she said, "You have really let yourself go, Carina."

"You are fine," retorted Kain, "A little meat in the bone never did anyone any harm."

"That is easy for you to say Kain," said Carina starting to stretch.

"I frankly prefer your current pinup version. Back in high school, you looked like a walking skeleton," said Kain assuming the warrior pose.

Carina frowned when she noticed that nearby woman was checking out her boyfriend. She was starting to regret suggesting the Yoga class idea. Her face turned red in impotent anger when she saw that woman attempting to start a conversation with Kain.

"I haven't seen your face around campus," said Carina's competition.

"I don't go to school. I do not see the point of wasting away the best years of my life in a classroom," said Kain.

"Do you work, handsome?" asked the maiden.

"Yes. I am employed. I give tickets to speeding drivers. It isn't an important job, but somebody has to do it," said Kain.

"Have you ever shot anyone?" asked the maiden.

"My Uncle Boss doesn't let me use guns with real bullets," joked Kain before assuming the reverse warrior pose, "When an incident does occur. I call for backup, and I hide behind the biggest rock I can find."

The maiden laughed heartedly. Carina extremely jealous asked, "What's the joke Kain? I want to laugh too."

"I told her that my uncle doesn't let me use guns with real bullets," said Kain.

"Is that a fact?" asked Carina.

"I don't know you tell me," said Kain reaching into his jacket to show Carina his revolver.

"Put that away!" hissed Carina, "Why do you even carry a loaded weapon?"

"It is not loaded, so relax," said Kain showing the empty

cartridge, "I keep the bullets in pocket, to avoid any accidents when walking around stupid civilians."

"You still didn't answer my question," said Carina.

The nun passed by, and she instructed Carina to assume the downward facing dog. This pose made the blood rush into Carina's face. This combined with the noon sun made her pretty dizzy. The interruption made her forget what she was talking about. When she transitioned to the upward facing dog, she was peeved when she noticed Kain still talking to the other woman. At the end of class, Kain had been cordially invited to a Sorority Party.

"We don't have to go, if you don't want to," said Kain, "I am not even a University Student, so I have no earthly business going there."

"It is just a party," said Carina giving a fake smile, "There is nothing wrong with going there just to have a couple of free beers."

"It will save me the trouble of cooking up something," Kain added giving a sly smile, "And aren't you always complaining that we do nothing fun together."

The night came and the two showed up at the party. Truth be told, Carina couldn't remember the last time she had been to a stag party. She had been so focused on her classes to bother with matters of the mortal world. Carina wore her skimpy Marlowe dress decorated with oranges and leaves. She had curled up her hair, and she had worn her cheapest, plastic Successories. With her white high heels, she was tall enough to reach Kain's shoulder.

Kain arrived a little later after sending his grandma to Uncle Gent's house. Since Esther had fallen once and broken her hip, it became the popular opinion that she should not spend her time alone. As much as Esther hated the chaotic household populate by Gent's twin daughters, she hope that Kain would meet a nice girl at the party. Kain came dressed in the first junk that fell from his closet. This being a green tank top, and orange shorts. He left the gun at home, and instead he brought a fully charged taser.

Carina saw the device sticking out of Kain's pocket. She commented, "Since when do you carry a weapon?"

"Since high school. Though back then, I was only able to sneak in a boxcutter knife," said Kain, "Of course nobody knew, since I never had to make use of it."

"Sometimes I feel like I don't know you," said Carina narrowing her eyes.

"You would know me, if you spent less time trying to change me. When have I ever nitpicked anything you have ever done?" said Kain before going to dance with another woman.

Kain tortured Carina by dancing with another woman for two hours. Carina boiled in her jealous rage, while she rubbed up against random guys. She tried kissing one within Kain's line of sight. Kain yawned, already used to Carina's childish tantrums. Kain turned his head to look at the skank that had invited him to the party. The woman was dressed in an outfit that left little to the imagination. Her shrill laugher deeply annoyed Kain.

"She even laughs the same," said Kain more to himself.

"What I can't hear you," said the woman. She took Kain's hand before saying, "I want to show you my room. We can talk more quietly there."

Kain allowed himself to be taken away by the woman. Trailing behind the two was the jealous Carina. If Kain slept with another, while the two of them were together, Carina was going to leave him for good. This is at least what she told herself, over, and over, while she simmer with murderous rage. Kain entered the woman's bedroom. She maiden was a ginger, skinny twig, with brown eyes, and a pasty face covered in freckles.

"What was your name again?" asked Kain.

"Eugenia," said Eugenia, "Were are you from?"

"From here," said Kain. Kain looked at her collage board, "Are these from all your trips?"

"Yes. I have been to Paris, to China, to Japan…" said Eugenia bragging about being well traveled.

"It must be nice being rich," retorted Kain.

"Rich! Please! I have more than 200,000 dollars in credit card debt, and don't even get me started as far as student loans are concerned," lied Eugenia laughing.

Carina had her face glued to the door, in order to eavesdrop. A guy tried to get her attention, but Carina pushed him aside. For one so petit, she had a lot of strength when she was in a rage.

"Who was that girl you were with? Is she like your little sister or something?" asked Eugenia.

"Carina is my pet cat. She comes and goes as she pleases, and during the rare occasions when she is in a good mood, she lets me sleep with her," explained Kain, "Carina hasn't been declawed yet, so try not to get on her bad side."

Kain opened the bedroom door and he smiled seeing Carina eavesdropping. Kain beckoned her inside, much to Eugenia's annoyance. Eugenia looked at the angry Carina over the top. She wasn't her type, but Eugenia didn't want to dismiss Carina out of fear of being called racist. Eugenia decided that a little moonshine was needed in order to make this threesome happen. Though truth be told, Eugenia was only interested in Kain. To get the private party started, Eugenia brought out the drinks. She added a little Acid into the mix, in order to liven the mood. Before Carina drank it down, Kain took the glass and he shook his head.

"Why is it that you people drug every person you run into?" asked Kain.

"I am sorry," said Eugenia, "I just assumed that you liked to run with the wild horses. Plus, you look a little tense…so I thought you could use a chill pill."

"You still didn't answer my question," said Kain with a hostile tone in his voice, "Why was your first instinct to drug me?"

"Well…look at you," said Eugenia laughing nervously.

"Just because I shop for clothing at the flea market doesn't make me a crackhead," retorted Kain.

"First of all, that wasn't crack. It was a micro dosage of ecstasy, studies have shown the positive benefits of micro dosage," said Eugenia folding her arms, while she defended her lifestyle.

"A century ago, scientists used to say that lead was good for you," said Carina interrupting the woman she perceived as a threat.

"Fine! Forget the chill pill!" said Eugenia before gulping down one of the drinks. Going straight to the point, she said to Kain, "Do you want to fuck me or not?"

"I will after you answer my question," insisted Kain.

"What answer do you want me give?! I don't know why I did what I did! Alright! That is just something I do every time I am about to sleep with someone at a party," protested Eugenia.

"Sounds like the ritual of a serial killer," said Kain, "If you don't remember why you do something, isn't about time to take a step back, and carefully evaluate such a compulsory behavior. Everybody is different. What would you have done if Carina suffered an overdose because of your so called micro dosage… which wasn't micro because I was able to see it."

"Get out!" yelled Eugenia pointing to the door.

"Not, until you provide me a satisfactory answer to my question!! I will ask you again? And this time pay attention! Why is your first instinct to drug anyone that behaves in a way that is slightly inconvenient for you!!" yelled Kain, "Do you also drug small children, Eugenia? What type of a monster does that to a small child? Answer me!!"

The commotion drew the attention of some frat guys. They entered the room with the intention of throwing out Kain out of the sorority. Before they had a chance to do so, Kain taser one guy, and he punched another. He brought out his badge from his pocket, and he called for backup. He got Eugenia arrested for possession of a "micro" dosage of an illegal substance. Carina had not expected for this night to turn out like this. Kain left quite satisfied with his work. Carina spent the rest of the night as quiet as a mouse. She had never seen Kain behave that way. As soon as Kain fell asleep, Carina left the bedroom and she went to call up Esther. She hanged up the phone immediately, when she realized the time. The house phone immediately started ringing.

"Carina, unplug the house phone!" complained Kain who had been woken up.

Carina picked the phone. It was Uncle Gent, "I was meaning to call you Carina."

"So you heard," asked Carina.

"I heard one version of the truth," said Gent, "What happened exactly?"

"This skank tried to drugs us. When Kain attempted a citizen's arrest, her coked up buddies attacked us, with beer bottles, knives and pitchforks," said Carina covering up for her man.

"I figured that was what happened," said Gent, "That addict... what was her name? Eugenia, she claims that Kain was threatening her?"

"No. He asked her a simple question, why are you trying to drug me?" said Carina, "She saw that as a threat because we dared to question her way of life. Plus, a person who is flying can get spooked easily."

Gent sighed and he went to his office to go deal with the problem that Kain had created. He allowed the University students to get out of jail, without any charges. If they didn't cause any problems for Kain, Gent wouldn't show their toxicology report to the University Police Campus.

"But that nut! He attacked me!" protested an injured student.

"From what his girlfriend tells me, you started it," said Gent, "And I have affidavits from seventeen other students collaborating her side of the story. If you bring this issue to court, I promise you that you are going to lose."

Gent allowed the rest of the students to leave, after giving them a slap on the wrist. Gent tended to be soft on drug addicts, because his little brother Jack was a former user. Eugenia returned to her dorm extremely perturbed by the night's events. Once, she was in her home element, she began the slow process of digesting what had occurred the night before. The only thing she learned from that experience was to never do drugs in front of a police officer. The morning came and Carina had fallen sleep on the couch, next to the phone. She saw that she had a pillow under her head, and a blanket that Kain had brought for her. At times like this, she remembered why she had loved Kain. The true Kain was thoughtful and considerate.

"Well...his police officer job is stressful," said Carina trying to rationalize Kain's unusual behavior, "He probably deals with junkies all the time. It makes sense that he no longer has patience for their nonsense. Next time that happens, I am just going to get him to leave."

Carina allowed for Kain to sleep off his fit. She went to the kitchen to make breakfast, but then she remembered that Kain didn't like her cooking. He was always stubbornly insisting on cooking everything himself. Carina returned to the bedroom and she lied down beside her friend. Kain was so close to the edge of the bed that it seemed as if he might fall off. Carina who wanted to cuddle waited till Kain was facing her. She then wormed her frame into his strong arms. Once she was comfortable, Carina immediately fell asleep. She awoke close noon when Kain left the bed. While Kain was showering, Carina entered the bathroom to watch Kain shower. Kain's bathroom had a clear glass standing shower. Kain chuckling proceeded to seductively pass the soap all over his thigh, his pectorals and his lovely neck. The seductive shower had the intended the effect. Carina pounced on him, in order to make love in the shower. After this morning workout, the two went to the kitchen. Carina sat down to wait for her breakfast.

Carina asked sighing, "Do you think I am fat, Kain?"

"Again with this…who called you fat last night?" asked Kain.

"A good number of guys, but it is not as if I care about their opinions," protested Carina.

"Sigh…How do you want me to make your pancakes?" asked Kain.

"Add strawberries and black barriers into the pancake mix," said Carina focusing on her food.

"Are you almost done with school?" asked Kain while making the pancakes.

"Almost, but there this one class that has two prerequisites, and…I am bullying my counselor to get her to count that Microeconomics class we took in high school," changing the subject Carina said, "What do you want to do today?"

"Oh! So, you are finally giving me a choice in the matter," asked Kain sitting down to eat his breakfast, "Tell me Carina, what activities am I allowed to suggest to you?"

"You make it sound as if I am a control freak!" protested Carina rubbing her temple, "Tell me what do you want to do. Whatever it is, I am going to say yes to it. I promise!"

"You promise to say yes to whatever request I have for you?" asked Kain giving a sly smile.

"Yes," said Carine shifting in her seat nervously, "We will do whatever you want today. No request is taboo. What is it that your heart longs for me to do?"

Kain gave a playful smile, after thinking about it, he said this,

"I want you to watch with me the latest season of Inuyasha. My computer just finished downloading the episodes."

"Can't we just watch the Sesshomaru episodes? He is the only character I actually care about," said Carina.

"The episodes are only numbered. I have no way of telling when the aristocratic assassin is going to make an appearance," said Kain, "But we can watch something else if you like."

Carina was about to suggest seeing something else, but she noticed that Kain had a bruise on his face from the night before. Carina brought an ice bag from the fridge and she placed it over his face. The two watched a couple of episodes from Season 6. Kain frowning with disappointment went to look for something else to watch. It felt to him that they were stretching the show in order to bleed more money out of the series. Whenever a series got in that mood, Kain immediately lost interest. Carina suggested they try watching new shows. Kain had downloaded the first episode of a bunch of new anime series.

After failing to find something new to watch, Carina asked, "Do you even like anime Kain?"

"Sigh…I need a new hobby…" said Kain sighing with disappointment, "For every Escaflowne, there are thousands of uninspired Eiken Clubs."

"It is usually the ecchi ones that are God awful," said Carina, "Somebody must like them. There wouldn't be so many, if there wasn't an audience of brain dead buffoons who are impressed by a pair of balloons fluttering in the wind."

"I sometimes wonder if the makers of those shows have ever seen a real woman? No matter." said Kain, "I got nothing else planned for my day. So, let's do what you want Carina."

"Do you want to go meet my new psychic?" asked Carina.

"Sure. Why the hell not," said Kain, "I have nothing better to do with my time on this Earth."

The two went to meet the infamous psychic. Carina had developed a taste for palm reading, tarot cards and other occult things thanks to Escaflowne. Irina was the first "true" psychic that Carina had ever met. She was curious to hear what Irina would tell her boyfriend. The pair showed up unannounced at Irina's home. When she knocked, a teenager with crazy hair opened the door. The crazy mane little maiden was Irina's granddaughter Lucero, and her successor. Irina's second sight always skipped a generation.

"If you are looking for grandma, she is in the Bucky Dent," said Lucero, "And no, she doesn't know the lottery numbers. If she did, do you think we would still be living in this dump!"

The two made their way towards the Bucky Dent. It had an Olympic sized pool, two slides and a kiddy pool with a jungle gym. They found Irina suntanning herself while reading Laughter in the Dark by Nabokov Vladimir. Kain couldn't help but notice the difference between Irina and his grandmother Esther. While Esther was shy about showing skin, Irina was a "cool" grandma, with her sunhat, her bikini, her heart shaped shades, and her large Cuban cigar.

When Carina showed up with her boyfriend, Irina said not bothering to look up from her book, "Here is a bag with two bathing suits. Instead worrying about your future, why don't you take a moment to enjoy the present?"

Kain got changed into the swimsuit, and Carina did the same. The two returned to pester the psychic. Even without a crystal ball, Irina was an expert at reading people. The former chess champion was always two steps ahead of every person she met. Kain had been skeptical at first, but Irina had shown with a simple action to be genuine article. While Carina changed, Kain checked her cellphone to make certain that she hadn't called the psychic beforehand.

"Wow! You really are real," said Kain with a childish smile on his face, "Are there others like you? Or are you like the last of your kind?"

"The Spanish Inquisition thinned down our numbers," said Irina dryly, while browsing a fashion magazine, "Unlike my ancestors, I know how to keep a low profile."

"Oh! I get it! My lips are sealed," said Kain winking.

"That's cute," said Irina, "If you want a professional card reading, do so during office hours."

"Can't you just give me a quick look," insisted Kain shoving his palm at Irina's face.

"Pay for the pizza and the sodas and then I will see," said Irina annoyed.

Kain paid for the food and the sodas for Irina's grandchildren Yanamaria, Lucero, Eufrasio and the youngest Marlene. While the kids where chowing down, Irina gave a cursory glance at Kain's palm. Irina commented, "Your life line has two interruptions."

"What does it mean?" asked Carina leaning forward on her seat.

Irina took both hands to examine them closely. The fact that she was looking at them so intently didn't inspire the lovers much confidence. Changing the subject, Irina said to Kain, "I see one marriage. Two marriages. Three…four…and…seventeen in total. With the most recent divorce taking…place two…months ago."

"Oh! You are looking at the times we have broken up," said Carina laughing.

"My mistake. I normally use the word marriage, but these lines can represent any type of romantic relationship," said Irina giggling. She seemed to want to say more, but she changed her mind, "Your hand tells me that you are quite content with your love life. This contrasts with Carina's hand, you see how this line starts in the pinky and it ends in the middle finger, this tells me that her love is egotistical."

Carina frowned not abused by listening to the truth. Irina laughing, said, "If you don't want to hear the truth, I could just tell you the sweet lies you long to hear."

Irina brought out her spectacles to look at Kain's hand more closely. She saw small marks on the heart line. These lines represented three different traumas. The way she was staring at the hand almost made it seem as if she was having a vision. Irina blinked twice and she went to focus on a different line.

"This straight line across the middle of your palm means that you are a realist Kain. You see the world for what it is and not for what it could be. See how it contrasts with Carina's wavy lines, your lover is dreamer. Her mental line shows that she has short attention span. Both have long lifelines. These interruptions in your lifeline show that you have experienced several changes in lifestyle. This trend is further reinforced by your luck line. Your lifestyle is dictated by external forces. And your girlfriend, her broken luck line shows that she is the master of her own fate..." Irina added, "Whether your life turns out for the better or for the worse, depends on you Carina."

"Grandma, you forgot to mention the elements," retorted Lucero.

"Ah...yes...the elements," said Irina, "My protégé, why don't you do the honors."

Lucero examined Kain's hand, and then she said, "This an Earth type hand, you are materialistic, and stubborn," Lucero added looking at Carina's hand, "And this is the hand of an egotistical fire type. You are also impulsive and optimistic. And...that's it for today. That will be 100 bucks."

"I bought the food," protested Kain.

"But not the dessert," retorted Lucero giggling.

Kain bought desserts for the brats. He then went to the pool to burn the empty calories. He swam laps while Carina played catch with the kids. Carina becoming tired of playing swam over to Kain's side to interrupt his workout. She protectively wrapped her arms around his handsome shoulders to have her boyfriend ferry her around the pool. Carina began to pondered why she was still with Kain. She thought on all her previous relationships. They all started nice enough, but once as soon as they dropped their mask, Carina ran for the hills.

"Kain why won't you marry me?" asked Carina.

"I have no guarantee that you won't divorce me as soon as you get bored or angry at me," said Kain being brutally honest, "You always leave me Carina. You always leave."

"If I stay for an entire year, will you marry me?" asked Carina.

"Well, you heard the psychic. You are the master of your own fate, and as for me, my life is always changing due to outside influences," said Kain.

"But do you love me?" insisted Carina.

"You are my best friend, so, I own you the truth," said Kain turning around to face Carina, "When you are with me, everything is alright in my world. When you leave me, I miss you. IF that isn't love, I do not know what it is."

"Let's go get marry right away!" said Carina happily.

"I think we should see other people," said Kain swimming away.

"Kain!! You jerk!!" yelled Carina splashing her friend.

The sunset over the Bucky Dent. The lovers wanted to linger, but the place closed at dusk. The lovers drove back home in order to wash away the pool water. When Kain entered within, he found his grandma and uncle Gent entertaining guests. The guests where Eugenia, her parents and the family lawyer. Eugenia was a rich princess, but she liked to cosplay as a pauper. When Kain entered the house, the guests regarded him with a look of pity. Gent had told the visitors a version of Kain's truth. Kain annoyed by the situation locked himself in his room. He putted on his headsets, and he blasted at full volume into his eardrums System of a Down.

"I was just telling our guests how Kain's mother died of an overdose," said Gent, "Such a tragic end to such a beautiful, kind loving woman. Like Eugenia, she fell for the micro dosage myth. Over time, the dosages grew bigger and bigger till she became a shadow of her former self."

"My grandson was only trying to help you Eugenia," said Esther making excuses for her grandson, "He saw the path that you were talking, and he is all too aware of its final destination."

"Do you know of any good rehab centers?" asked Eunice, stepmother of Eugenia, "We weren't aware that our daughter was using again."

"Mom! That won't be necessary. That was a onetime thing," lied Eugenia. She added, "And if Kain wanted to help me, he didn't need to be a psychopath about it."

"Well to be fair, Kain told you he was a cop. You have to be pretty stupid to do drugs in front of a police officer," said Carina trying to shame her competition, "She just poured her little micro dosages into our drinks, without even asking. I mean, what kind of a psycho does that to a person they just met. I would think twice about eating or drinking anything that this woman prepares for you."

"Is that what really happened?" asked Michael, the father of the Eugenia, "You little liar!"

The parents and the lawyer had a hardy laugh at Eugenia's expense. The laugher was echoed by Uncle Gent and Carina. Eugenia annoyed said, "Now that bygones are bygones, I wanted to ask Kain out on an official date. I promise to leave the Roofies at home. Scouts Honors."

"What are Roofies?" asked Eunice.

"It is the date rape drug," translated Gent.

Eunice in anger dragged her daughter out of the house. Eugenia was going to a rehab center, whether she wanted to or not. Eugenia said laughing, "I was kidding mom. Sheesh!"

"Bye, bye!" said Carina closing the door. She opened it one last time before saying, "And don't come back."

"Phew...I hope that is the last time we see that degenerate," said Gent sighing with relief. He reached into his pocket and he handed Carina a key, "Use it to enter the boy's bedroom. For the love of God, do not ask about his mother. I do not want Kain to fall into despair again."

"Can I talk to him about his father?" asked Carina curious.

"That subject is also taboo," said Gent departing the house, "Just leave well enough alone, woman!!"

Carina entered Kain's room. He had a dull expression on his face. She removed his headsets, and she gave him a comforting hug. She looked through the items in his bedroom, and she turned on the PS2. After browsing through the disks, and she picked out Tony Hawk Pro Skater 3. After watching her epic fail in that game for a half an hour, the light returned to Kain's eyes.

"Do you want to play that new game that comes with the plastic guitars?" asked Kain getting up from his bed.

"I would love to," said Carina giving a fake smile.

Carina ended up liking Guitar Hero, in spite of herself. The weekend came to an end with a bittersweet taste to it. Things hadn't gone the way Carina had planned, but at least, she thought she had gotten to know Kain a little better. Kain had also told her in his own weird way that he loved her. The two went to sleep close to midnight. Carina wanted to stay up a little longer, but she knew that Kain had a fulltime job. She figured that while he worked, she might as well hunker down and study for her finals. Once she got her diploma and a day job, she would see about bullying Kain into marrying her. Or maybe they could move in together... Carina fell asleep while making plans for her future with Kain. While she slept peacefully, Kain spent the night tossing and turning in the bed. He didn't manage to consolidate sleep, until it was 3 a.m. Come morning, he felt extremely sleepy, but at least, he had forgotten what he was angry about in the first place.

CHAPTER 2

The Hangman

◆ ◆ ◆

The weekend came to an end and the lovers went their separate ways. Carina had her finals, and Kain had to report for duty. Kain did his morning workout, performed his libations, ate breakfast and he drove to work. His Uncle Gent managed the Islandia Miami Police Department. Since it was summer and tourist season, the crime rate spiked. Gent had manned this post for almost two decades. He didn't make waves, nor was he a crook. His priority one was keeping his men safe. Gent looked at the noticeboard with all the reported crimes of the day.

Frowning, he said, "The natives are restless, today."

Gent Sanson was the current patriarch of the Sanson household. He was in his late 40s, and what little hair remained in his head was completely white. Due to his administrative job, he was somewhat portly, and he had a propensity for stress eating. His most distinguishing feature where his cold, black eyes. His father claimed to be a direct bloodline descendant of Charles Sanson. Their infamous ancestor had been a French executioner. His eldest son Gabriel had faked his death, and he moved to American. To feed his family, Gabriel had no other option, but to become a Hangman. Gabriel considered lynching a painless alternative to the hours of public torture that were fashionable in France. When Raphael died of a heart attack, it fell on Gent to manage the two black sheep of the family: Kain and Jack.

Jack was Kain's father. Jack was a recovering addict. He had managed to stay clean for the last five years. As of lately, Jack wanted to reconnect with his son Kain. It was Gent's role in the family to make certain that never happened. Kain was only at peace when his father was out of sight, and out of mind. Gent looked at the map with all the violent crimes being reported today. He looked at the tracker he had placed in Jack's molar. Based on the last pinback, Jack was driving around the Police Department trying to work up the courage to go speak to Kain. Gent called Kain before his nephew reached his workstation.

"I need you to go patrol the…" said Gent looking at the map, "Planned Parenthood…I am going to text you the address."

"But I haven't checked, yet," protested Kain, "And my lunch, I need to put it in the refrigerator."

"I will refund you the spoiled food! But I need you there right away! It is an emergency," lied Gent, "There protestors are growing restless. I need you there to keep them from turning violent."

"If they are turning violent, just send the SWAT team," said Kain pocking holes into Gent's lies.

"Alright, you got me. I think my Kyle got a chick pregnant.…" said Gent trying to think of a lie, "And…I need you to keep an eye on who goes in and out today. If you recognize his girlfriend, call me…"

"If Kyle doesn't want to be a father, you should just let him pay for the abortion," protested Kain, "I wish grandpa had paid for my mother's abortion…I wish…I had never been born."

"Don't go to that dark place again, son," said Gent scratching his bald head, "Look. The truth…is…that…Internal affairs is sniffing around our station. So, I want you to look busy. Trust me son, you don't want to be here today."

Kain turned his car around and he drove to the Planned Parenthood Clinic. He left his car and he took out his sketchbook in order to pass the time. Standing in front of the clinic were the usual protestors, for and against the work being done in the clinic. When he got bored of sketching, he returned to his patrol car to play Megaman NT Warriors in his Gameboy Advance. He sat down under a shaded tree, and with the summer breeze the hours rolled lazily by. He was snapped out of his reverie when he noticed that someone took his photograph.

"Is this what you do all day Mr. Police officer?" asked Eugenia laughing.

"Among other things," said Kain, "Though at night, I take great pleasure in arresting University students."

"Don't you have a partner or something?" asked Eugenia.

"It is more economically efficient to have one cop per car. This arrangement also maintains the flexibility of sending officers to more locations," explained Kain, "And if I run into any trouble, only one officer will die, instead of two. This saves a ton of money on pension."

"Wow…who is the cheap bastard that decided that?" asked Eugenia.

"The constituents. They want security, but they don't want to pay for it. Some even want to defund the police to punish the many for the sins of a few," said Kain, "But that is not my prerogative. I am just one man. And I know a lost cause, when I see one. Speaking of lost causes, are you for or against it?"

"I support a woman's rights to choose what to do with their bodies," said Eugenia, "Do you want to protest with me? I have a blank sign that you can decorate however you like."

A bored Kain agreed to protest for Eugenia's cause. He wrote on his sign: Spay and Neuter your Humans. Eugenia got a good chuckle out of Kain's sign. The other protestors finding the poster amusing, began to chant Spay and Neuter Your Humans. Eugenia took a few candid photos of Kain among her people in order to show that the police was pro-choice. A Priest annoyed with the situation went to give a sermon to Kain. Kain's face turned blank as he tuned everything out. When it became obvious to the priest that he was preaching to a wall, he went to bother someone else.

"There is nothing I hate more than rude people telling me what to do," said Kain, "Had he bothered to ask nicely, I would have gone over to champion his lost cause."

"So you don't believe in a woman's reproductive rights?" asked Eugenia deflated.

"I don't believe in peaceful protests," said Kain, "The world only truly changes through violent means. If you are not willing to kill for your cause, why are you wasting your time under the blistering sun?"

The two got into a heated debate about violence and peaceful protest. For every peaceful Gandhi that Eugenia brought up, Kain had thousands of bloodthirsty Robespierre.

"You...you are a lot sharper than I gave you credit for," said Eugenia amused by the intelligent conversation.

"I was the captain of the debate team back in Middle School. Everything was fun and games till I made the mistake of debating about Stereotypes. A rich chick in the audience felt alluded to, so she sue my family because I accidently made her feel insecure about her weight. The court ruled in my favor, but I was still boycotted from ever competing. At the end of the day, only rich pricks like you, Eugenia get to have an opinion!" said Kain becoming passive aggressive again.

"I am not rich! My parents are rich," protested Eugenia.

"That is such a rich bitch thing of you to say," retorted Kain dryly, "Instead of wasting your time protesting, why don't you do something useful with your time and buy food for the homeless? That makes an immediate difference in someone's life."

"You what, Kain! Fuck you!!" yelled Eugenia pocking at Kain's chest with her index finger.

"If want someone to agree with you, go bother someone else," said Kain going back to sit under his tree.

Kain brought out his headsets to drown out the noise from the world. Around noon, the protestors decided to go for snack break. Eugenia invited Kain to dine with them. As much as the debate had angered her, Eugenia had found it mentally stimulating. Since she was paying for the food, Kain agreed to tag along. Back in the station, Jack had finally worked up the courage to go see Kain. Jack was a skinny twig, who resembled a walking skeleton. His long face and wispy mane combined to give him the perfect horse look. He made his way through the station, with none of the officers paying him any mind. They were all used to him.

Jack was holding his briefcase protectively while he dodge around the other knaves and low lives. He eventually made it to Gent's office. Gent finished his donut in order to feign good humor. Gent hugged his skinny little brother and he beckoned him to sit down.

"Do you want a donut?" offered Gent.

"No. I am not really hungry," said Jack.

"Eat it," insisted Gent.

Jack ate the pastry at first without much enthusiasm. Eventually, his hunger awoke, and he demanded more food. Gent went to his minifridge and he gave his brother a sandwich.

"Did he like it?" asked Jack.

"Did who liked what?" asked Gent confused.

"The game. I sent Kain that silly Guitar Hero game," explained

Jack.

"Since when can you afford things?" asked Gent suspiciously.

"My Sponsor got me a job, a real fulltime job. So, that gift is my way of showing you that I am no longer a financial burden," explained Jack. Jack opened his briefcase to show his brother all the pertinent information. He added, "Here is the name of my workplace, and the information of all my employers. So, you can investigate them till your hearts content."

Gent looked at the material over the top. Gent pretending to give his brother the benefit of the doubt said, "Everything looks legitimate. So, you sell used cars now."

"If I can sell tic-tac's as Fentanyl, this salesman job is going to be a piece of cake," said Jack giggling. Most addicts are on others drugs, so they experience a placebo effect from the tic-tac's they ingest.

Gent sighed with frustration, before forcing a fake laugh. Gent changing the subject said, "How are you feeling today? You look skinnier? You can move back with me if you want to."

"Your wife Stacie hates me," said Jack as if stating a fact.

"If it makes you feel better, she also hates me," said Gent returning Jack's papers, "It is just that I am worried about you Jackie. I don't feel comfortable with you living by yourself. I was meaning to stop by your apartment later, but since you are here, happy birthday little brother."

Gent gifted Jack his first cellphone. The battery life of Jack's molar tracker was almost dead. Gent needed a new way of keeping track of his brother's movements. The minutes rolled by with Gent showing his brother everything that the cellphone could do.

At the end of the tutorial, Jack asked, "So, how do I make a phone call?"

"That's right. How stupid of me," said Gent calling his little brother, "And now, my number is saved on your cellphone. This way you no longer need to bother to memorize everyone's numbers. This one is mom's number. And don't forget to put your therapist's number in the cell as well. And that's everyone."

"What is Kain's phone number?" Jack asked.

"I don't know..." lied Gent, "His cellphone got hacked. So, he is in the process of getting a new number and a new phone that is virus free."

"Is he still playing with computers?" said Jack smiling warmly, "I remember the first computer we ever owned, Kain ripped it apart to see if he could understand how it worked. When he is not running your little errands, what is he doing with his life?"

"Since when do you care about what happens to your son!?" exploded Gent before he could stop himself. Jack's turned as a pale as a sheet and his eyes widened. He then proceeded to ball his eyes out. Gent left his seat and he hugged his brother, "I am sorry Jackie. Please don't cry."

"For a moment there, you sounded just like dad..." protested Jack when he could talk.

"Don't joke like that, little brother," said Gent laughing nervously. Gent added turning seriously, "All his barking and tough love never did anyone any good. Don't tell mom, but I am actually glad that the big brute finally kicked the bucket."

"You don't really mean that," said Jack hugging his brother tightly.

"Well...I knew him longer than you. By the time you were born, he had softened. He no longer had the energy to whip you into submission," said Gent being brutally honest, "I am kidding little brother alright. You need to lighten up. Here, have another donut. This one comes with flan on the inside. I do not know were Kain buys these donuts, but they are to die for."

"...I don't want any more food," said Jack pushing aside the donut, "If Kain isn't here today, I will come back tomorrow, and tomorrow, and tomorrow."

"Jack, tell me what this is truly about? Are you dying? Do you need a kidney? I can give you one of mine, if you don't mind that it is a little diabetic," said Gent sitting down to face his brother.

Jack turned his gaze and then he said, "I was talking to my therapist about Kain. I told her how he shuts down whenever anyone so much as mentions my name or his mother's name. Maybe…he should visit her…as well…"

"Kain is…fine," said Gent hesitating.

"What did he do this time?" asked Jack trying to assert his ownership over his son.

"He accosted this hippie broad. I do not know the exact details, and the dumb bitch barely remembers what happened that night. Carina said that Kain wanted to know why her first instinct was to drug the drinks of every person she brought into her bedroom," explained Gent.

"Maybe she just assumed that Kain was like her, seeing as though he insist in dressing like a hobo. He must earn at least 50K, he should be able to afford nicer things," guessed Jack.

"Maybe he is saving up to go to college," said Gent, "OR maybe he is going to marry Carina."

Father and uncle spent an hour ranting about what was Kain saving up for. Kain on the meantime was at a vegan restaurant called Planta. Since Eugenia was paying for the food, Kain's stomach and cheapness had dictated his priorities. The others felt uncomfortable with Kain tagging along, but since Eugenia was paying for the grub nobody bothered complain. After ordering the food, a few attempts were made to start a dialogue. The conversation began to flow as soon as the others learned to ignore the blue elephant in the restaurant. With some glucose in her blood, Eugenia realized that she should have been more emphatic with the less fortunate.

Eugenia asked Kain, "Do you still remember your stereotype

speech?"

"I memorized it by heart," said Kain, "I would be happy to repeat it, if you write me a contract that guarantees me that you will not sue me, should you feel offended."

"I didn't want to sue you," said Eugenia, "It was all my stupid stepmom's idea. She has been wanting to get rid of me since the minute she walked through the front door. I have to account for every penny I spend, and if I want bigger allowances, I always have to grovel to that woman. My mom…my real mom, she was the one with all the money. I shouldn't need that succubus's permission to spend something that rightfully belongs to me, and only me!"

"I could investigate her," offered Kain, "It is not as if I have anything better to do with my time."

"If you find anything that will help me keep that woman in check, I will buy you lunch for the rest of your life!" said Eugenia happily.

"While you are in a working mood officer, I wanted to file a noise complaint," said the waitress who was eavesdropping.

Kain went to the car and he came back with his laptop. He typed up the reports as they came up. He was going to hop to it, as soon as he got back to the office. Kain collected everyone's leftovers in a box, before driving back to the station to print and file those reports.

On his way out, the waitress said to Kain, "When can I expect you to visit my noisy neighbors?"

"My uncle will send someone over, eventually," said Kain.

"I much rather you go there right now," insisted the waitress.

"You are here, so clearly, the noise isn't a problem for your at this moment," said Kain, "I will stop by later."

"My children haven't slept in a week," said the waitress, "Can you go come before 8 p.m.?"

"I will go quiet down your neighbors in time to put your kid's to bed," lied Kain.

Kain never worked the nightshift. Kain drove back to the station. He filed the reports and petty complaints. Gent read the new reports that his nephew had dished out. For someone out on a fool's errand, he had actually done actual police work. Gent looked at the noise complaint report. He ran the files of the waitress that had asked Kain for help. The waitress had given a name that belonged to an old woman, whose children lived abroad. Gent suspected that the waitress was working without a Green Card. If she lied about her name, she probably lied about everything else. After meditating things, Gent decided to have his trigger happy rookie, Zidanta investigate this noise complaint. Zidanta had only been in the force for a month, and he had already shot 7 civilians. The kid was setting a State Record.

"It's a trap!" said Gent before giggling.

"What's a trap?" asked Kain waiting for his next assignment.

"Don't worry about it," said Gent. Changing the subject, he said, "Carina called a few hours ago to announce your engagement. Congratulations."

"We are not getting married. I told her that if she stayed with me for an entire year, then I would propose to her," explained Kain, "I don't expect her to keep her end of the bargain."

"I get why you don't want to marry her. She always leaves, and yet she has the gull to claim that you are the one not ready to commit," retorted Gent laughing.

"The thing is…uncle…Carina. She has all these plans and all these dreams. She has her perfect life planned out in her head, and when reality doesn't match her expectations she becomes frustrated with me," said Kain.

"I blame the Telenovelas," said Gent, "You should get her to watch something with a bit more substance."

"That is going to be easier said than done," said Kain, "They just remade Betty La Fea, so I will probably have to sit through that for the next couple of months, but it is a small price to pay since she watches anime with me."

"The pieces are all there Kain. Can you tell me the real reason why you don't want to marry Carina?" insisted Gent.

"I don't want children. She wants children. End of discussion," said Kain.

"Not all children are as annoying as Tweedledee and Tweedledumb," said Gent pointing to the photographs of his seven year old daughters, Hanna and Anna. Gent then pointed to his eldest son Kyle, age 13, "Kyle is nice. He is a little stoic, but that is because he was born a little old man."

"I don't know uncle...it is just...society says that..." started saying Kain.

"I am not in the mood to hear about orphans and overpopulation, Kain," said Gent, "I chose to have children with my wife because I loved her, and I wanted a physical manifestations of our love in the form of little children. I didn't do it to make my parents happy. Or to make society happy. I did it because I wanted to! Now, I want you to tell me why you don't want to! Don't hold anything back son. Tell me the truth."

"...I...just...don't want to...uncle...what do you want me to say?" said Kain shrinking into himself, "And it is not that I hate kids. They are great in micro dosages. It is just that I do not see myself as the type of person that can dedicate his life to another. And children, they are a lifetime commitment. Even when they are grown up, you might end up taking care of them forever. Till his last days, grandpa was forced to take care of my father..."

"He was atoning for his sins," explained Gent.

"What?" asked Kain looking up.

"My dad... he only bothered to get involved when the problem known as Jack grew too large to be ignored. When Jack fell from grace, my father lost complete interest in my brother. Jack was a broken toy my father wanted nothing to do with. Not only didn't he help Jack, but he interfered every time I tried to help my little brother," protested Gent, "You can hate your mother as much as you want, but not my Jackie. I am not asking you to like him, but please, be civil to him."

This was the first time Gent had openly spoken about the hatred he felt for his father Raphael. Gent brought out a little miniature he had of little Jackie. Gent spent the rest of the workday telling Kain stories about his little brother. The workday came to an end. While he drove back, Kain digested this new piece of information about his father's past. His father Jackie had been negligent, because his father Raphael didn't take care of him. As an only child, Kain didn't emphasize with the strong bond Gent shared with his little brother. Even if Kain couldn't understand it, he had to respect it. While driving back, Kain mussed about what his life could have been like if he had a little brother or sister. The closets person he had to a sibling with was his girlfriend Carina. Even if she got married, Kain hoped that she would remain a part of his life. When Kain arrived home, he saw Jack's humble little mini cooper parked outside. Sitting inside waiting to build up courage was Jack. Kain parked beside the car, and he noticed Jack was crying while talking to himself. Kain worried tapped on the window.

Jack rolled it down, and he said trembling, "Is there a problem officer?"

"I am going to need you to step out of the vehicle," said Kain.

"I…my son lives here," protested Jack, "And I am…oh…Kain… hehehe…hi…"

"You can come inside," said Kain opening the front door. He was about to add "Don't Steal anything" but he chose not to.

"Kain, welcome home," said Esther hugging her favorite grandson. The smile immediately faded when she saw the pitiful creature standing behind him.

"It is fine grandma," said Kain, "He bought me a new game. Inviting him over for a nice homecooked meal is the least I could do to repay him."

Jack entered the house, uncertain. He had always seen the place from the outside, but never the interior. This house was emptier than what Jack had expected. Like Gent, Jack assumed that the house belonged to his mother Esther. Kain had bought the house with Esther's help. His grandma had provided the down, while Kain paid for everything else, including the utility bills. The room décor contrasted with the cluttered mess that was Esther's true home. Esther was a bit of a hoarder, and her garage was filled with everything including all of her children's school works, family albums, their toys, clothing, as well as a colony of roaches living inside the mess.

Since Kain owned the property, his grandma had placed him in charge of the decor. Kain wasn't too fuzzy with the look as long as the furniture was cheap, and comfortable. He had gone for a milky white look, for all his furniture, following the trends he had seen in the Fixer Upper. Kain only had two televisions, a big flat screen TV in the living room, and a fat old TV in his bedroom. From the open living room, the house flowed towards the dining room and the small remodeled kitchen. Kain's house had four bedrooms and two bathrooms. Though one bedroom was technically a garage turned into a bedroom. There was the bedroom Esther slept in when she visited, as well as second guestroom with a sofa bed, instead of a bed. Kain began dinner, while he did Esther silently judged her good for nothing son Jack.

To break the silence, Kain turned on the TV and he handed the remote control to Esther. Esther began to flip through all the channels of Kain's hacked cable service. A movie was eventually found and it helped dissipate some of the darkness. Come seven, dinner was served. With Jack visiting, Kain made his father's favorite meal, spaghetti with bacon. Kain sliced up some hard bread in order to reheat it, and garnish it. When it came out of the oven, the old bread had transmuted into garlic bread.

"I don't have beer, but I can get you a soda, an orange juice, or maybe some carbonated water," said Kain opening the fridge.

"Soda is fine, thank you," said Jack politely.

When the food was placed before Jack, he proceeded to munch on it before it got cold. Kain normally talked during his meal, but instead he focused on eating. Esther couldn't believe her eyes. Father and son were eating together at the same table. It had been ages since Kain had tolerated his father's presence. Kain was still uncertain about the situation. At the moment, he wasn't angry or sad because of his father's presence. This was a good thing. Kain didn't want to continue feeding those negative emotions if he could help it. Kain looked at his scrawny father, and he fancied that his presence would be tolerable if he thought of Jack as his little brother.

"You smell a little funny," said Jack sniffing Kain. Jack was already far too full to take another bit.

"Some of the guys mentioned that when I got back," said Kain smelling his uniform, "I need to get changed and shower after I rest my food."

Jack drew closer and he smelled Kain's hair. Nodding happily Jack said, "I recognized that smell! It is Reefa!"

"Reefa?" repeated Esther worried.

"It is just a cigarette brand," lied Jack, "It is no different than those Camels you smoke when nobody is looking."

"You can't prove that I still smoke," said Esther defensively.

"Whatever it was, that restaurant stunk of it," said Kain, "But at least the food was delicious, even if it was all vegan."

Kain looked at his phone and he noticed that he had 17 messages from Eugenia. They were all different versions of the same command call. She wanted Kain to drop everything and investigate her mother Eunice. Kain was about to text her to tell her to bother someone else, but even that seemed like too much a bother. The problem was that the psycho bitch knew where he lived. Kain reluctantly went to his room to get started on that little side project.

"What are you doing?" asked Jack looking over Kain's shoulder.

"A random woman asked me to find dirt on her mom," said Kain.

"Did she promise to pay you?" asked Jack.

"No," said Kain pouting, "But she knows where I live, and I do not want any more problems from her psychotic parents and their lawyers."

"Let me help you with that problem, son," said Jack handing a towel to Kain, "Go take your shower."

Kain stripped out of his officer uniform and he finally took his bath. While he showered, Jack took Kain's cellphone. He found Eugenia's phone number and he marked that wench as spam. He also marked as spam a couple of unfamiliar numbers. Jack then left the room, and he informed his grandma of the problem called Eugenia.

"Those two haven't even mated and she is already asking for big favors mama. That Eugenia is nothing but bad news," said Jack, "Kain is going to get in trouble because of that mooch."

"Takes one to know one," retorted Esther dryly, "Still, this whole evil stepmom scenario is a little too cliché, for it to be true. And Eugenia might be a user. Her parents restricted her finances for a good a reason."

Once Kain was relaxed, he lied down on his bed to read a book. He looked at his phone for a second. He realized the type of help that Jack had offered. After thinking things through for a bit, he realized that Jack was right about Eugenia. She was nothing but trouble. Kain shouldn't be so eager to help a bimbo that he met less than a day ago. A torrential rain began to fall. Jack made a motion to leave under the stormy weather, but his mother Esther insisted that he stay the night. The morning came and much to Esther's surprise, everything was where it should be. She was even more surprised to see that Jack was getting dressed for work.

"I wasn't lying about having a real job," said Jack, "I am really trying to do things right this time."

"I believe in you Jackie," lied Esther hugging her son.

Jack smiled sadly. He could always tell when his mother was lying. Jack walked to his car and he attempted to turn it on. Since it kept stalling, Kain gave his father a lift to work. Jack nervously got inside the patrol car. The two rode out in utter silence. Jack looked at the laptop on the dashboard.

"If you want to see your criminal record, you do not need to ask for permission," said Kain turning the laptop to make it face Jack, "Only, do not ask me too many questions, because I get distracted if people talk to me while I am driving."

Jack gave a cursory view at his record. From there, he began to amuse himself by looking up the criminal records of people he went to high school with. After a 20 minute ride, Kain arrived at the used car store. Jack left the police car clutching his briefcase for dear life. Kain stopped him and he made Jack hold the briefcase like a normal person. Kain straightened Jack's tie, and he combed his hair with his saliva.

"Just because your friend got you this job, doesn't mean you can slack off. As long as you look busy and professional, you are going to be able to retain this job for years to come. And if you need to boost your sales, don't forget craigslist exists," said Kain, "And if you start talking to yourself, put your cellphone to your ear. It makes to look a little less crazy."

"I don't listen to voices, if that is what you are implying," retorted Jack, "It is just...when nobody is around my apartment I have gotten into the habit of speaking my thoughts out loud...I can't live by myself, Kain. I am not used to it. I don't like it."

"Then go back to uncle Gent's house," said Kain.

"I can't. His wife hates me," said Jack, "And Nathan is apparently staying in Abu Dhabi forever. And Elizabeth doesn't have room for me in her New York shoebox apartment. And…"

"So, that just leaves me, then?" said Kain rubbing his temple, "I don't have time to deal with your nonsense, dad! Go to work. Call me when you get fired."

Kain got in the car and drove away from the situation. Once he got to the first red light, Kain punched the dashboard while cursing. Kain saw the light turn green, and he pressed down the gas pedal. He didn't get far before a speeding vehicle T-bone him. His patrol car rolled and rolled, as his life flashed before his eyes. The vehicle that struct him drove backwards and fled the scene of the crime. It was one thing to T-bone a random car. It was another matter to crash into a police car. Kain was hanging upside down, tied by the seatbelt. He could smell gasoline. It was only a matter of time before the car would explode. Kain went to remove his seatbelt, but at the last moment he chose not to. He closed his eyes, while he waited to leave this cruel world with a big bang. This plan was short lived. Kain heard the footsteps of someone rushing over, and franticly opening the door.

"Help! Help! Somebody call the police! Somebody call an Ambulance," yelled Jack hysterically, while he struggled with the seatbelt.

Kain wearily stopped playing possum, and he reached for the seatbelt. One of the drivers that had stopped reached from the other side of the patrol car to help drag Kain out of the vehicle, and not a moment too soon. The patrol car exploded in a spectacular fashion.

"Careful with his head," said Jack while his son was slowly carried to the sidewalk, "Don't worry son, the ambulance is coming. You are going to be alright. Ok. Ok. Ok. Everything is going to Ok."

"I am fine," said Kain sitting up. This mere act made him dizzy, as the world started spinning around him. He leaned forward and he rested his head on his hands.

"It will pass son," repeated Jack petting Kain's back, "You are in shock. You are alright. Everything is fine. Everything is fine! Ok. Ok."

Kain began to collapse again, only this time Jack was nearby to offer his lap as a cushion. Weary of the effort of struggling against destiny, Kain accepted the help from the father that he didn't want. The man who had assisted Jack handed him Kain's revolver. It wouldn't do well for it to be left lying around in the pavement for any random person to pick up. Jack stashed it in his coat pocket, before immediately forgetting that it was there. The ambulance came. Instead of going to the hospital, Kain asked to be taken to IFA America. Carina's mother Unla worked there. She would be able to get him an MRI at a cheaper value. While the two waited, Kain started feeling a little better, in part thanks to the first aid he had received in the Ambulance. His head was bandaged up, and the cut he had received on his wrist was threated.

"Dad...your hand is burnt," said Kain looking at one of Jack's hand.

"Hahaha...I didn't notice," said Jack, "When the car exploded I used this hand to protect my face."

A medical assistant sent by Unla summoned the two to enter her office. An ointment was applied to Jack's burnt hand, and it was bandaged up. It was a good thing too. Now that Jack was aware of the burn, it hurt like bloody hell. After removing all the metal from his uniform, Kain got his MRI. There was no concussion or damage. Unla noticed the purple bruise on Kain's left arm. The car had struct him from the driver's side. An X-Ray showed that there were no broken bones. Unla provided an arm bracer and some ice to reduce the swelling. They were then released from the clinic with all their booboos threated.

While the two waited for Carina to pick them up, the two spoke. Kain spoke first, "Sigh, dad...why didn't you love me? When I was small, you rarely spent any time with me."

"I was working. I couldn't keep an eye on the baby, while trying to compose music. If I wasn't playing with you all the time, you would throw yourself into hysterics," said Jack scratching his hair, "I just didn't know how to manage. I didn't have any experience taking care of children, and I was a child myself. I was only 12 when you came into this world, Kain. And when mom took you to live with her, it was a relief. I no longer needed to be responsible for you."

"If you didn't want me," asked Kain starting to cry, "Why did you bother to save me?"

"I am sorry!" said Jack realizing what a terribly thing he had just said, "I didn't mean it!"

Carina arrived around noon to take Kain home. She found Kain crying next to a creepy, thin man. Kain saw Carina and he went to cry on her shoulder. The girl guessed that her boyfriend was still a shacky from the accident. Carina turned to look at the news. There was a helicopter view of the accident, as well as some eyewitness reports of the heroic rescue. Carina walked Kain to her car, while he kept crying uncontrollably. She was about to drive away, when Kain noticed that there was someone missing.

Taking control of his emotions, Kain said, "…sob…you forgot my father…sob…"

Carina returned to the clinic and she looked about for someone that resembled Kain. It was then when the thin man approached her. Jack was clutching nervously the ends of his buttoned shirt. Since the strange man was following her, Carina guessed that this lanky creature was Kain's father. He was not what Carina had imagined.

Jack looked at his phone and he said, "This thing has been vibrating for hours. I think it is broken."

"When it vibrates it means that you are getting a call," said

Carina, "Is this your first cellphone?"

"Hand it over, dad," said Kain gesturing with his hand, "We better not distract Carina while she is driving, and put on your seatbelt."

Carina and Jack buckled up. Kain texted to his uncle Gent to tell him that he was fine. The patrol car had exploded, but he did not. Kain took a selfie with the phone, and he sent it as visual confirmation that he was more or less in one piece. Carina arrive to Kain's home. Kain looked for his house keys, but he frowned when he realized that they had blown up with the car. Jack realizing the problem removed one of his hairpins. After breaking it, Jack was able to pick the lock, and all were able to get inside the house. Kain went to the beeping house alarm and he tried to type in the password. With his head still foggy, he kept getting the 4 key combination wrong. Jack after thinking for a second, typed in Raphael's birthday. This made the alarm stop beeping.

"I want to stay," said Carina, "But I have finals in two hours. I really need to get back to school. As soon as I finish, I am coming back, I promise. Are you going to be ok, Kain?"

"With my father taking care of me, everything is going to be alright," said Kain giving a fake smile.

Carina couldn't tell if Kain was being serious or sarcastic. She looked at the time, and in the end her ambitions dictated her priorities. Carina drove back to school in order to finish her finals. With her gone, Kain went to collapse on the couch. Jack went to the bathroom, and he came back with a cold, moist towel. He placed it over Kain's eyes, before sitting down nearby.

"I have a proposition for you," said Kain, "I am going to let you live with me. As long as you don't cause me problems, I am willing to tolerate your presence."

"Do you really mean that Kain?" asked Jack smiling happily.

"You better go get your things before I change my mind," said

Kain, "And go to work already!"

Jack lingered in the house till Carina returned from her exams. With someone keeping an eye on the big baby, Jack ran to his car and it turned on without a problem. Jack drove to his workstation and he reported to his boss the reason why he had been extremely late for work. The remaining four hours passed without incident. Jack mentioned the existence of Craiglist, and this became his new role in the company. It was his task to take photographs of the cars, and create listings for it in Craiglist. Jack's boss was a failed drummer that insisted on being called by his stage name: Arjuna. They only needed a failed vocalist and songwriter in order to form a new rock band. Jack returned to his Plan 8 apartment, in Opa Loca. He frowned when he noticed that someone had broken into his home again. This was another reason why he wanted to move out. Jack cautiously opened the door. He saw that the thief was still there, tearing at the floor and walls looking for anything of value. Jack tiptoed to the neighbor's house. He knocked a few times in morse code. His good neighbor allowed Jack to hide out there, until the thief left. His neighbor and landlord was an old man in a wheelchair. He would allow Jack to visit him, whenever he was feeling particularly bored and lonely.

"If your brother is a police officer, why don't you call him?" asked his good neighbor.

"I don't want to cause him any more problems," said Jack, "While I am here, I wanted to terminate my lease. I am moving in with my son."

"There are penalties for early termination…" started saying his landlord, before laughing and adding, "I am just messing with you. I will wait a few months before getting a new tenant, just in case just son throws you out of the house."

"That won't happen," said Jack, "We have come to an understanding."

The noise in the other apartment went away. Jack breathed in a sigh of relief. Just when the coast seemed clear. The door was kicked down. At that moment, Jack regretted not calling the cops. The thief screaming hysterically punched Jack and the harmless old man. He dragged the tenant by the hair and he demanded he showed him the money. Jack was lying on his side, and he felt something hard and metallic pressing up against his thigh. When his hand reached for it, he saw that he had Kain's revolver. With a trembling hand, Jack brandished the revolver. The thief took a cautious step back, and another and another. He then fled the apartment to avoid getting shot at.

"If you had that revolver you should have brought it out sooner," complained the landlord, "I don't know about you, but I am calling the cops. Help me back on the wheelchair."

Jack assisted the old man back on the wheelchair. Once everything was in working order, Jack returned to his small apartment. Everything was a mess. Jack called his brother Gent to inform him that he had gotten robbed. Gent held his hand over his chest. He just couldn't handle any more bad news, for today. Gent sent over the nightguards to investigate the robbery, before taking an aspirin as a preventive measure. Jack looked through his apartment. He picked up a few articles of clothing, the guitar he had hidden inside the roof, his pillow, and the cash inside the toilet bowl. The rest Gent could send for, or sell it. Jack locked closed the door on the way out. He drove back to Kain's home. During the time Jack had been away, Kain had been considering telling his father to go to hell. When he saw him return all beaten up, Kain softened. The night was spent with Jack ranting about getting mugged by an addict.

"I guess I finally got a taste of my own medicine, eh, Kain," said Jack laughing nervously.

"I need your help in the kitchen," said Kain changing the subject.

And just like that, Kain and Jack started to reconnect with one another, whether they wanted to or not. Acting as mediator for the two was grandma Esther. She had heard from Kain that Jack was going to be moving into his home. She was uncertain about the situation, but she felt that this was how things should have always been.

CHAPTER 3

The Moon

◆ ◆ ◆

Carina drove back to FIU after dropping off Kain and Jack to their home. When she had sent Jack that anonymous letter, she hadn't expected for Jack to seek his son so quickly. Carina didn't know what to expect of Jack's father. All she knew of the guy was that Jack was a failed rockstar, and a recovering addict. As someone who was impulsive by nature, Carina was starting to second guess her decision. When she arrived to FIU, she came to this conclusion. Families where supposed to stick together, both on the good times and specially in the bad times. This was how her family rolled. She smiled gleefully, thinking that she had done a good deed, by forcing father and son to reunite.

Carina ran to her classroom, in order to cram for her finals. Once it was finally over, Carina breathed in a sigh of relief. Whether she did good or bad, it was irrelevant. Even with a D, she was still going to pass. She went to pester her counselor after this examination. The counselor gave Carina the good news. She had met all the requirements to graduate. It was finally over! This summer Carina finally became a Pediatrician. Now, she just needed to complete the minimum one year of Residency, in order to get her medical license. With her education concluded, Carina could now devote more time into turning Kain into her perfect husband. The alternative was to return to the dating scene. It could take months, even years before running into a decent man. Carina drove to Kain's home to tell him her good news.

When she got to the parking lot, she saw a green Plymouth fury. She backed up a bit and she waited to see who was going to come out of the house. When she saw that it was Eugenia, Carina's blood began to boil. She simmered for 10 minutes. As soon as her competition drove away, Carina breathed in a sigh of relief. Carina knocked and Jack opened the door for her. The two didn't have time to chat, since Jack was extremely late for work.

Carina entered the house to see how Kain was doing after his accident. Kain was in the shower cleaning off the dirt and grime. Carina picked up his dirty uniform and she threw into the laundry. Since she was nervous and insecure, Carina started to clean Kain's home, starting off by dusting his bedroom. She noticed that his computer was running a long process. She read an open composition book. Kain was running a background check on Eunice's finances using the information Eugenia had given him, just to be safe, he was also going to investigate her husband. He was doing the bare minimum working with under the confines of probably cause.

Carina didn't understand why Kain was helping out that woman who had tried to sue him. She looked at her reflection in the vanity, and she didn't like it. She sighed before returning to clean the house. Kain had never cheated on her. He was too lazy or comfortable to go find himself another woman, whenever she was around. Carina repeated this to herself while she fastidiously worked. The shower closed and Kain stumbled back into his bed.

"What did the bimbo want?" asked Carina.

"She begged me to find dirt on her step-mother Eunice,"

explained Kain, "It is a little cliché, but she promised to pay me for my work."

"What is she going to pay you with?" asked Carina chocking her broom.

"With a donation for my coworkers," said Kain wearily, "Unlike me, they work really hard. They deserve to see proper renumerations for putting their life in danger, for the sake of citizens who see them as the enemy. She also promised not to bother me ever again, regardless of the results of my investigation. After all, she is but a stranger, who expects men to become her little lapdogs because of her beauty."

"Ahah! You admit it!" hissed Carina, "You think she is prettier than me!!"

"Carina. Everything hurts. I don't feel well. Please!" protested Kain placing a pillow over his head.

"It will take more than a bump on the head to kill you Kain!" said Carina before going on one of her jealousy rants, "What does that bimbo have that I don't have?"

"Get out of my house! Carina," yelled Kain sitting up.

Carina turned as white as a sheet. Kain rose from the bed, the color from his face was completely gone. Carina took a step back, and Kain walked towards her. Carina closed her eyes expecting the worst. Instead, Kain had staggered towards the bathroom to throw up his breakfast. Carina ran for the phone and she called her mother.

"The adrenaline surge must be going down," said Unla, "His accident was really bad Carina. Why were you arguing with him? What is wrong with you?"

"I wasn't arguing," lied Carina meekly.

"Don't you think I don't know my own daughter. Seriously, Carina," said Unla, "Give the man time to decompress."

Carina hung up the phone. She tiptoed back to the bedroom. She opened the door slowly. She found Kain still throwing up, even though his stomach was still empty. Carina brought him a glass of water, and got him back on the bed. She proceeded to sanitize the bathroom, starting with the toilet. She had inherited from her mother, the compulsion to clean everything whenever she was nervous. While she cleaned, she pondered why Kain had offered to help Eugenia. In her jealous fury, the only conclusion she kept coming to was that Kain had feelings for Eugenia.

"Carina…I didn't ask you to clean the bathroom," moaned Kain, "I want to sleep, and the noise you keep making is worsening my headache."

Carina picked up the cleaning supplies and she made the extreme effort of being as quiet as a mouse. She got bored of seeing Kain sleeping, so, she saw herself out. She needed to prepare for her graduation ceremony, and there was the after party. Carina went through her entire contact list to inform her parents, uncles, aunts, cousins and distant relatives that she was graduating. She started walking around the front yard, and the backyard while ranting on the phone. Carina noticed that the grass was a little tall. She went to the storm shed and she brought out the lawnmower. Kain awoke as soon as he heard the lawnmower sounding. He wanted to tell Carina to keep it down, but he was far too weary to leave the bed. Resigned to his fate, Kain reached for his headset. He turned on some classical music in order to drown out some of the noise. With this measure, he was able to fall asleep again. Carina finished cutting the grass, and she even trimmed the edges. She looked at her gardening work, and saw that it was good.

With nothing else to do, Carina returned to the house to see if Kain was still breathing. Since he had his headsets on, Carina returned to fastidiously clean the house. She saw Esther driving up the house. Since her man was no longer going to be alone, Carina return home in order to begin the preparations for her graduation party. Carina lived in a small house, behind a large mansion owned by the matriarch of the family, Barbara.

Her mother Unla was the little sister of the Matriarch, and therefore she lived in the smaller, three bedroom house. In the center of both properties, there was communal garden, with a thatch roof Gazebo, a trampoline a tree house, a pool, and a variety of fruiting trees. Her house was mainly where Carina slept. Throughout her youth, Carina seamlessly moved between the two houses. Barbara owned two clinics. Every member was expected to fill a spot in the family business. When Carina was born, all the spots were full, so she was allowed to "follow her dreams". Carina tried a bunch of different career paths while in high school. She eventually decided to become a pediatrician.

The first thing Carina did when she got home was inform her relatives that she was graduating. That night her family did an impromptu party. Barbara was always looking for an excuse to throw a big party. Just a few days ago, they had celebrated the wedding of their pet macaws. Nobody bothered to inquire why Carina's boyfriend was not at the party. Since Barbara saw that Carina's relationship was stagnant, she decided to interfere. Her interference came in the form of Bruno. He was a lawyer friend of her eldest son, Rodrigo. Rodrigo and Bruno had been roomies and they had played College Football together. Rodrigo felt that his friend would be a good match for his cousin, since both were allergic to casual relationships.

Carina drank, danced and was merry. She looked at Bruno over the top, and she thought that her aunt Barbara had excellent taste in men. There was something particularly charming about his discount Che Guevara beard. She also liked his intense green eyes. His entire being emanated strength and determination. Taking the initiative, Bruno invited Carina to dance. Bruno ranted about his work as a defense attorney. Meanwhile, Carina bored him with her medical jargon. Both where talking, but neither of them where having a real conversation. Carina didn't know anything about laws, while Bruno couldn't find his prostate to save his own life.

"You seem like a sharp individual, what are your plans for the future?" asked Carina.

"For the time being, I am on the prowl," said Bruno.

"And when you find what you are looking for, what do you plan to do?" asked Carina drawing closer. Bruno answered Carina's question with a kiss.

The two exchanged numbers and they planned for a future date. Carina didn't felt guilty about kissing another man. In her mind, Kain had already replaced her. When the party died down, Carina went to lie down on a hammock to stargaze and to feed the mosquitoes. Even with the anti-mosquito lanterns, the little critters were biting. Carina stoically ignored them, while she stared at the three Quarter moon. She had until Saturday to decide to bind herself to Kain. Carina thought on the events of the night. How quickly had she jumped into the arms of another. She traced with her finger the lines on her palm. Irina was right, Carina was a selfish lover.

"Why did I kiss Bruno?" said Carina to herself, "I just met that man…he was awfully pretty. Aunty really knows the types of men I like. Why did he have to have green eyes?"

Carina reached into her pocket and she brought out her cellphone to check the time. Kain was probably asleep. With the distraction of school out of the way, Carina finally had time for self-reflection.

"Why am I always self-sabotaging?" asked Carina, "I wasn't able to be faithful for one year."

"If you are done feeding the mosquitoes, please come inside Carina," said Unla, "There is something important we need to talk about."

Carina went into the house to speak with her mother. The moment she entered within, she became aware of the mosquito bites. Carina took a quick shower and she changed into her nightgown. While Carina had been busy fooling about, Unla had gone to tend to Jack's newly acquired wounds, and she gave

Kain something to help him sleep through his nauseas. When Carina faced her mother, she had the feeling that she had done something wrong.

"Do you know what it means to be married?" asked Unla removing her wedding band, "Marriage is a promise. A promise that you will support one another, in sickness and in health. I stayed with your father, until the bitter end. You couldn't even spend a single night with your ailing boyfriend."

"His grandma was there…" said Carina meekly, "And he told me to leave, because I wasn't letting him sleep."

"What where you doing while he was trying to sleep?" asked Unla.

"I was cleaning the house," said Carina.

"Sigh…Carina," said Unla, "What were you thinking about while you were cleaning the house?"

"I was thinking about this ginger bimbo that is wasping around my man," protested Carina.

"Honestly, Carina, your man is ill and you are thinking about your competition," said Unla shaking her head sadly, "Kain has never cheated on you. If after all this time, you do not have faith in your bond, why are you still together?"

"I would have more faith in him, if he agreed to marry me," pouted Carina.

"A wedding ring won't cure you of your jealousy," said Unla, "While your father lived, I never doubted the strength of his devotion to me."

"But that was because he was always so devoted," said Carina, "Dad was always doing cute romantic gestures. He showed you every day that he loved you. But Kain…he…"

"He isn't the romantic type," said Unla, "Every person is different, Carina. It isn't healthy for you to look for your father in every man you date."

Carina yawned to illustrate her desire to hit the hay. She wasn't in the mood to talk about her dead father. When she was five, her father was diagnosed with Cancer. He battled with the illness for two years, before succumbing to it. During that time, his health fluctuated like the waxing and waning of the moon. There were days when he seemed good as new. During those days, life returned to normal. There were nights when he spent it coughing up bloop. In order to get her away from that situation, Barbara would take Carina out. She would only bring the girl home, when he father's negative symptoms subsided. Carina knew that her father was having a bad day, whenever she saw her mother fastidiously cleaning the bathroom. And then one night, Carina's father was gone. It was his last wish that Carina wouldn't see him dead. Carina wasn't even allow to go to the funeral. She only found out that he was dead, after he had been buried. Since Carina never saw his corpse, there were nights where she would forget that he was dead. During those delirious night, Carina would suffer major tantrums, while she demanded to see her daddy. The solution that Unla found was redecorate the house, to have it serve as a visual reminder that their life was never going to be the same way again.

That night Carina dreamt she was cleaning the toilet. She looked up to the window and she saw the blood moon. Blood began to seep through the tiles. Regardless of how much Carina cleaned, more and more bloodstains manifested. Carina turned her head and she saw the open bathroom door. Resting on top of the bed hooked up to machines was the shape of a man. Carina walked towards the sick bed, but regardless of how much she walked she couldn't seem to reach it. The man turned his head to look at Carina.

Carina awoke after screaming, "Papa!!"

Carina was bathed in a cold sweat. With a trembling hand, she looked for the lamp light. When its gentle glow bathed her bedroom. She breathed a sigh of relief. There was something childish about her choice room décor. Everything was a combination of soft pastels, pinks and yellows. Her bookshelf was dominated by her medical tomes. Beneath it, there where artbooks, fashion magazines, and other visual mediums. Carina wasn't much of a reader, though she liked to browse through Artbooks. The only totems from her childhood that she kept was her dollhouse. It would amuse her to redecorate it. The current resident of her dollhouse was a her tiny white bunny plushie, named Nana. Nana was the last gift Carina had gotten from her father.

Carina left her bed and she opened her dollhouse. She brought out Nana from her home. Carina petted her little bunny nervously. Her mind was still filled with distorted visions of her nightmare. Carina saw a strong pale light sipping through the window. When she opened the blinds, Carina saw the moonlight shining down on top of her pillow. Carina moved her pillow to the other side of the bed. That way the moonlight would fall on her feet, instead of her face. She closed the blinds again, and she attempted to fall asleep again.

"Nana. They say that a little bunny lives on the moon," said Carina talking to her plushie, "The bunny is constantly grounding herbs needed to make the elixir of immortality for the Gods."

"They sure keep him pretty busy," said Nana. Nana didn't speak, rather Carina altered her voice to make what she thought was a cute bunny sound.

"Nana…do you think Kain is alright?" asked Carina.

"Why do you care? Aren't you more interested in Bruno?" asked Nana.

"Bruno? That man is such a bore," said Carina, "I truly do wish he didn't have green eyes. Green eyes are my favorite…"

Carina fell asleep thinking about Bruno's green eyes. Carina awoke an hour before noon. She had overslept. She left her bed and she started to look for Nana. After flipping the bed and all the covers, she saw that the bunny had fallen from the bed while she tossed and turned at night. Carina returned the bunny to her dollhouse. Carina wasn't in the mood to go residence hunting right away. She decided to take the rest of July as a sabbatical.

Carina took her morning bath, and she had a light breakfast. Carina went to the main house to see if her stay at home aunt Mira was around. There was a note on the fridge that said that she had taken her kids, and their cousins to the beach. Since nobody was at home, Carina checked her messages. Bruno had not called to check up on her. If she called him first, Bruno was going to have all the power in the relationship, or so Oprah claimed.

Carina's boredom overcame her common sense. Carina called up Bruno, and he didn't answer. A few minutes later, she got a text saying: Court is in session. Carina feeling stupid remembered that Bruno worked for a living. He wouldn't have time to entertain her for a while. She would call him back at 5 p.m. Carina after examining her options decided to join her nephews at the beach. She drove to Miami Beach, and she parked beside her aunt's van. Once she found her family, she stripped down to her bikini and she laid down her burden beside her aunt, who was reading a book. Carina swam in the ocean for a bit, but the water was choppy. The waves kept tossing her about like a ragdoll. When she got bored of swimming by herself, she went to assist her nephews in forming a sandcastle.

"I saw in the morning news about what happened to your boyfriend," said Mira putting down her book, to switch to gossiping mode.

"Did something happened to Bruno?" asked Carina.

"Sheesh, Aunty. A guy kisses you once at a party, and suddenly you change allegiances," said Jennifer, age 13.

"It isn't my fault that I like Bruno. He has green eyes!" protested Carina, "You know I have a weakness for green eyed men."

"Eye color isn't a strong foundation to build a relationship Carina," said Mira sadly, "What else do you like about him?"

"I like the way he dances," said Carina, "He must move well in the bedsheets. I wager."

"If you were at least of a lustful nature, then we would understand," said Mira, "But you always leave, sometimes for the right reason, but most of the time you leave over petty things."

"Are you afraid of commitment, Aunty?" asked Jennifer. She was soon joined by others nitpicking Carina's past relationships.

"Pile it on! Pile it on!" protested Carina. Her cousin George in answer to her request piled sand on top of her head.

Carina checked the time and she saw that it was five. She texted Bruno to see if he was done with his case. Bruno again claimed to be busy at work. Carina went to the public bathroom and she dusted her hair, and she changed out of her swimsuit. She drove to Court to see if her boyfriend was lying to her. Bruno was just getting out of the courtroom when he saw Carina asking the receptionist to see him. He laughed heartedly seeing her barking orders at the poor receptionist. He couldn't decide if Carina was desperate or psychotic. Bruno began to silently judge Carina.

Carina recognizing that judgmental look said pouting, "They are like that because I am not wearing a bra."

"I wasn't looking at that," said Bruno lost in contemplation, "I was merely taken by your presence. It was only a kiss. It is far too early for you to be stalking me."

"I am not stalking you!" said Carina offended by the accusation.

"Why are you here then?" scoffed Bruno. He started pacing around Carina as was his habit, whenever he wanted to intimidate a witness.

"I came to...would you stand still! It is pretty hard to have a conversation with you circling around me like a vulture," protested Carina closing her fist, and stomping on the floor.

"I am still in work mode," said Bruno carefully measuring his words. He stopped pacing the floor, in order to stand uncomfortably closed to Carina, "Please excuse my poor manners. It wasn't my intention to make you feel uncomfortable."

Carina placed her hand on Bruno's face to push him back. Bruno took that hand and he kissed it with reverence. Carina's unpredictability amused him. Carina giggled at this romantic gesture. Bruno's coworkers and his client chuckled seeing the contrast between the sandy, boho looking girl and the sophisticated lawyer. Bruno walked past Carina in order to return to his work. The case was still being decided, and Bruno was not the type of man who liked to lose. Bruno went to his office to ponder on the problem he had created for himself. The problem could easily go away if he told Carina that he wasn't interested.

"What is going to be my next move," said Bruno starring at the chessboard he had in his office.

Carina left the court extremely embarrassed to be there. She had made a scene over a guy that had only given her a kiss and a phone number. Carina felt her cellphone vibrate. She had gotten a text message from Kain: Congratulations on your Graduation. I hope all your dreams come true.

"Aw…that's so sweet," said Carina. She texted back to her friend, " :) "

The two proceeded to communicate with emojis. Kain eventually mentioned that he had the rest of the week off. His uncle Gent needed to get his nephew a new patrol car, or so he claimed. Gent wanted Kain off the street because he had yet to catch the guy who had rammed into his patrol car. After texting for 20 minutes, Carina felt like driving back to her house. When the light was red, her cellphone vibrated. Since she was a responsible driver, Carina continued to drive home without reading her messages. While she drove, she made mental plans.

She was going to shower, and then she was going to take her boyfriend Kain out for dinner. Since he didn't have work, Carina fancied that the two could make love all night long.

"Maybe I can convince him to let me tie him up again…" said Carina giggling, "Or…maybe we could try something new. Uh… what haven't we done yet?"

Carina arrived home, and she prepared for herself a bubble bath. She was going to exfoliate herself, in preparation of the long night she had ahead of herself. With the candles lighted and her face cream applied, she entered the steamy hot water. She thought of all the things she had yet to do to her boyfriend Kain. She dozed off in the bath for an hour. She could have easily slept for longer, but she had a nightmare. Carina dreamt she was at the beach. The only illumination came from a ridiculously large moon. Carina looked down and she saw that her hands where fat, with tiny fingers. She was a little girl again. She felt someone taking her hand. Carina turned to look at the stranger. The stranger was so tall that she couldn't see his face. His green eyes shimmer under the moonlight.

The man moved his mouth but Carina wasn't able to hear what he said. The crashing waves drowned out the sound of his voice. The man began to walk towards the ocean. Carina was left behind in the safety of the shore. Carina saw the man walking deeper and deeper, till he disappeared beneath the waves. The waves retreated before crashing right on top of Carina. When she awoke, her head was submerged underwater. Carina rose to the surface of the water and she coughed up a lung. She checked the time on her cellphone. It was then when she noticed two text messages from Kain. The first message was deleted.

It was followed by a second message that read: My father was playing with my phone. Pay no mind to the stupid photo he sent you.

"Don't worry about it," texted Carina, "I saw nothing."

"Phew," texted Kain.

"Was it a dick picture?" texted Carina curious.

"Something like that," lied Kain.

"Is he bigger than you?" texted Carina giggling.

" :(" replied Kain.

Carina was distracted from her texting when she heard a knock on the door. She heard her mother opening the door. Carina left her bath and she peeped outside. Her mother informed Carina that her boyfriend Bruno had brought roses. He was waiting in the living room for her to get dressed. He was going to take her to eat at his favorite restaurant. Carina taken aback by the romantic gesture left her bath. After browsing through her evening dresses, Carina chose for herself a crimson knee-length, satin cocktail dress, with applique lace at the end of the skirt. She dried her hair as quickly as she could. She curled it up with a bit of gel. Once she felt herself presentable, she left her bedroom. Bruno was still sporting the same blue tuxedo, and Carina thought that he looked very handsome, and sophisticated.

Bruno opened the car door for Carina. Her red dress was the same color as Bruno's Porsche Carrera Convertible. The two drove away with the top off. This allowed for the warm summer breeze to finish drying Carina's hair.

"Where are we going?" asked Carina.

"It is going to be a surprise," said Bruno giving a sly smile.

"I don't like surprises," said Carina shifting in her seat, acting all bashful.

"Neither do I," said Bruno.

Instead of driving Carina to a fancy restaurant, Bruno pulled up to the North Pole Restaurant in Hialeah. Carina saw the establishment, and she saw that she was overdressed. She was even half afraid of being mugged. Since she was starving, she decided to see were everything was going. She figured that Bruno was probably angry for her showing up at his job, uninvited. Bruno went to the counter, and he checked for his "reservation". Bruno pulled up the chair for Carina, and he took a paper napkin from the dispenser and he draped it over his date's lap. Bruno looked at the menu, and he pretended to carefully consider his options.

When the waiter came, Bruno ordered, "We will have two strawberry milkshakes and a Crema de Queso, with Bacon for appetizer."

"Wow! Big Spender!" said Carina sarcastically.

"I am going to make you eat those words," retorted Bruno, "And two personal cheese pizzas."

"I take it that you are still angry at me," said Carina with a hostile tone to her voice.

"If I was angry at you, why would I be feeding you?" asked Bruno.

"Look, mister! I know your game. You got me all dressed up, and instead of taking me to a nice, place, you took me to the cheapest restaurant you could find…" protested Carina.

"I didn't tell you to dress up," said Bruno sipping his milkshake, "You did that all on your own. IF I was taking you some where nice, I would have bothered to change out of my sweaty tux."

"Yeah…I did notice the smell," said Carina. She finally took a sip from her milkshake before exclaiming, "Wow…This is a really good milkshake."

"Nothing but the best, for my little lady," said Bruno giving a fake smile.

The appetizer arrived. Bruno leaned forward, and he proceeded to chow down on his meal. Carina was amazed by how quickly he ate. Smiling candidly, Carina said, "The cream is not going to escape your plate."

"I don't like to eat cold food," said Bruno.

Carina tried the appetizer, and she had to admit that it was delicious. When she added the cookies to it, it became even better. The two chit-chatted about the food and the restaurant. When the pizza arrived, the conversation immediately died down. Both where ravenous, and it was such a delicious pizza.

"Your cousin Rodrigo warned me about Kain," said Bruno at a certain point, "It do not know why he made such a big deal about you having a guy for a best friend."

"We date sometimes," said Carina nibbling on her pizza, "People say that one should marry one's best friend. But me and Kain function better as friends."

"Did he cheat on you?" asked Bruno.

"No," said Carina, "But he is disinterested. The element called passion is completely absent from our relationship. In all the time we have been together, he has never sent me flowers."

Bruno gave a sly smile before saying, "She walks in beauty like the night, of cloudless climes and starry skies…"

Carina giggled and blushed while she heard the recitation. This was the first time Carina had been recited romantic poetry. If it wasn't for the setting, she would have consider this the perfect dinner date. The dessert came. The two shared a Copa Lolita. It consisted of two scoops of ice cream, and flan in the center. Carina's ice cream ball was made of dulce de leche, and it was decorated with sprinkles and crushed cookies. Bruno's strawberry ball was decorated with gummy bears, and little pieces of cheesecake. The flan in the middle harmonized all opposing elements. Carina leaned back on her chair, feeling overstuffed. When the bill came, she reached for it.

"For a cheapskate, you have a way with words," said Carina dishing out her credit card, "And it is only 50 bucks. I can spare 50 bucks."

"Thank you. I will pay for the next one," said Bruno.

Bruno walked Carina to the car and he opened the door for her. Carina sighing said, "I really need to get back to regularly working out. Do you have a home gym?"

"Something like it," said Bruno before turning the car on, and driving away, "My condo has something that it calls a gym. Wouldn't recommend it."

"I used to work out in the university, but now that I am no longer a student, I lost access to the gymnasium. I was thinking of getting a gym membership," said Carina.

"Wouldn't recommend it," said Bruno, "If you want a place to work out, I know a good spot, and it won't cost you a dime. I can even get you a person trainer if you so desire it."

"Alright, Mr. Cheapskate. If you are not too busy with work tomorrow I want you to hook me up with your personal trainer," said Carina.

"The thing is that I am going to be busy tomorrow, and the day after, and the day after," said Bruno, "If you don't believe me, you are welcome to visit my office to watch me work overtime."

"Alright. I give you the benefit of the doubt, this time," said Carina shrinking into her seat.

Bruno drove back to Kendall, and he delivered Carina to her mother. Carina lingered by the door. She was feeling itchy, and she wanted Bruno to split her in half. Bruno limited himself to embracing Carina, while delivering a passionate kiss. The man left her thirsty and wanting more. Carina extremely frustrated went to her room to daydream a little. She looked at the mystery bag with the spell to bind herself to Kain. It was right on her nightstand to keep her from forgetting. She thought of her most recent nightmare. She pondered why she had dreamt of Bruno drowning. She thought that the person in her dream was Bruno because he had green eyes.

"Maybe my contact with a real psychic has awoken my latent magical abilities," said Carina sitting up.

"That's the stupidest thing I have ever heard," said Nana, "There is no such thing as magic. Our world has never been that interesting."

"Yeah. You are right Nana," said Carina turning to stare at her doll house.

"IF you don't believe that magic is real, why did you buy that spell from that sketchy witch?" asked Nana.

"She seemed sharper than the average psychic," said Carina, "It was almost as if she could read my mind."

"You are a normal girl, who wears her heart on her sleeve," said Nana, "It was child's play for Irina to guess your backstory."

The door to Carina's room opened slightly, and then it closed again. Unla was worried because Carina was talking to her bunny plushie again. Carina tended to do that when she felt lonely. Carina started talking to Nana after her father died. She would talk to the bunny, and then she would speak in a different voice. For a while, Unla feared that Carina had a dissociative personality. Unla realized that this wasn't the case when Carina returned to school. Carina only spoke to the bunny, when there was literally nobody else to talk to. Carina looked at her cellphone and she checked the time. She left the bed and she got changed into her pajamas. She had gotten all dolled up for nothing.

"You don't need to talk to your plushie when I am at home, Carina," said Unla entering the room.

"Sorry mom, force of habit," said Carina giggling.

"Do you want to watch El Clon with me?" asked Unla entering the room.

"I have already missed a lot of episodes," said Carina sitting up.

"I can fill you in on the details," said Unla smiling benevolently.

Unla was almost fifty. She had married her childhood sweetheart. After much trial and error, she had managed to give birth to her only daughter Carina. Unla was of a darker copper tone, with brown eyes, medium built. She had a face filled with laugh lines and eyes marked by deep suffering. Aside from being devoted to her daughter, she religiously took care of her dyed blonde hair. The two watched the telenovela. In between commercials, Unla interrogated her daughter about her date.

"He probably has a lot of student loans," said Unla, "Becoming a lawyer isn't cheap."

"Other than being Rodrigo's friend, what else do you know of Bruno?" asked Carina.

"Bruno isn't originally from Florida. He is from Kansas, like Dorothy. He came to Miami to play College Football for the University of Miami. He became friends with your cousin Rodrigo, since both played on the same team, and they were roomies for a spell…he drives a Porsche. He plays chess," said Unla, "He is employed and he is well mannered. Why don't you like him?"

"I don't know mom…he seems too good to be true," said Carina blushing, "Can you believe that he recited me poetry? What type of a guy recites poetry these days?"

"There are good men out there Carina," said Unla, "I was married to one. If Bruno went as far as to recite you poetry, and to buy you flowers, that means that he likes you."

"If he likes me, why didn't he sleep with me?" said Carina shifting on her seat.

"It is only your first date," said Unla, "I didn't sleep with your father till we got married."

"That was a different time mom," said Carina, "These days it is normal for men to sleep with you on your first date."

"And look how well that has gone for you, Carina," said Unla tentatively, "I know that you are nervous. This time you are dating an adult, and not an immature man child. Bruno respects you enough not to try to worm himself into your bedroom. He is a little on the poor side, but nothing that a few years of back breaking labor won't fix…"

"Sheesh mom! If you like Bruno so much, you should be the one to date him," said Carina laughing.

"Give him an honest try, and while you date him, you are not allowed to see Kain," said Unla.

"But Kain is my friend mom, and he got run over by a car," said Carina.

"Fine. You can see your friend," said Unla, "But you have to tell him that you are seeing another."

"Fine! Mom! Sheesh," said Carina.

Carina texted to her lover, Kain, "I found myself a new boyfriend."

"I am happy for you," texted Kain. He added, "I made a new friend. I think you already know her."

"It better not be Eugenia," texted Carina, "It is Eugenia, isn't it?"

"You guessed it," texted Kain, "I was helping her look through her family's finances. It turns out that her father has an illegitimate child. I am not going to bore you with the details. The overall point is that this information helped her regain control over her inheritance."

"Good for her," texted Carina after writing and rewriting her message. Unla saw on her daughter's face, that jealous pout Carina had whenever Unla kissed her husband. She leaned over to spy on the conversation her daughter was having with her friend.

"The two of you should go on a double date," suggested Unla.

"Mom! I don't want to meet Kain's new girlfriend," protested Carina.

"You can't keep Kain on lockdown while you go off smooshing someone else," protested Unla, "It isn't right. It is one man or the other! Not both! So, decide already!"

"I know mom, but I can't help feeling jealous. I know it is a stupid, irrational feeling, but it is an aspect of myself that I have difficulty controlling," said Carina sadly, "Today...I showed up to Bruno's work uninvited and I made a scene, all because I didn't believe him when he told me that he was working."

"I think the root cause of your jealousy problems is separation anxiety," said Unla trying to diagnose her daughter, as doctors often do with their offspring, "You feel that Kain will stop being your friend, if he finds himself another. Friendships between men and women are complicated by the expectation that they must grow into something else. What you have is a beautiful friendship. Treasure it for what it is, and stop trying to make it something else."

"You are right mom," said Carina agreeing with her mother, "The thing I had with Kain is nothing more than a faraway dream. He changed, and I changed too, but our friendship somehow survived our metamorphosis into insufferable adults. That is something to be thankful for."

"That's a good girl," said Unla hugging her daughter before kissing her on the forehead, "Next time you are feeling jealous, call me. We will talk through your emotions."

Carina went to bed after having a heart to heart conversation with her mother. She saw the mystery bag with the spell inside of it. She threw it in the garbage can. Carina resolved to deal with her issues like a normal person. Come morning, she sprung out of bed with the intention of using the spell on Bruno, instead. When she checked the garbage can, she frowned when she noticed that her mother had taken out the trash. Carina ran out of the house in her pajamas to make it to the curb before the garbage truck stopped at their house. After dumpster diving, Carina fetched the mystery paper bag that was now coated in leftovers, and other nasty stuff. She cleaned the exterior of the bag as best she could. Much to her dismay, the mystery bag came apart. The bag wasn't supposed to be opened. It was supposed to be thrown into the river on the new moon, completely closed.

With the spell broken, all that was left to do was look inside the paper bag. There was a sheet of paper inside of it. The paper read: A spell to bind the destiny of Carina and Bruno.

CHAPTER 4

Swords

Carina returned to her house in order to shower and eat breakfast. Her mother frowned when she saw Carina covered in garbage juices. Carina removed her pajama, and her mother placed it inside a trash bag to throw it away. There was no salvaging it. After scrapping the grime for one hour, Carina succeeded in removing the garbage juices from her hair and body. She was a little peeved, but her mind was also filled with childlike wonder. Irina was the genuine article.

"Mom. I want to show you something," said Carina leaving the shower.

"If it is something you fetched from the garbage can, please keep it to yourself," said Unla shaking her head sadly, "Do you want pancakes?"

"Always," said Carina, "On second though no. I ate way too much last night."

"I polished up your resume while you slept," said Unla, "We can start looking for a Residency when you are ready."

"Next month, mom, next month. I am in vacation mode! When you are in vacation mode, we speak about literally anything else," said Carina.

Mother and daughter ranted a bit about possible activities. Unla wanted to linger a little longer, but unlike her big baby, she had to work. A bored Carina finished her breakfast. She saw the time and she decided to go upgrade her wardrobe. She looked through her contact list. It was a Wednesday and everyone was at work. The only person not doing anything was Kain. Carina texted him to see what he was up to.

"I am busy. My father exploded his work computer," texted Kain.

"How?" asked Carina giggling, "With dynamite?"

"His computer is infested by Blaster Worm," texted Kain, "It is going to take me a while to fix this mess!"

In the car dealership, Kain was struggling to repair the computer. Kain protested, "Dad? What did you do? Were you looking at porn?"

"I wouldn't even know where to look for that," said Jack meekly, "I am not computer literate."

"Tell me step by step what happened," said Kain rubbing his temple.

"I don't know what happened," said Jack meekly, "I was adding products to craiglist just like you taught me, when the computer started acting up, and then, it got worse and worse. Till it exploded."

"Blaster Worm takes days to fully infect the computer," said Kain, "The other PCs in this establishment are probably infected too."

Sure enough, other coworkers started reporting that their computers were malfunctioning. With Kain busy, Carina decided to give Eugenia a call. She was a University student, and if she hadn't graduated yet, she was probably busy. Eugenia looked at the unfamiliar number. Her curiosity got the better of her.

"Hey, Eugenia, it is me Carina," said Carina.

"Kain's girlfriend? Nothing happened," said Eugenia.

"It's fine. Don't worry about it," said Carina, "Kain and I, we used to date in high school, but that is about it. I was thinking that we could go on a double date. I will take my new boyfriend Bruno, and you can go out with Kain."

"We are we going exactly?" said Eugenia.

"I don't know yet. That is why I need you here to help brainstorm an activity," said Carina.

Eugenia after examining her "busy" schedule agreed to go shopping with Carina. She hoped to get intel from the maiden in order to make it easier to get into Kain's boxers. Kain was the first man that had been immune to Eugenia's Super Model Body. Eugenia looked at her face with her compact mirror, and she frowned when she saw imaginary wrinkles. The two maidens rendezvous in the Dolphin Mall. Their first stop was at Victoria Secrets. They picked out 20 different items, and then they went to share the same dressing room, in order to critique each other's bodies, while they gossiped.

"So, who is Bruno?" asked Eugenia removing her dress.

"He is a friend of my cousin Rodrigo. We met at my graduation party," said Carina.

"Is he sexy?" asked Eugenia.

"I wouldn't know," said Carina, "I still haven't sealed the deal."

"That's a shame," said Eugenia, "If it makes you feel better, your Kain is giving me the roundabout. How did you get into his pants?"

"When I first had Kain, he was a sweet little virgin," said Carina smiling at that happy memory, "I was more experienced, more experienced in heartbreak and disappointment. My first boyfriend was a real jerk. He cheated on me with practically every girl in school. Sigh…Kain is the only man that has ever been faithful to me."

"You still love him?" said Eugenia looking at her reflecting. She was trying to decide whether this red undergarment would work on Kain.

"I still love that Kain," said Carina, "Kain…he changed. And I do not know what happened. Kain never talks about what bothers him. He bottles it all up, until he explodes."

"Not violently?" asked Eugenia worried.

"Nah! If there is one thing I like about Kain is that he barks, but he never bites. And even when he barks, he is polite about it. Like that night he interrogated you. When he gets like that, I just stop talking to him, until he calms down," said Carina trying to squeeze into her a pink undergarments, "Does this lingerie make me look fat?"

"Define fat," said Eugenia, "There are different standards of beauty…and…"

"If I wanted someone to lie to me, I would have gone shopping with Kain," said Carina, "I want an honest critique of my body. Does this this ensemble make me look fat or not."

Eugenia reached into her purse and she brought out her reading glasses. She pretended to examine Carina like one would do a piece of artwork. At the end of her careful examination, Eugenia came to this conclusion, "The thin bra compresses your flesh too much. It gives the illusion that you have boobs on your back."

"Thank you for the honest critique," said Carina removing her bra, to try on a different ensemble.

"So, how was your first time with Kain?" asked Eugenia trying on a different lingerie set, "I have never slept with a Virgin before. What was it like to be the first of someone?"

"Let me paint you the scene: I had just caught my boyfriend cheating on me, so, I went home with Kain in order to sulk. With his help, I removed from my room all mementos of the life I had tried to forge with the first man I fell in love with…I vented to Kain for hours about all my shattered hopes and dreams. I was wrapped inside his strong muscular arms, while he petted my hair lovingly, and then…" said Carina while she passed her hand over her lips.

"He kissed you," said Eugenia giggling.

"I kissed him," said Carina sighing.

"Did he kiss you back?" asked Eugenia.

"No...no, he didn't," said Carina, "Sigh...That was the night I tainted our beautiful friendship."

Eugenia was quiet while the digested everything Carina had said. Changing the subject, Eugenia said, "Have you ever been to Faena?"

"Is it expensive?" asked Carina.

"I am friends with one of the showgirls," said Eugenia, "So, we can sit up front, for 80 bucks a head."

"Showgirls?" asked Carina.

"Hey! Get your head out of the gutter, Carina!" protested Eugenia getting dressed in her street clothing. She set aside the lingerie she had liked, "Faena is like an Ecchi version of Cirque du Soleil. It is the perfect marriage of artistry and eroticism."

"No need to oversell the place," said Carina, "If anything, your double date idea seems like the most inspired one."

"What were you going to suggest we did together as a couple?" asked Eugenia.

"I was going to suggest we go roller skating," said Carina.

"OMG! I love roller skating!" said Eugenia, "Whenever I walk my dogs, I always do it while wearing roller skates."

The shopping day passed peacefully enough. Eugenia was naturally charismatic, and not prone to hold grudges for very long. She seamlessly integrated with Carina's other friends. On Friday, the maidens got together at the hair salon to gossip. The guys were already on board with the double date idea. On Saturday, Carina visited Kain to make certain he had something nice to wear. When she drove up to the place, she was greeted by the sound of drumming and the electric guitar. Arjuna and Jack were jamming together in the back porch. Carina texted Kain in order to get him to open the door. Kain jogged back to the house.

"Are you having a party?" asked Carina.

"Nothing of the sort," said Kain entering the house, "My father was driving me crazy, so, I told him that he could jam with his friend. When he plays his music, he completely forgets that I exist."

"How was he driving you crazy?" asked Carina.

"By paying me too much attention," said Kain, "If I so much as even sneeze, he is calling 911. The way he babies me, it is irritating. He irritates me."

"He is probably trying to make up for lost time," said Carina smiling warmly, "Now that he is cured of his addiction, he can finally be a father to you."

"He took too long to get cured of being a selfish asshole," said Kain clenching his fist, "I am an adult, I no longer need a father."

"Come on, Kain! Don't be like that," said Carina, "You have no idea how hard it is for a person to conquer an addiction. Withdrawal symptoms hurt Kain. Do you remember how you felt after your accident? Do you remember the dizziness, and the pain you felt in your limbs? Well, imagine feeling that all the time…"

"You didn't just come here to play Devil's Advocate?" asked Kain changing the subject.

"I came to help you pick out clothing for the double date," said Carina going to Kain's bedroom to look through his closet, "Do you have a tuxedo?"

"Just the one I wore for my grandpa's funeral," explained Kain sitting down on the bed.

Carina looked through Kain's closet. She brought out the funeral tuxedo and just looking at it made her feel depressed. She thought a moment and then she came up with this idea. She was going to have Kain borrow one of Bruno's tuxedos. Carina went to porch and she informed Jack that she was taking

Kain. Carina got inside her car and her friend sat down beside her. She had been itching for an excuse to see Bruno's living arrangements. Bruno did not disappoint. His small Condo was a total pigsty. There entire living room was littered with file boxes. There only reason why there weren't dirty dishes was because Bruno survived on junk food. Bruno led Carina to his bedroom. The maiden frowned when she saw the cluttered mess was also present in the bedchambers. The apartment stunk of dust. Bruno opened the closet door and there where his tuxes. They were religiously kept safe inside plastic bags.

"Wow! You really are poor!" said Carina thoughtlessly.

"I never said I was rich," said Bruno nonchalantly, "Your family just assumed that I was rich because of my profession. This place may pale in comparison to your castle, but it is all mine."

"My Auntie's Mansion isn't that big. And you can afford a big place when everyone works and lives together," said Carina.

"It must be nice to have a big family you can rely on," said Bruno with a hint of envy in his voice. He brought out a blue tux, and then he changed the subject, "Try this on...This fits a little tight on me, so it should be a perfect fit for you. And don't worry, the tux just came back from the dry cleaner."

Kain undressed and he tried on the tux. While he was busy as thus, Bruno opened his drawers to look for a tie that complimented Kain's grey eyes. Carina observed these proceedings with mild curiosity. She was relieved that Bruno had accepted that her best friend. In order to look busy, Carina tidied up Bruno's bed. Carina then took out the vacuum from the closet, and she got to work on the living room.

"She only cleans when she is nervous," translated Kain.

"I figured as much," said Bruno coming over with a tie. Once it was set just right, Bruno patted Kain's shoulders before saying, "You are all set. Carina, if you are done disorganizing my things, come over and see if you like how this tux looks."

Carina stopped cleaning for a second and peeped her head into the bedroom. Kain looked extremely handsome in his deep blue tuxedo. The silvery ash tie completed the look. Now, all that Kain was missing were the shoes. Bruno brought out a pair of shoes. He took Kain's feet and he frowned when he noticed that the shoes were too big for Carina's friend. Kain decided to wear his funeral shoes. With the problem of the wardrobe out of the way, all that remained was to wait till nightfall. For logistics' sake, all were going to go ride in Eugenia's car. She lived in a beach front property close to the Florida Keys. It would be easy for her to pick up the others on the way to Miami Beach Faena Theater. The first person to be picked up was Bruno. He lived closets to Eugenia's house. Instead of driving herself, Eugenia had dusted off the family limousine. Eugenia was dolled up with her war paint and her most expensive jewelry. As part of her peacocking strategy, she wore a golden sequin dress that left little to the imagination.

During the drive to Kain's house, Bruno and Eugenia made small talk. Bruno did most of the talking. He ranted about his work as a defense lawyer. He gave the perfect impression of someone that cared about justice. Eugenia was impressed that Carina had managed to get herself such a handsome, eloquent devil. She began to wonder what was Carina's appeal. Her competition was short, chubby, and whenever there was a bit of humidity Carina's hair went crazy. Eugenia went to cross her legs, and she waited to see if Bruno paid any attention to this action. Much to her surprise, the man maintained eye contact.

"How old are you Bruno?" asked Eugenia.

"I am 32," lied Bruno. His true age was 27. Bruno was flexible with his age depending on whom he spoke to.

"Ah…that explains it," said Eugenia.

"What does?" asked Bruno pretending to be confused.

"Nothing," said Eugenia, "We are already here. Go get Kain."

Bruno walked up to Kain's house and he rang the bell. When he opened the door, a cadaver looking a man answered the door. Jack said, "Who are you?"

"I am here for Kain," said Bruno.

Jack looked at Bruno over the top. His face turned pale and then he went to call up his son. Jack knocked on Kain's door. He said nervously, "El Che is looking for you Kain."

"Ah…it is almost time then," said Kain finally leaving his bedroom.

"Look at you son! What a handsome devil! Here, let me fix this for you," said Jack smiling happily seeing Kain in his blue tux. Jack took a moment to fix his son's tie. Before Kain could flee from the situation, his father brought a bit of hair gel from the bathroom, and he styled his son's hair the way he liked.

"I am going to be late for my date," said Kain moving away from his father.

"There is no food in the fridge," protested Jack.

"Yes, there is," said Kain.

"I don't know how to cook," said Jack, "And I don't want to eat chips or cereal."

"Here is some money," said Kain opening his wallet to give his father a few twenty dollar bills, "And I have a few takeout menus in the pantry. See if there is something you like."

"How long are you going to be out?" asked Jack.

"I don't know. It depends on how the night goes," said Kain running towards the front door.

"Wait Kain!" yelled Jack running after his son, "Take this camera! Take lots of pictures.

"Alright dad!" said Kain accepting the gift.

Once Kain was out of the house, he breathe in a sigh of relief. Bruno opened the door for Kain to help him enter the limousine. Jack saw the scene and after putting all the clues together, he came to the conclusion that his son Kain had come out of the closet. He called up Gent to tell his brother what he had seen. Gent didn't want to jump to conclusions, but the signs were there. Jack called his sponsor Arjuna, and the guy also agreed with him. The gossip was picked up by Gent's wife Stacie, and it circulated among all those within her social circle.

Kain sat down beside Eugenia, completely indifferent to her beauty. His last interaction with his father had left him extremely irritated. Eugenia brought out a club soda and she placed it against Kain's face to get his attention. The cold brought him back to the present. He turned to look at Eugenia and he blushed when he saw the getup she was sporting. Eugenia liked this reaction, and she laughed with glee at her success. Kain's sudden infatuation with Eugenia immediately died when he heard her laughter. The woman laughed the same as his mother. Kain started to remembered how his mother used to give him Nyquil to make him fall asleep. She would do so whenever she wanted to leave the house, to go party with her friends.

"What's the matter?" asked Eugenia placing her hand in Kain's knee.

"Nothing…it is just…your laughter is the same as my mother," said Kain bitterly.

"Aw…you poor guy," said Eugenia hugging Kain lovingly, "There. There. Feel better?"

"A little," said Kain smiling shyly.

He accepted the cold soda Eugenia had offered. He opened the can and he gulped down the bubbly drink. The awkward silence lasted until Carina was picked up. The manic pixie entered the limousine bringing with her joy and merriment. She handed her mixtape to the driver, and then the speakers began to blast at full volume these lines: "Suavemente, besame!"

Bruno taking the hint embraced Carina and he slobbered her face with kisses. With her arrival, Kain's melancholy immediately dissipated. With Carina there, everything was alright in his world. Kain brought a camera from his coat pocket and he took photos of all of them having fun. The good vibrations carried them all the way to Faena Theater. They left the limousine and they walked through the entrance of the hotel. Thanks to traffic, they only had 20 minutes to look about. Outside in the pool area, there was a golden mammoth. Carina lingered a little looking at the creative piece of artwork. Kain brought out his camera and he took a photo of Carina and Bruno. Bruno placed his arm around Carina's waist. The maiden was sporting a green, draped collar wrap satin dress, the same hue as Bruno's green eyes. She wore her hair naturally curly, with her body punctuated by golden Successories. Bruno's tux was a stoic, wine colored ensembled.

"We better get going," said Carina looking at her watch.

Eugenia walked ahead, leading the way. The interior of the theater had a cozy cabaret feel, with the small stage with red curtains. The party sat on a round table that faced the stage. Bruno pushed the chair for Carina, while Kain sat down without bothering to be chivalrous to his date. Eugenia was not used to this polite indifference. She thought of Kain's dead mother, and she figured that he was still moody because of the stiff. The menus came and Bruno frowned when he noticed that all meals costed more than 20 bucks. Eugenia ordered a little bit of everything, for her date. She owned Kain that much.

"I am a bit of a lightweight," said Kain looking at the drinks, "What do you recommend?"

Bruno asked, "Do you like sweet drinks or do you like the taste of alcohol?"

"I rather taste it as little as possible," said Kain.

"For you my friend, I recommend," said Bruno browsing through the menu, "The Caribou Lou."

"Oh!! That sounds sexy!" giggling Eugenia, "What do you recommend for me Bruno. I for one fancy the taste of lemon in my drinks."

"Then order a corpse reviver," said Bruno, "And for my little lady, I suggest a Havana Beach, and I will order the Strawberry-Coconut Daiquiri."

Bruno had chosen strong drinks for Kain and Eugenia. For himself and Carina, he had chosen light drinks.

"How do you know so much about drinks?" asked Carina.

"I learned all about them from my father," said Bruno.

"Was he a bartender?" asked Carina.

"He was an alcoholic," said Bruno. He complimented that truth, with a lie, "He died in a car accident."

"Do you miss him?" asked Carina.

"No," said Bruno dryly, "Why would I? He is an alcoholic."

The topic died when the curtain rose. The theme was Midsummer Night Dream. Titania entered the scene in a dress covered with stylized flowers. Titania was the main singer, who presented all the acts. For two hours, the friends forgot about their personal baggage. They enjoyed the music, the show, the food and the drinks. Just like Bruno had planned, Kain and Eugenia got really drunk. With both uninhibited and happy, they became boisterous and loud. Eugenia got on stage and she danced about with the other chorus maidens. At a certain point, she tripped due to her ridiculously high heels. Bruno caught her before she splattered against the floor. Eugenia giggled and she returned to her seat. Kain had become quite the shutterbug. He took plenty of photos to use as reference for his drawings.

"Stop playing with the camera, and watch the show," protested Carina.

"Let the kid have his fun," said Bruno placing his hand on Carina's knee.

The show came to an end and Eugenia paid for everything. Just like Bruno had planned. The party wabbled over to the front of the hotel to wait for the limousine to pick them up. Carina looked at the time, and she said, "It is only ten. Let's go do something else."

"Let's go night swimming!" suggested Eugenia.

"Let's not," said Carina remembering her dream.

"Aw! Come on! Carina! Stop being a party pooper!" protested Kain shacking Carina by the shoulder, "I wanna go swimming too!!"

The driver took them to the beach near Manolo restaurant. In the darkness, the four of them tiptoed towards the seashore. Due to the turtles, the beaches didn't have any lights at night. Even the moon didn't provide any light. Carina looked up at the sky and she saw that it was almost New Moon. Kain and Eugenia undressed and the two went for a night ducking. The cold water helped sober them up a bit. With both bodies locked in an embrace, Eugenia and Kain finally shared a kiss. Carina looked at the pair with a hint of envy in her eyes.

"Bruno! Stop being a gentleman and fuck me already!" commanded Carina.

"As you wish," said Bruno embracing Carina.

The two only got as far as third base. Just when Carina was finally enjoying herself, a scream in the darkness totally ruined the mood. Kain left the water carrying Eugenia who was in tears. For a moment, Carina thought that Eugenia had been bitten by a shark. In the darkness, Carina couldn't tell what was wrong. Bruno picked up the clothing and purses that had been left behind. With the baggage out of the way, the four of them made their way towards the limousine.

"It burns! It burns!" protested Eugenia, "Somebody do something!"

Kain stumbling back fell on something hard on the sand. This hard object made a clicking sound, thus hinting to the fact that

Kain had sat on a broken bottle. Bruno who was the only person that was somewhat sober picked up Eugenia to allow Kain to rise to his feet. In a whinny tone, Kain said shacking Carina by the elbow, "My ass hurts. Do something, Carina!"

"One problem at a time," said Carina, "First, let's make it back to the limousine."

The four of them made out of the darkness. Under the hale of the streetlamp, Carina saw what was wrong with Eugenia. She has been stung by a jellyfish. Carina brought out a tweezer from within her purse and she removed from Eugenia's back the long piece of tentacle. Based on the shape of the tentacle, the poor maiden was attacked by a Portuguese Man of War.

"Should I pee on it?" asked Bruno seeing the sting.

"No! Don't be stupid," protested Carina, "We need some hot water. Let's get inside the car."

"Carina! I need help too!" protested Kain crying.

Carina went to see about Kain. The back of his undergarments was bloody. When she lowered it, she saw a small piece of glass embedded in his left caboose. Carina removed the piece, and she sprayed some hand sanitizer over the tiny wound. This was going to have to do for now.

The driver awoke and he drove his wards to the nearest CVS to get hot water and some medicine. With the hot water, Carina was able to threat Eugenia's jellyfish wound. She gave a painkiller to Eugenia, and she added some antiseptic ointment on her back. Carina wrote down some instructions for Eugenia, and she left handed it to the driver. Kain's wound required two medical tapes in order to close up the gap. Once the patients were taken care of, the party made their way back home. The patients were lying down, waiting for the pain and the dizziness to pass. To cope with the sting, Eugenia had brought out the tequila from the cooler. She proceeded to get even more hammered with the hope that it would cure her of her pain.

"Impressive!" said Bruno giving a true smile.

"What is impressive?" asked Carina smiling coyly.

"You are impressive Carina," said Bruno before praising Carina's skills as a doctor.

"Flattery will get you everywhere mister!" said Carina giggling.

The limousine arrived at Carina's house. Bruno said, "I am going to make certain these two make it to bed. We can pick up where we left off tomorrow."

Carina kissed Brone and she said, "Tomorrow it is then!"

The next stop was Kain's house. Bruno placed his coat over Kain's shoulder. After fumbling with the keys, he was able to open the front door. The alarm sounded and thus waking up Jack. He ran to the door with a bat and he went to bash the head of the intruder. Before he got a chance to do so, Kain's hand reached for the light switch.

"What did you do to my son!" protested Jack still holding the metal bat.

"He drank...he drank a little bit too much," said Bruno unprepared for such a hostile reception, "And then he went night swimming."

"It's fine dad," said Kain trying to stand on his two feet.

Between the two, they got Kain into the bathroom. Kain turned on the shower in order to wash away the seawater. When Bruno became certain he was alright, he returned to the limousine to deliver Eugenia home. The cold shower helped Kain recover some of his senses. He emptied his bowels on the shower. Kain forgetting to turn off the shower left the bathroom completely in the nude.

Trembling in the darkness, Kain said, "Dad. Can you get me a towel?"

Jack was already ready with the Towels. He tried Kain as quickly as possible, and he wrapped a towel over his head. As soon as

Kain's head touched the pillow, he immediately fell asleep. Jack went to the bathroom to tidy up. He frowned when he saw blood droplets on the floor. Kain's wound had reopened during his car ride. He had fixed the stitches while he bathed, before returning to the bed. The blood droplets didn't inspire Jack much confidence. He picked up the bloody underwear and he chugged it into the garbage can. Once everything in the bathroom was clean, Jack went to see about his son. Kain had a happy smile painted on his lips.

CHAPTER 5

Pentacles

The following morning came and Kain awoke with a serious hangover. He looked at the clock and he frowned seeing that it was almost noon. He found by his nightstand a can of coconut water, a banana and a Tylenol. Kain guessed this was his father's home remedy for a hangover. After drinking the water, and eating the banana, he felt as if life was returning to his sore limbs. The medicine also helped. While he ate, he looked through the photos he had taken with his new digital camera. He laughed seeing all the nudie photos he had taken.

He saved all the photos into his computer. He then sent to Carina all the tasteful photos he had taken of his friends and the show. In the photographs, he saw that he had gone to the beach. He didn't remember swimming in the ocean, nor did he remember kissing Eugenia. He smiled as he remembered other bits and pieces of the night before.

Since he was feeling better, he decided to show up for work. Kain went to the driveway and he frowned when he remembered that his patrol car had gone up in smokes. Without his father home, he needed someone to give him a ride. His first instinct was to bother Carina, but he felt that he had abused her kindness enough. After hesitating, Kain called up his father Jack.

"Dad, I need a ride to work," said Kain.

"Maybe you should continue resting," said Jack answering the photo, "You do not know how awful you looked when you came home last night."

"Was it that bad?" asked Kain.

Jack lowered his voice, "You came home with your undergarments, completely covered in sand, and blood. I was worried sick about you!"

"Carina's new boyfriend played a mean prank on me. I asked him to suggest me a low alcohol drink, but he did the complete opposite…hahaha…We got super wasted, dad. After, the show we went night swimming in shark invested waters!" said Kain giggling as he remembered more of the night before. He added turning serious, "I think one of us got bit. I don't remember who. Thank God Carina was there to provide first aid."

Jack said, "If you had a crazy night, that is all the more reason to rest."

"I feel fine," said Kain, "If you are not going to take me to work I will just call someone else."

"Have it your way, son," said Jack, "I will go pick you up right… boss…I am taking my lunch break now."

Kain waited twenty minutes. It was convenient that his father worked so close to home. During the ride to the police station, Kain ranted about what he remembered of the show. The two were going to look through the photos after work. At a certain point, Jack asked about Kain's date. The two had a hardy laugh over the misunderstanding.

"Whether you choose to be with Eugene or Eugenia, you have you father's full support," said Jack still giggling.

"Don't even joke about that, dad," said Kain, "You know how

people are."

"Yeah," said Jack sadly, "I need to make a lot of calls, to tell them that it was a false alarm."

"Don't bother," said Kain, "Let them think whatever they want about me."

"But Kain…" protested Jack.

"Fine. For the sake of peace, I am going to send you this photo. You can forward it to grandma, and everyone else who doubts my masculinity," said Kain sending a photo of himself and Eugenia.

Jack looked at the photograph of Eugenia and he began to drool. When the two arrived at the police station, there was a PR Event. Eugenia's father was there with a big check donation for the Men in Blue. Jack drove to his work, while Kain went into his office to clock in a few hours. While he was busy with paperwork, Eugenia entered with her father into the Police Station. Gent was giving their benefactors a tour. He was explaining to them how they were going to use the money they had donated. Eugenia smiled when she saw Kain.

"Good afternoon, Kain!" said Eugenia, "You actually made it to work today."

"Barely," said Kain, "My skull is split in two, but other than that I am more or less in one piece."

"I was thinking that maybe after work, we can pick up where we left off," said Eugenia smiling coyly.

"Truth be told, I only agreed be your date because Carina pressured me into it," said Kain.

"Oh, bother. So I am not your type?" asked Eugenia.

"You are very beautiful woman Eugenia," said Kain stating a fact, "What little I remember of last night was quite amusing."

"How old are you Kain?" asked Eugenia.

"I turned 23 recently," said Kain.

"Then why do you talk like an old man?" asked Eugenia.

"I was mostly raised by my grandpa," explained Kain.

"Mostly? And before your grandpa, who raised you?" asked Eugenia.

"I lived for two years with uncle Nathan, but then he got a job offer he couldn't refuse, so he dumped me with my grandparents. And before Nathan I lived with Uncle Gent, until his born son was born. And before uncle Gent I lived with Aunty Elizabeth for five months. I spent a year with an old lady whose name I don't remember," said Kain, "And before the old lady, I lived with my parents."

"Wow! And I thought my family sucked," said Eugenia smiling warmly, "After my mother died, I saw an endless parade of secretaries that father insisted I call mom. Eunice is the only one that stayed, and mainly it was because she got pregnant."

"I truly wish you wouldn't aerate our dirty laundry to every degenerate you meet," said Michael butting into the conversation.

"Dad...you know Kain," said Eugenia.

"Right...your date," said Michael, "The one who couldn't be bother to escort you home."

"It is hard to escort someone, when you can barely walk yourself," retorted Kain.

"Great! Just wonderful!" yelled Michael, "Now instead of a drug dealer, you are dating a drunkard, but I suppose I should consider this an upgrade!"

With the glove thrown, Eugenia began to bicker with her father completely oblivious of all who were watching. As soon as they heard the clicking of a camera, they settled down to continue their argument in the privacy of their home. The two left in a huff both going their separate ways, in separate cars. With the distractions gone, Kain returned to his paper work. Just when he was finally making progress, he had a new interruption.

"Is this yours?" asked a reporter holding a sketchbook with the book binding partially burnt off.

"Yes! Yes it is!" said Kain recovering his sketchbook, "I was afraid it had gone up in smokes with my patrol car."

"If you have artistic tendencies, why did you become a police officer?" asked the reporter sitting down before Kain. He was looking for a fluff piece, and interviewing the artist police officer who almost went up in smokes seemed like an easy topic.

"And you are?" asked Kain.

"I am Alexia. I am a reporter," said Alexia, age 25. His true name was Alexander Warren, but he preferred to be called Alexia. He also preferred to wear women dresses when not working, and at night he preferred the company of men. He had a medium built, had dyed blonde hair and the type of boring face one never gives a second glance to.

"Nice to meet you Alexia," said Kain shacking his hand, "Thank you for recovering my sketchbook, but I have a lot of work to do."

"I have something else for you," said Alexia digging into his satchel. He brought out a yearbook, "We went to high school together. We were in my same journalism class. Do you remember me?"

"Not really," said Kain being honest, "I only took that class because all the other electives I had chosen were full."

"It figures that you wouldn't remember me. We only spoke whenever we had to collaborate on an assignment. I want to interview you, Kain," said Alexia. The way he said the name Kain had an almost silky inflection to it.

"Why?" asked Kain, "I haven't done anything with my life worth knowing. If you want to get to know a real hero, go bother Detective Farley."

Kain brought out his headsets and he played Korn at full volume. The music drowned out the noise of the world. If it wasn't for uncle Gent, Kain could have easily stayed there working till the following morning. The two chatted a bit about last night's date. He insisted on getting all the sordid details. Sadly, Kain remembered very little of the night before.

"I know that your new girlfriend is a hot piece of ass, but don't let her pressure you into becoming a drunkard," said Gent sternly.

"I didn't mean to drink so much," said Kain, "It won't happen again."

"It better not happen again," said Gent sternly, "In order news, we are having a little get together this Saturday to celebrate mom's birthday. Everyone is going to be there. You can bring your new girlfriend over, but only if she promises to behave."

"Or we could just not invite her," said Kain, "This is a family affair after all."

"Too late," said Gent, "I already invited her. You hit the jackpot Kain! Eugenia is hot and rich! Good things are finally coming your way!"

Kain sighed with frustration. He didn't want anything to do with Eugenia, but the entire world was conspiring to ram her down his throat. Before departing, Gent gave the keys to Kain's new car. Kain went to the new car and he tried it on for size. He circled around the parking lot a bit, before driving home. He stopped at the red light. When the light turned green, something unexpected happened. He started suffering from shortness of breath. This was followed by heart palpitations. With a trembling hand, Kain called Carina.

When she didn't answer, he called Unla. Unla always had her phone nearby, for her patients would sometimes call her at odd hours of the night. Unla only needed to hear Kain's breathing to guess what was happening to him. Together, they did breathing exercises till the panic attack passed. He tried to get past that street, but he wasn't able to. Instead, he turned towards a nearby gas station. He called his father and he told him that his new car had broken down. He needed a ride home. Once Kain was in the safety and security of his house, he breathe in a sigh of relief. Kain gave himself a cat bath, and then he started making dinner. Sitting down in the living room waiting for his food was Jack. He was busy watching reruns of Buffy the Vampire Slayer.

"Unla called," said Jack, "She told me about your panic attack."

"I guess the HIPAA Laws don't mean anything to her," said Kain while seasoning the chicken.

"Those laws only apply to official patients," reasoned Jack, "And it is not as if she has your medical record."

"If she did, she would probably suggest I spend some time in the madhouse," said Kain starting to fry it, "Still, it is refreshing to see a doctor that truly cares about the wellbeing of others."

"True doctors are few and far between," said Jack agreeing with his son. He sighed for a moment, and he said, "What's going to happen if you are never able to drive again?"

"I went an entire week without driving, and it didn't changed anything about my life," said Kain.

"Driving a car is about having freedom, Kain," insisted Jack.

"Freedom to do what exactly?" asked Kain dryly, "Dinner is ready by the way."

The topic died as soon as the food was served. Jack ranted about selling his first car. Once dinner was concluded, the two settled down to watch television. At a certain point, Kain said, "I go to sleep around ten. If you want to practice the guitar a bit before going to bed, I don't really mind."

"But then you won't be able to watch television," said Jack meekly.

"I can play video games instead, or I can read a book, or I can draw. Unlike you, I have more than one hobby," said Kain coldly.

"For me, it isn't a hobby. Playing the guitar makes me happy. When I play my music, all the problems in the world ebb away. Gent's wife doesn't let me play the guitar when her kids are around. She doesn't want her children to follow in my footsteps. Whenever Gent isn't around, she treats me like a piece of furniture," vented Jack.

"That frosty bitch hates everyone that didn't come out her vagina," said Kain.

The two bonded over their mutual disdain of Gent's wife Stacie. The following day came and Jack drove his son to work after their morning routine. While Kain was busy with his paperwork, Jack went to speak to Gent about how to help Kain get past trauma. Unla had suggested for Kain exposure therapy, to help threat his anxiety.

"...I don't know Jackie," said Gent, "Your son is allergic to therapy."

"But he trusts Unla. When he wasn't feeling well, he called her up first," said Jack, "So, maybe she can give him the help he so desperately needs."

"I don't know...Jackie," said Gent sighing.

"Maybe, she can give him therapy without him knowing that he is seeing a therapist," suggested Jack trying to be clever.

"I don't know...maybe..." said Gent, "I don't know...Jackie. I don't know..."

Jack's watch began to beep. He needed to head back to his work, "I need to go now. Text me when you finally know."

"Look at you, finally being responsible! When do you get paid?" asked Gent.

"On a weekly basis," said Jack, "Plus commissions whenever I am lucky enough to sell a car."

The hours rolled lazily by. Close to noon, Kain was bashing

his head against the table. He was bored to tears of doing paperwork. After brainstorming an activity for his nephew, Gent came up with this idea. He could go on patrol with one of the rookie cadets to show him the neighborhood. He needed to pair up Kain with someone dull, but enthusiastic, someone who would obey his nephew's orders without questioning him.

"Officer Zidanta Adel report for duty," said Gent.

Zidanta had ebony skin, a perfect beefcake body, brown hair, and intense copper eyes. He claimed to be Egyptian, but he was in fact born in the States. As an orphan, who grew up in hundreds of foster homes, he wasn't the most sociable. Zidanta did an army salute, as soon as he entered Gent's office.

"At ease, soldier," sighed Gent wearily, "Why do they send all the weird ones to my department? You are going on a ride along. My nephew is going to show the extent of our jurisdiction."

"Sir, yes, sir!" said Zidanta with a fake smile painted on his lips.

"Just get out of my sight, and stop it with that stupid salute," said Gent, "We are the police force, not the army."

Zidanta went over to Kain's workstation to inform him of the ride along, assignment. The two went to the parking lot. Zidanta frowned when he noticed that Kain sat in the passenger seat. Zidanta realized that his true mission was to be the chauffeur of Gent's Golden Child.

"You can drop me off at Camillus House. I will call you when I am ready to return to my workstation," said Kain meekly.

"That accident really messed you up, didn't it?" asked Zidanta punching in the address for the nearest Camillus House.

"I am sorry I am such a burden," said Kain sadly.

"It's fine," said Zidanta starting to drive, "You don't need to apologize for something you cannot control."

The two spent the rest of the ride in silence. Kain went inside Camillus House and he made his way towards the kitchen. Back when his grandpa was alive, the two would go once a week to Camillus House to make food for the homeless. Since Kain was missing his grandpa, he decided to visit the place on a whim. Due to his officer's uniform, the homeless inside the eating area became tense when he walked into the room. He received the same lukewarm reception in the kitchen area. The moment he putted on an apron, all those assembled relaxed. The police officer wasn't there to arrest anyone.

He took over soup duties. Once it was seasoned to perfection, he served all those waiting in line, before serving a bowl of soup for himself. When one of the oldest residents tried it, the light of recognition fell upon his face.

The man exclaimed with his toothless mouth, "You are Kain! Raphael's grandson! We haven't seen you in ages. How have you been? How is your grandpa?"

"He died three years ago," said Kain, "Today is the anniversary of his death."

"How did he died?" asked a very gossipy maiden.

"Heart attack. He was angry that I was wasting my so called potential working as a mechanic. While he was arguing with my uncle and grandma about my lack of a future, he started feeling ill, and then he dropped dead," said Kain dryly, "Grandpa had a very short fuse. He would still be alive if he hadn't wasted so much energy being angry all the time."

"Did you have potential Kain?" asked Eugenia sitting down beside him to gossip, "Fancy meeting you here."

"Hi…stalker. Don't you have anything better to do than chase me all over Miami?" asked Kain.

"My pride will not allow me to leave you alone," protested Eugenia, "Today you will be mine! I have my Volkswagen parked outside. After you finish your soup, you can come over to have dessert."

"Sigh…duty calls," said Kain getting up to leave with Eugenia.

"It was nice seeing you again, Kain," said a homeless man.

"Don't be a stranger," said a little old lady.

Kain entered Eugenia's hot pink Volkswagen. She closed the pink curtains, and she turned on a Pink Floyd Vinyl Record. More specifically, the it was The Wall album. The song being playing was "Hey You". Despite Eugenia's best efforts, she wasn't able to get a rise out of Kain. He simply laid there with a blank expression on his face, waiting for it to be over.

"Why don't you like me, Kain?" whined Eugenia.

"Being rejected is not the end of your the world," said Kain getting dressed, "A beautiful, rich heiress like you should have no problem in finding herself her own prince charming."

He left the car and he closed the door before Eugenia had a chance to protest. Eugenia stopped with her crocodile tears. When she felt herself alone, she grabbed onto the car seat, and she started kicking and screaming. Once her fit subsided, she went to the driver's seat. She looked through the rearview mirror and she saw Kain starring at her door.

She lowered the window, and she said, "Do you need a ride officer?"

"Yes. My coworker had a family emergency, so he won't be able to pick me up," said Kain coming over to sit beside Eugenia. The two rode in silence. During a red light, Kain asked, "So when you do not get your way, you throw yourself into hysterics?"

"Pretty much," said Eugenia extremely ashamed of her childish behavior.

"Does it work?" asked Kain.

"It used to," said Eugenia, "Now, my tantrums just annoy people. My stepmom wants me to spend some time in the sanitarium."

"Sanitariums only work if you perceive your behavior as a problem," said Kain.

"I take it you are a frequent visitor of such establishments?" said

Eugenia giggling.

"Nah. Rehab centers are more my style," said Kain, "When my father's career began failing, the chill pills he used to take before each concert because his main coping mechanism and the rest is history."

"Are the rehab centers bad?" asked Eugenia.

"Everything depends on the customer service. I can give you the name of the center that cured my father, but more than anything, you need support from your friends and family," said Kain.

"My father's idea of support is to yell my ear off. My real momma never raised her voice. She was kind, soft and gentle. Papa used to be nice, before she died. Now, the only two emotions he can express is bitter or angry," said Eugenia sighing sadly.

The conversation came to an end when Eugenia arrived to the Police Station. Kain gave his uncle a full report of his activity. Gent smiled happily seeing that his nephew had done something productive for his community. If he made it a lunch time habit, this could help erase some of the negative reputation that Police Officers enjoyed thanks to a few rotten apples. Kain concluded his shift. He smiled warmly seeing his father already there waiting to pick him up. The fact that his son was happy to see him meant the world to Jack. The two drove to the Senior Activity Center that Grandma Esther frequented. The three went to the cemetery to put flowers on Raphael's graveyard.

On the drive back, Esther said, "I spoke to a nice reporter today. He wanted to do a story about you, grandson."

"My life isn't that interesting," said Kain, "It is boring even."

"That is for the readers to decide," said Jack.

The three arrived to Kain's home. Waiting outside like a penitent was Alexia. The interview was merely an excuse for Alexia to get to know Kain. The two had met during Kain's Junior year. The old Kain was sociable, and always willing to lend a hand to anyone who asked. In his last year, Kain was often seen roaming the hallways. He spent more time in Carina's classes, than his own. He went from being the Valedictorian to a lackluster C student. Like his grandpa, his teachers mourned the fact that he was throwing away his future.

Kain began dinner, while he answered Alexia's questions. His biggest accomplishment was that he owned a house, and he saved some stupid kid from drowning. He talked about his hobbies, his favorite food and his workout routine.

"Are you a Democrat or a Republican?" asked Alexia.

"Is there a difference between the two?" asked Kain dryly.

"Please, let's not get into a political debate before dinner," protested Esther while she was watching Wheel of Fortune with Jack. From time to time, the two would try to guess the puzzle.

Alexia changing the subject said, "IF you are good at drawing, why didn't you got to art school?"

"These days being a good draftsman isn't enough to be considered an artist. You have to be what the art critics and the collectors consider original," said Kain adding the final touches to his Greek salad, "All I can manage is a soulless mimicry of the world."

"Is that what Mr. Peters told you?" asked Alexia, alluding to their art professor.

"Nah, he encouraged me to continue with my art education. So, I did my research and I came to the conclusion that Collage is for suckers. By the time you reach the last classes, they are worth an arm and a leg, and the teachers don't speak a lick of English, so you are basically paying to learn absolutely nothing. And don't even get me started with Tuition differentials..." said Kain before going on a long rant about everything that is wrong with the US education system.

"Wow...you really did research that topic Kain," said Alexia smiling sadly.

"So, you didn't go to college because you thought we couldn't afford it," said Esther sadly, "We could have dipped into the family savings to help pay for your education, Kain."

"That wasn't the only reason I chose not to bother with collage, grandma. Take aunty Elizabeth for example. After all her studying, the only high paying job she managed to get has nothing to do with her degree. She got her job thanks to a friend, not because her education. Without connections, your degree is worth the same as toilet paper," said Kain concluding his big speech.

The topic died when dinner was served. Alexia was impressed by Kain's wit. His old classmate was still as sharp as ever. Back when they were in high school, Kain's main contribution to the school paper were his cartoons. He illustrated whatever stupid idea popped into Alexia's mind. The first time Kain was ordered to write about a topic, his opinion piece gave the teachers and the students plenty to think about. Alexia still had a cutouts of Kain's articles and his original political cartoon drawings in his office, to inspire him to write with passion.

"Sigh…such a waste of potential," commented Alexia while eating dessert, "You could be doing so much with your life."

"You sound just like Carina," said Kain narrowing his eyes, "She too is only interested in the type of person that I could be. But we don't live in Could world! WE live in the REAL world. And in the REAL world, only the lucky few have their dreams come true!"

On this dour note, dinner came to an end. Kain left the table and he went to take his rage out on the unfortunate plates. It didn't matter how much he scrubbed the frying pan, the black stains just wouldn't be washed clean. Jack collected the leftovers and he handed them to Alexia, before opening the door for him. Alexia taking the hint left. The encounter with his old classmate had left Alexia really depressed.

"I am sorry Kain," said Esther apologetically, "Please don't be sad."

"It's fine grandma. You didn't do anything wrong," said Kain smiling sadly, "I am just sick of people looking down on me because I didn't get a College Degree."

"Do you want to go play with Carina?" asked Esther.

"Carina is busy with her new boyfriend," said Kain when he finished watching the dishes, "For the time being, she will only be able to hang out when we go on double dates."

As if feeling alluded to, Kain got a text from Carina, "I convinced Bruno to watch Betty la Fea with me. I want you to see it as well. Text me whenever there is a scene you like."

"She can't be serious," said Esther raising an eyebrow, after reading the message.

"You should watch it with me Grandma, you might grow to like it," said Kain.

"I will watch your telenovela with you," offered Jack.

The three settled down to watch Betty la Fea. While seeing the show, Kain reclined on the couch, and he rested his head on a pillow. The pillow happened to be beside his father Jack. Jack remembered that when Kain was small, he would always watch his shows while lying down. Almost by reflex, Jack proceeded to pet Kain's short hair lovingly. At first, Kain grimaced. The cold, delicate musician fingers succeeded in calming Kain's anger. Esther couldn't help but silently cry a little. She was just so happy to see father and son finally getting along. The moment lingered past the telenovela. With the two in perfect harmony with one another.

"Dad...when you fell from grace, why didn't you come back home?" asked Kain, "You didn't have mom. You didn't have fame. You didn't have money, but you had me father. I would have received you with open arms."

"I was ashamed. I sacrificed so much, and when my band split up, I just couldn't bring myself to face you...I kept thinking, once we are all millionaires, all the pain and humiliation is going to be worth it. Being a musician is not as glamourous as they make it seen in the movies. The record labels eat most of the profits. Going on tour is the only way we make money..." said Jack, before explaining all the factors that contributed to his failure.

Esther changing the subject asked Jack to play something on his guitar. Jack played an old Sesame Street tune that baby Kain used to find so amusing. The little jingle succeeded in dispelling the darkness that was weighting down their family. The following morning Kain awoke extremely early and in a good mood. He did his morning workout, and he baked cookies. He noticed that he was missing sugar for the frosting. He took his father's keys, and he drove to the nearby Publix. It was only when he returned home that he realized that he had managed to drive. In a good mood, he finished his baking project in time to make breakfast. Jack drove his son to work. Kain in a good mood attempted to drive his patrol car. The same anxiety attack manifested far worse than before. He called up Unla immediately.

"It's alright Kain. Breathe with me," said Unla.

Carina who was beside her mother opened her mouth to in inquire, but Unla placed her index finger to her mouth. Carina took the hint that her mother was busy working. Once Kain felt better, Unla finally answered Carina's inquisitive gaze.

"Your friend Kain is my new patient," said Unla flatly.

"What is wrong with him?" asked Carina pestering her mother for answer.

"It is called doctor patient confidentiality, and your specialty is small children. Which reminds me, I have already lined up for you a few interviews in clinics that will offer you a high paying residency," said Unla changing the subject.

"Fine. If you are not going to tell me, I am going to find out myself," said Carina calling Kain.

When Kain picked up the cellphone, Carina heard was her friend sobbing. Carina instead of going over to see her friend, she went to her first interview. This didn't surprise Unla in the slightest. Unla figured that her daughter was neglecting her friendship to avoid thinking of her dead father. Unla sighed wearily. As soon as her daughter left, she went to the attic to look at all the things belonging to her dead husband. Normally, she limited herself to looking through the old family album. This time Unla looked through everything. She found a box filled with the medical records of her husband's patients. He was always taking his work home. When she moved the box, her husband's name card fell to the floor.

Unla said his name out loud, "Juan Carlos…"

She repeated his name again, only louder. It felt nice to say his name, for it made her feel that he was still alive. Unla smiled sadly and then she brought downstairs the box with the medical records. She wanted to read them over the top, only to quench her medical curiosity. She had never bothered to actually read those files. Juan Carlos was a General Surgeon, who specialized in operating in small children. She discovered that Kain was a former patient of her husband.

"Let's see Kain, what were you brought in for…" said Unla raising an eyebrow, "Punctured lung caused by a broken rib…"

Unla saw the file photo of four year old Kain. He had gotten a major beating that had landed him in the hospital. Unla remembered a case that had gotten Juan Carlos extremely upset, so much so, that he had called Child Service. Unla was going to sit on that information, for the time being.

Back in the Police Station, Kain was filing documents and sorting through evidence. On top of his desk, he had two plastic boxes filled with his homemade cookie sandwiches. From time to time, Uncle Gent would check up on Kain. What Gent really wanted was a cookie, but he was too ashamed to ask for one. After hearing his belly rumblings, Kain finally guess what his uncle truly wanted. He opened one of the box of cookies and he handed one to uncle Gent.

"I need a ride uncle," said Kain meekly, "I was able to drive just fine this morning…but I don't know why I had that panic attack again."

"I spoke to Unla about it," said Gent, "She theorizes that the patrol car gives you bad flashbacks. Or maybe driving while sporting a uniform reminds you of your accident…she is currently devising an exposure therapy for you. According to the research she forwarded, it has been successful in reducing phobias…"

"How much is it going to cost us?" asked Kain dryly.

"Your work insurance should cover it," said Gent, "The therapy sessions will only eat away one hour of the day, and it mainly involves driving. She visits a lot of her patients in their homes, so, you can drive while she catches up with her paperwork."

Gent saw Kain clench his fists. With a defeated tone in his voice, Kain agreed to do exposure therapy. Lunch break came, so, Kain went outside to wait for his shrink. Instead of forcing Kain to drive his patrol car, Unla insisted that he be passenger instead. This would remove some of the immediate tension from the experience. At first, Unla was all business, but then she started to fiddle around with the controls of the patrol car. When she succeeded in turning on the siren, she had a hardy laugh when all the cars moved aside to let her pass.

"If you wanted to play with the patrol car, you didn't need to come up with such a convoluted scheme," protested Kain.

"You need to enjoy your happy moments, wherever you find them," said Unla, "Now, were did you want to go?"

"The Miami Herald. I printed out the directions from MapQuest," said Kain looking at his notes.

Along the way, Unla asked, "Did they ever catch that speeding driver that crashed into you?"

"Not really. Everyone saw everything and nothing at the same time," said Kain, "Which works just as well. I feel that our scarce resources are better spent elsewhere."

The two arrived at the Miami Herald. Unla decided to tag along. She figured that she might as well give her business card to every distressed person she ran into. The two caused quite the commotion when they entered the establishment. It was an uncommon to see a police officer and a doctor walking together. Kain asked the receptionist to speak to Alexia. Alexia was in the middle of adding the final touches to his article. Based on his malevolent smile, he was writing something awful. He saw a shadow looming over his shoulder. He jumped out of his skin when he saw Kain in full uniform. Kain attempted to speak, but he wasn't able to. Unla wrote in her notepad the words: Selective Mutism. Since things were becoming awkward, Kain delivered his Tupperware filled with cookies. He had taped a note to the bottom of the box that explained the nature of his gift. With the delivery concluded, Kain ran away from the embarrassing social situation. As soon as Kain left, all of Alexia's coworkers started crowding about him.

They all wanted to see what was in the box. Alexia guarding his present jealously went to lock himself up in the bathroom in order to get some privacy. This privacy was short lived. His boss who had the master key opened the bathroom, and he demanded that Alexia not keep any secrets from his coworkers. Florida Reporters by their very nature were a gossipy bunch, and most didn't believe in privacy. Alexia opened the box and he showed his boss the cookie sandwiches. Alexia remembered that Kain used to offer those boxes as tribute, whenever he missed a day of school. Alexia's coworkers jumped at his loot, only leaving a single cookie behind. Alexia tried the cookie sandwich.

Based on the warmth and texture, he realized that the cookies had been baked just a few hours ago. He pondered on the meaning of the offering. The cookies couldn't just be a simple apology for being rudely dismissed. Deep down, Alexia wanted the cookies to mean something more. Alexia returned to his workstation with the empty box that still had the letter hidden underneath. He read through his article about Kain's accident, and felt that it was a little mean spirited. He reedited the article to focus on Kain's positive qualities. When he lifted the box, he felt the letter. When the coast was clear, he read what he hoped was a love letter:

To my former classmate Alexia,

I wanted to apologize for my rude behavior last night. Ever since my accident, I haven't been feeling well. Every time I try to cross a red light, I am overcome by a shacking fit, followed by shortness of breath. The stress of these panic attacks have made me irritable. Even so, it was wrong for me to me to yell at you. I hope that you can forgive me.

Sigh,

Kain.

P.S: This weekend we are celebrating my Grandma's birthday. I would like for you to come, but you don't have to. We can talk about old times. And yes, there is going to be cake.

A childish smile manifested in Alexia's lips. He was reading too much into Kain's heartfelt apology. Alexia gave another polish to his article. He photocopied the letter he had received. He left visible the lines were Kain described how the accident had negatively impacted his life.

After visiting Alexia, Unla took Kain to Eugenia's house. When they arrived, the person who answered the door was Eugenia's half-sister Dorothy. The girl saw the police officer and the doctor, so, she naturally assumed that they were coming take Eugenia to Rehab. Kain sat there, and he waited for Eugenia to manifest. He guessed that Eugenia was tracking him somehow. He got confirmation of his suspicion when Eugenia waltzed into her home.

"I came here to apologize for my rudeness yesterday. I haven't been feeling well since my accident. I have even started seeing a shrink," said Kain as his ears started turning red, "So, I baked you a box of cookies, with the hope that things go back to normal."

"Give me those cookies," said Dorothy jumping at the present. She ate one and then she said, "That's strange…"

"What's strange?" asked Eugenia alarmed.

"I am not seeing anything. That is why it is strange," said Dorothy giggling.

"The only secret ingredient that you will find in these cookies is Sugar Cane," explained Kain.

Kain looked at an imaginary watch, and then he left the mansion. Like Alexia, Eugenia began to overanalyze the simple apology. She imagined that the cookies meant that Kain was in love with her. The sisters spent the rest of the afternoon gossiping about Kain. When Michael returned home from work, he frowned when he heard the topic of conversation. His first impression of Kain was terrible, and now he had both daughters gushing over the handsome police officer. At times like this, Michael felt like he was being punished through his daughters, for his womanizing ways. He called up his private detective to find dirt on Kain. The detective already had the information. Eugenia was paying him to stalk Kain and to investigate his past.

"Have you found any dirt on him?" asked Michael.

"A little," said detective Dave Parker. Parker was a former Agent Romeo, who got too old and fat to continue that line of work. Now that he was "retired" he amused himself by spying for the rich American socialites, "His father is a recovering addict…"

"I already know that! Everyone knows that," scoffed Michael.

"He illegally downloads movies and music," added Parker.

"So do I, and I am in the Fortune 500," hissed Michael.

"Fortune 600, last I checked," said Parker dryly.

At the age of 58, Parker was a short, bald, chubby man. His most distinguishing feature was his white mustache that contrasted with his watery raven eyes. He would often cosplay as a treasure hunter with a metal detector, in order to blend with the other retirees and vacationing tourists. His detector instead of listening for rare metals recorded all the conversations near his proximity.

"If you are done interrupting, let me tell you the rest..." said Parker before ranting about everything he discovered about Kain's past, "There are still some mysteries left to unravel. The one that intrigues me is the circumstances of his mother's death. How did a drunkard die of a Fentanyl overdose? Fentanyl has only become popular in recent years."

"I am not paying you to solve a cold file," said Michael, "Just answer me this one question. Is Kain a drunkard or an addict like his parents?"

"Based on his Publix receipts that I found while dumpster diving, he isn't a drunkard. He follows a strict daily routine, and this routine doesn't include buying drugs," said Parker, "If I had to find a fault in him, is the fact that he doesn't do anything as a cop. Though, I suppose that can't be helped, his uncle overprotects him."

"Does he hit women?" asked Michael.

"According to Carina, no. I also spoke to some of his past little girlfriends. All unanimously praised his manners, his tidiness, his beauty and his cooking skills. He rarely barks, but he never bites. As long as you do not pressure him, he is quite amicable," said Parker, "They all unanimously complained about his lack of passion, his miserly ways and his terrible fashion sense."

"Why is Eugenia chasing after Kain?" asked Michael.

"He is the first man that has ever rejected your daughter. The more he flees from her, the more she chases," said Parker, "The two were even in bed together, and she failed to get a rise out of him. Hahahaha..."

"And just how do you know something so intimate?" asked Michael visibly enraged.

"Wouldn't you like to know," said Parker before departing. Parker had a hidden camera inside Eugenia's van. It would amuse him to see the maiden engage in casual encounters.

After listening to Parker's tirade, Michael began to relax with the Kain situation. With some luck, she would get bored of chasing after Kain. Saturday came, and with it the end of summer. On the first day of August, Esther was going to be another year older. The party was done in Gent's house. What it lacked in size, it made up tenfold with the ridiculously large backyard populated by mango trees. Gent made a healthy surplus by selling the extra mangoes in the farmer's market. Gent rented a Pergola, some tables and a catering company to provide most of the food. This was the first time they were all going to be together as a family, in a long time. Jack arrived early with Kain, and Esther, the birthday girl.

The next guests to arrive were Carina and her boyfriend Bruno. After closing his case, Bruno finally some time to unwind. Despite being so busy, he made time to send Carina flowers, poems or little trinkets. They were not expensive gifts, but they at least showed Carina that he was invested in the relationship. Carina smiled seeing Kain with his father.

"I made that happen," whispered Carina to Bruno.

"What did you do?" asked Bruno worried.

"You make it sound as if I did a bad thing," giggled Carina before resting her head on Bruno's shoulder. She told Bruno how she had gotten Kain to make peace with his father. At the end of her tirade, she said, "The psychic told me that if I forced Kain to confront his father, he was going to lose his fear of commitment."

Carina felt her phone vibrating from an unknown number. When she answered it, a familiar voice said, "I said no such thing."

"Haaa!!" yelled Carina dropping the phone.

Bruno picked up the phone and he asked, "Who is it?"

"Wrong number," said Irina hanging up.

"Hehehe...I guess the psychic can sense when people are spreading lies about her," said Carina giggling, "All she said was that my actions were going to have unexpected consequences. I think I did a good thing. Without outside intervention, father and son were going to continue avoiding each other till the end of the days. Families are meant to be together. They help each other out, and they work together for a common goal."

"That may be true for your family Carina, but not all families operated under the same way," said Bruno. Changing the subject, Bruno said, "Look. There is Eugenia. Let's go say hi to her. We should go on another double date with her and your friend."

Carina saluted Eugenia and Michael who had self-invited to the party. Michael was there to observe and silently judge all the party guests. More and more guests started to arrive, and then the appetizers were brought out. The flow of the conversations was broken when an unexpected guest arrived fashionably late. That guest was Alexia. Alexia came sporting an elegant supper dress, painted nails, high heels and makeup. His short hair had been curled in order to give it a more feminine look. As soon as he let himself into the backyard, all stopped talking and they turned to look at him.

"It's fine. I invited him," said Kain breaking the silence, "We went to school together."

The conversations resumed immediately with nobody paying Alexia any mind. Alexia looked for Kain with his eyes, and he went to sit down at his table. Sitting beside Kain was Eugenia and Jack. Sitting in front of the young man was Bruno and Carina. Alexia sat in the only empty seat. The one that was beside Carina.

Carina was the one to address Alexia first. She asked the pertinent question, "When did you start wearing dresses?"

"Around the time when I discovered that I was a man in a woman's body," said Alexia shyly. He was always less confident whenever he went out into the world as his true self.

"We always knew that you liked men, Alexia," said Kain, "What we want to know is when did you start wearing dresses?"

"Hahaha…you always knew," giggled Alexia blushing.

"We knew," said Carina, "But we decided not to make a big deal about it."

"I don't have anything against men like you," said Esther, "It is a lifestyle choice, that I respect."

"I didn't choose this," said Alexia sadly, "I tried to be normal. I really did try, but I wasn't able to."

"Define normal," said Jack.

"What is considered normal changes with each generation," said Kain before going on a rant about all the horrible things that were considered normal back in the "good" old days.

"Thank God we don't live during the middle ages," said Alexia after listening to his old classmate's tirade.

Night fell and the music began to play. When it came time to bring out the cake, Jack made a quick stop to the car to bring out his guitar. He played Happy Birthday to his mother. Jack's family felt a little iffy about the situation, but since it was Esther's Birthday they tolerated his music. This is not to say that Jack played the Guitar badly. Rather, it was a visual reminder of the problems that followed after he tried to make a career out of his hobby. Jack was happy to be playing to an audience, even if it was a small audience of family and friends. Jack looked at his son and he was happy to see that Kain was also cheering for him. Everything was perfect, just as it should be.

After cake was served, Kain went to dance with Eugenia, while Carina danced with her Bruno. A bored Carina proposed a dance duel, and Eugenia decided to obliged. The first song they danced to was Cha-Cha-Cha. Over the years, Jack had expanded his repertoire. Back when he was still trying to make it, he learned other types of guitar styles to play for non-rock bands. These days he learned new songs to fill with music the emptiness he carried everywhere he went. Carina and Bruno won the first round. Eugenia wasn't too familiar with Latin dances, so, she was naturally at a disadvantage. When Eugenia botched the Merengue and the Paso Doble, Alexia tagged in order to try to help Team Kain. When Jack started to play mambo, Alexia and Kain were able to keep up with Carina and Bruno. This match ended in a draw. Eugenia took over for the breakdancing round, and she was able to win the Charleston. The priceless competition lasted for an entire hour, with some of the guests placing bets to see who was going to win each round. Due to their early lead, Carina and Bruno were the definite winners. Still, Alexia, Eugenia and Kain, made Carina work hard for her victory. At the end of the dance off, the competitors drenched in sweat went to collapse at on the first chair they found.

"You made me lose 1000 bucks Eugenia," protested Michael, "I was betting on you to win."

"Thank you for believing in me, daddy," said Eugenia hugging her father.

Michael reached into his pocket and he handed Uncle Gent the money he owned him. Michael smiling warmly added, "This was fun. We should have competitions like this in all our get together."

"Any excuses for you to gamble, am I right daddy?" said Eugenia teasing her father. Eugenia removed her heels, and she petted her wounded little toes, before commenting, "That Carina is a beast! She does not hold back when she wants something really badly."

"Her determination is admirable," said Michael, "You could learn a thing or two from your new friend. She already graduated. When are you going to finish your Thesis?"

"My Thesis is going to get done, when it gets done, daddy," protested Eugenia. Her Thesis was the one thing that was keeping her from getting her Master's Degree.

"Have you even thought of a topic?" asked Michael pressuring his daughter.

"We are at a party," said Kain intervening, "The last thing a person wants to do is talk about work or school. I finally caught my second wind, Eugenia. Do you want to continue dancing?"

"My hero!" said Eugenia jumping from her seat, to get away from the conversation.

"What are you writing about?" asked Kain while slow dancing with Eugenia.

"I am writing a personal narrative about my ancestry," said Eugenia, "But after digging for information, I found absolutely nothing. My dad is a descendant of Potato Farmers, and my mom's ancestors made their fortune by selling Alcohol during the Prohibition...other than that, I haven't found anything amusing about my ancestors."

"My family descends from French Executioners. One Sanson even had the privilege of decapitating the King. My Grandpa was quite curious about his past. He descends from a man that supposedly died while displaying a severed head. A year later, my ancestor Gabriel Sanson pops up in Maine, along with a bunch of French citizens escaping the poverty that Maria Antonietta had created with her reckless spending," said Kain, "It is funny if you think about it. Gabriel traveled halfway across the world to change his fate, and in the end, he ended up doing in America the same type of job he was doing in France. Lo que esta pa ti, nadie te lo quita!"

"Come again?" asked Eugenia.

"It means that some people regardless of how hard they struggle, they are not able to escape their fate," said Kain.

"Your ancestors sound like a far more interesting topic to write about," said Eugenia resting her head against Kain's shoulder.

"If you want to write about them, I can show you all the memorabilia that my grandpa collected over the years. Studying Gabriel was like his main hobby," said Kain, "We would spend a lot of time researching Gabriel, going to museums, yard sales and auction houses looking for pieces of our past. Yes...my grandpa and I, we spent a lot of time together."

"I totally vibe with you. When my mom died, there was nobody left who spent all their time with me. My dad's attention was always divided between his work, his new wife and daughter. And now, it turns out that he even has a secret family. Even when mom was alive, dad and I never truly bonded because I wasn't born a man," said Eugenia embracing Kain while she danced.

From far away, they looked like a loving couple. The reality was that they were two wounded animals licking each other's wounds. The two spent the rest of the night talking about their dead loved ones. While they were wallowing in despair, Carina and Bruno were happily chatting about their work. Carina was starting her Residency on Monday. Bruno was reciting the closing statement he gave last trail. He was truly proud of it.

"But was your client innocent?" asked Carina.

"Every person is innocent, until proven guilty," retorted Bruno, "There would be a lot more innocent people in jail, if it worked the other way around. I want to believe that my clients are innocent. If I don't believe, there won't be any way for me to convince the jury that they got the wrong man."

"What did your client do?" asked Carina.

"He was in the wrong place at the wrong time," said Bruno, "Those cases are my specialty. In this country, you can easily get in trouble for being in the wrong location..."

Bruno was about to elaborate, but Carina became distracted by Kain approaching. The friends began to chat like parrots about telenovelas. Bruno was annoyed by being completely left out of the conversation. He made a mental note to study up on Carina's interests.

Carina at a certain point said, "Kain…I finished my studies."

"I know. Congratulations," said Kain smiling warmly.

"You are smarter than me, Kain…If money is an issue, I am willing to lend you some," insisted Carina, "I still have all my notes, and workbooks."

"I don't need a degree. I have a house. I have a car. I have health insurance. I have a job. It isn't the most glamorous job," said Kain, "But I am trying to make the best of my situation."

"Kain…if you don't want to spend a lot of time in school. Online classes are available. I was reading about this IT Degree…you like fiddling with computers. So, maybe you can turn your hobby into a career," suggested Carina.

"Computers are just a means to an end. And I don't spend nearly enough time with my PC to want to turn a career out of it," said Kain.

"How about a teaching degree?" suggested Carina, "Back in High School, you were always tutoring. You know a lot about art, and you draw very pretty pictures. You could be a great art history teacher! You do not need to spend the rest of your life, as Uncle Gent's errand boy."

"That ship has sailed Carina," said Kain sighing, "I do not want to invest 4 years of my life getting a degree for a future that will not materialize. I don't even know if I will like being an art teacher. Or whatever other stupid career you have picked for me."

"Sommeliers make good money," suggested Carina.

"Cops make more than sommeliers, and our career doesn't cost us anything. And we even get health insurance," said Kain, "But if me having a degree is so important to YOU, I am willing to make the sacrifice for the sake of maintaining our friendship."

"I am sorry. Never mind. It was a stupid idea," said Carina laughing nervously.

"I have to drain the eel. With your permission, Carina," said Kain departing.

Kain ran to the house to get away from the situation. Carina went to sit down beside Alexia. She wasn't amused by how the conversation went. She turned her eyes and she frowned when she noticed that Bruno wasn't sitting down beside her. Bruno caught up to Kain in the hallway.

Kain frowning said, "What do you want Bruno? Did you come to pressure me into conformity?"

"I will do no such thing. Instead, I am here to express my admiration," said Bruno.

"That's a good joke," said Kain laughing sarcastically, "Tell me another one."

"You are a bigger man than me, Kain," continued Bruno, before placing his hand on Kain's shoulder, "You did the one thing that I was never able to do."

"And that is?" asked Kain pouting,"

"You made peace with your father," said Bruno.

"Oh…that. I don't really consider that a major accomplishment. As a Christian, I am obligated to forgive a repentant sinner. And besides, it is hard to make peace with somebody who is already dead," said Kain.

"When I said that my father was dead, I mean it, metaphorically," said Bruno accidently dropping his mask for a second, "More importantly, have you truly made peace YOUR father?"

"I don't know…" said Kain, "It is hard to say. I am no longer angry at him. When I was small, I used to think that he was having the time of his life working as a rock star. Now that I am older, I understand that he sacrificed so much because he wanted to give me all the luxuries that he didn't have when he was growing up."

"Luxuries are overrated," said Bruno, "But those who never had any naturally tend to overvalue them."

"I take it you came from a family of means?" asked Kain.

"I did," said Bruno dropping his mask, "We were not as rich as Eugenia, but we lived well."

"Why the sudden interest in the relationship I have with my father?" asked Kain.

"I consider you my friend Kain," lied Bruno, "And as your friend, I worry about your wellbeing. As a lawyer, I know the true power of words. It isn't enough to show a person that you love them with your actions. People crave certainty. Why do you think I am constantly expressing the affection I feel for Carina. If you have forgiven your father, you need to TELL him that you have forgiven him. Don't keep him in suspense."

CHAPTER 6

Judgement

The birthday party came to an end. Kain had spent most of his time chatting with Eugenia and Alexia. Esther stayed the night in Gent's house. Kain went with his father to the car.

Jack who was half asleep said, "Do you want to try driving son? Yawn…I can barely keep my eyes open."

Kain sat on the driver's seat. After taking a deep breath, he attempted to drive home. When he arrived at a red light, he asked his father, "Dad…do you remember the address of our original home?"

"There is…yawn…nothing left of that house…" said Jack with his eyes closed.

"Did you visit our old house recently, dad?" asked Kain.

"I did…I shouldn't have bought such a large house, so early in my career. It gave your mother the illusion that we were already rich and famous," said Jack sadly.

"She was fond of recklessly spending on herself," said Kain bitterly, "Every time we went to the mall, she would buy hundreds of dresses and jewelry for herself, and all I got for my trouble was a cheap plushie…but I got the last laugh in the end."

"Yes…I remember…" said Jack sadly, "When dad told me that your mother almost killed you because you tore up her favorite dress, I was beside myself. I couldn't believe that a woman was capable of doing something so monstrous, all because of a stupid dress."

"Mother and I were always at odd. When she told me that she hated me, I took her words to heart. I resolve to hate her as well, and to make every moment of her life a living nightmare," said Kain, "That day…she just snapped."

"Don't make excuses for that monster," said Jack, "You were only four years old. If you were driving your mother crazy, she should have just sent you to my grandparents for a weekend."

"She tried that for a while, but it didn't change my behavior," said Kain coldly, "Like my Grandpa, I am the type of man who holds a grudge."

"Hehehe…that's good to know Kain," said Jack on the verge of crying, "If you want to go to our old house take a left here."

Jack guided his son to their old house. The structured had caught fire four years ago, and now the lot was abandoned. The bank was still trying to find someone to sell that piece of property to. It was so rundown, that not even the roof provided sufficient cover for squatters. It was Midnight and a warm breeze was coming in from the ocean. Kain walked towards the front steps of his house. It was the only thing that remained of the original construction. He took 19 steps westward and 8 steps northward. He then began to dig on that spot. When he found nothing, he recalibrated the steps to account for his increase stature. Jack observed his son with a mixture of pity and curiosity. After some trial and error, Kain was able to dig up his buried treasure. Kain opened the box, and he sighed with relief. Everything he had buried was still there. He closed the mystery box, before returning to the car and driving home. All that time, the curiosity was gnawing away at Jack.

On the drive home, Kain stopped for a second and he began to speed up the car. Jack said, "Slow down. You don't want to get a ticket for speeding."

"We are being followed dad," said Kain, "I am going to try to lose him!"

Jack trying to reassure his son, said, "Maybe, Michael hired a guy to investigate you Kain. He is not going to let just anyone near his daughter."

"Yes…that makes sense," said Kain slowing down.

When the driver saw that it had been noticed, it turned a corner and left. With the stalker gone, the two breathed in a sigh of relief. The two arrived home around 3 a.m. Jack was so tired and sleepy, that he immediately fell on top of his bed. While he was dozing off, Kain religiously took off his father's shoes, and socks. He also removed his belt to help him get comfortable. Jack smiled in his dreams quite happy for the attention.

Back in Carina's house, she had finally slept with her boyfriend Bruno. He wasn't as big as Kain, but he was at least passionate. Since Bruno was more experience, he was superior in the bed chambers. The two languidly rested in each other's arms.

Carina at a certain point asked, "What are your plans for the future?"

"I am going to work in the bar for a couple of more years. When we get married, I want to become major of Broward County. Once the kids are born, I expect that we will be ready to become governors and once they start school, we will all be living in the White House," said Bruno voicing his plans.

"Wow! You want to be President! Why?" asked Carina laughing.

"I want to make the world a better place," lied Bruno.

"That is such a Presidential Answer! You little Liar!! Tell me the truth, why do you want to be President?" asked Carina.

"When I was in Primary School, I did a report on what I wanted to be when I grew up. When I told my classmates that I wanted to be President, they all laughed at me. Even the teacher laughed at me. She told me that a Mexican couldn't be president," said Bruno, "And I told her, that I was born in the States. This gave the right to one day Lord over all you pieces of shit! Pardon my language. I didn't mean to curse."

"It's fine," said Carina, "I too curse sometimes."

"Ever since then, being President has become my obsession," said Bruno, "As long as I reach my goal, nothing else matters."

"Boo…and for a second, I thought that I mattered to you," said Carina pouting.

"I included you in my plans, didn't I?" asked Bruno, "For every great President, there is a skillful First Lady, right behind him, cleaning up all his messes."

"You better clean after yourself mister," protested Carina pressing her body tighter against Bruno's hairy chest.

"If you were first Lady, what changes would you like me to make to this great nation?" asked Bruno.

"So, you are going to let me rule your world?" asked Carina.

"If you travel this path with me, I will do everything you say during my presidency. Through me, you will be able to turn your dreams into a reality," said Bruno trying to con Carina into helping him achieve his lofty ambition.

"What will I have to do?" asked Carina, "To make it all happen?"

"Nothing. Just continue being your perfect self," said Bruno petting Carina's face lovingly.

"How many children do you want to have?" asked Carina changing the subject.

"As many as you can handle," said Bruno, "IF it was up to me, we would have 15 kids, enough to fill an entire basketball team."

"That many?" asked Carina shocked, "Sheesh! I would have to be pregnant every year in order to reach that high number."

"Not if you take fertility treatments to give birth to twins," said Bruno giving a sly smile, "Or we can just adopt to fill up the rest of the team roster."

The two fell asleep while dreaming of the bright future that was ahead of them. Bruno slept like a log, with his mouth open, snoring like a tuba. More than once, his snores awoke Carina. Carina pushed Bruno to his side, and she placed a pillow on his back to keep him sleeping sideways. This immediately solved the snoring problem. Once the noise died down, Carina was finally able to get some Zzzss. In the dream world, the green eyed man whose face she didn't recognize manifested itself again. The two were in the beach. Carina was burying that man under the sand. When she got to his face, she added sand till he was completely buried. After a time, Carina tried to remove the sand from the person she had buried. When she removed it, instead of uncovering a person made of flesh and blood, all she found were piles of bones, and a human skull. Carina held up the skull towards the sunlight. Just at that moment, green eyes manifested inside the skull. Carina awoke yelling again. Bruno fell out of the bed with a start.

Frowning he said, "Do you have night terrors every day? Or just with me in specific?"

"I am sorry Bruno. Ever since I asked that witch for a Spell I have been getting Night Terrors," said Carina apologetically.

"Maybe the witch hexed you for not giving her a big enough tip!" said Bruno making spooking gestures with his hands.

"I guess...I don't know," said Carina.

"You could get a different witch to break the spell. Or maybe we can ask a priest for an exorcism," said Bruno giggling.

"Hahaha...very funny," said Carina dryly.

"When did the nightmares begin? Did you see a scary movie?

I still have Alien nightmares, till this very day," said Bruno smiling warmly, "That movie scarred me for life."

"The nightmares started on the day that I met you," said Carina.

"Now, I am the one who is offended," said Bruno folding his arms, "I have been a complete gentlemen. Pray do tell, what about my behavior inspired those dreams?"

"Those dreams are not really about you. I thought they were about you at first…but the man with green eyes that I see in my dream doesn't have a beard, he isn't beefy, he is skeletal even. Trust me Bruno. The man in my dreams isn't you," said Carina.

"He could be your father," suggested Bruno trying to spook Carina.

"That creature in my dreams is not my father!" protested Carina. Carina reached into her nightstand and she brought out a photograph of her father before he was ill, "See. This is what my father looks like!"

Bruno looked at the portrait and he commented, "I don't know what your ghost look like, so, I can't have an opinion on the matter. If you want to, I can hold you until you are able to fall asleep."

"Thank you," said Carina resting her head on top of Bruno's chest. Bruno proceeded to pet Carina's hair, while his mind was elsewhere.

"Tomorrow…there is a Yoga class in FIU. Do you want to come meditate with me a little?" asked Carina.

"Alright. Afterwards, we can go sailing. A friend of mine has little boat in Islamorada. He lets me borrow it sometimes," said Bruno.

"Sounds fun…" said Carina starting to fall asleep again, "Can you believe…that after all this time… I have never gone sailing…"

When Carina fell asleep, she dreamed about sailing. The following morning came. Jack awoke to the sound of someone knocking on the door. It was Carina. She had come to pick up Kain in order to force him to do group Yoga with her boyfriend. She had already conned Alexia and Eugenia into tagging along. Kain wearily left the bed and he opened the door while wearing only his undergarments. Alexia giggled nervously at the sight of quite the magnificent specimen. Bruno too saw it, and he frowned with jealously. Kain now fully awake saw what he was wearing and he ran to his room to make himself decent.

"We came here to take you to group Yoga," said Carina.

"That Yoga class isn't for two hours," protested Kain from his room.

"We know," said Eugenia, "We also came here to eat breakfast."

"So, you don't call us moochers, we bought the ingredients," said Bruno coming inside with a bag of groceries.

Kain went to his room and he got dressed. Kain entered his father's bedroom, and he tidied up the place over the top. Jack opened his eyes long enough to order his breakfast. Kain brought the mystery box into Jack's bedroom. He sat down beside his father, and he gave him a hug.

"I forgive you father," said Kain.

"I know son," said Jack, "I read your letter."

"Yes…my letter," said Kain narrowing his eyes.

Jack sat up and he opened his nightstand. He petted lovingly the letter that Carina wrote. Jack with a trembling voice said, "Every time I start sinking, I reread it."

Kain took the letter from his father's trembling hands. He immediately recognized Carina's handwriting. In a fury, Kain went with the letter to face Carina. Carina turned as pale as a ghost when Kain shoved that letter into her face.

Carina giggling nervously said, "But everything turned out for the best didn't it? You made peace with your father thanks to my intervention. So, your welcome, Kain."

"How could you do this to me Carina!" yelled Kain, "Do you have any idea how painful it was for me to see my father again?"

"If he didn't care about you, he would have just ignored the letter," reasoned Carina.

"Why did you do this to me? Have I ever forced you to do something that you don't want to?" asked insisted Kain.

"But…but…the psychic…she said that if I made you confront your father, you were going to lose your fear of commitment," lied Carina.

"Get out of my house Carina!" said Kain pointing towards the door.

"Stop being a big baby!" protested Carina, "Calm down, and make us breakfast."

Kain ran out of the house in sandals with no clear direction where he was going. Jack wearily took the car keys and he drove out of the house to find his son. Carina had not pictured her morning starting out that way. Her first instinct was to displace blame.

"Bruno! Did you tell Kain about the letter?" asked Carina.

"Had I told him about it, he would have made a scene yesterday," said Bruno dodging around the question, "If you doubt me, you can check my messages."

Carina took Bruno's phone to check all his messages. She also picked up Kain's cellphone to verify that he hadn't received any text or calls in minutes before finding out the truth. Bruno had also spent the entire night with Carina. There was absolutely no way he could have communicated to Kain the existence of such a letter.

"Ok. So, it wasn't you," said Carina folding her arms.

"Should we go after Kain?" asked Eugenia.

"When he gets like that, I just leave him alone till he calms down," said Carina.

A few blocks away, Jack had caught up to Kain. His son had collapsed due to a major Panic Attack. Regardless of how much he tried, Kain was unable to breathe. He was even starting to turn blue. Jack left the car and he called Unla. He placed the cellphone to his son's ear. At the sound of Unla's soothing, calming voice, the attack subsided. Kain wearily rested his head against his father's thin chest.

Crying he said, "Tell me daddy…if Carina hadn't written you that letter, you were never going to try to see me again?"

"That isn't true son," lied Jack. He hugged his son before adding, "Why do you think I got cleaned up? Why do you think I got a day job? I did it all for you, son. I did it to be worthy to stand beside you, once again."

"I never despised you for being an addict, dad. I never hated you for being unemployed. The only reason I grew to despise you was because you abandoned me. You have no idea how much I used to love you daddy…" said Kain before his sobs comply drowned his voice.

Jack stood up and thankfully Kain did the same. Jack guided his son back to the car. Jack turned on the car and he began to drive. Instead of returning home immediately, Jack circled around the neighborhood a few times to give his son enough time to calm down. When Kain entered the house, it was obvious to everyone that he had been crying. He went to the kitchen and he started to making breakfast. He served first his father. Bruno was the second person to get fed much to the ire of Carina. Eugenia was the next person to be fed, followed by Alexia. Once Carina was served, Kain went to his bedroom to sulk. Jack left his the table with his food.

Jack would take a bite from his eggs, before trying to get Kain to eat. Jack smiling sadly, said, "Here comes the little airplane. Brrr. Please open your mouth, before we crash land against your nose. Bop! Let's try to land this plane again. Vrrrr!!"

Kain opened his mouth and he took a bite to eat. Carina had

never seen this side to Kain and she didn't know what to make of it. This was not how she had pictured her day starting. Carina's cellphone started ringing. She turned pale as a sheet when she saw that it was her mother calling. Carina answered the phone and she before she even had a moment to response, Unla was yelling her daughter's ear off. Once she was allowed to speak, Carina told her mother about the letter.

"Carina…Your friend is not well. STOP Pressuring him!!" ordered Unla, "Stop pressuring him to go to College! Stop pressuring him to make peace with his relatives! If Bruno breaks up with you, I better not catch you sleeping with Kain ever again! Kain is your friend, not your ragdoll!"

"I am sorry mommy," said Carina meekly.

"Don't apologize to me. Apologize to Kain!" barked Unla before hanging up.

Unla was in the beach with her sister. Unla felt terrible immediately. She didn't like being strict with her daughter, but the Kain situation was getting out of control.

Unla asked her sister Barbara, "Was I too harsh on her?"

"You were just about right," said Barbara looking up from her book, "I love that girl to death, but her relationship with Kain is something I don't approve of."

"It is a classical, toxic codependent relationship," said Unla agreeing with her sister, "I should have seen the signs sooner."

"From far away, the two seemed like your typical friends with benefit," said Barbara.

Back in Kendall, Carina was apologizing to her "best" friend for her thoughtlessness. Since Kain was extremely lonely, he immediately forgave Carina. Someone who didn't instantly forgive Carina was Jack. Kain went to his room to get dressed to head out with his friends. Jack got dressed as well in order to chaperone the experience. He was going to their activities to watch and silently judge all those who surrounded his son.

The eight of them drove to FIU to participate in the Yoga class. The breathing exercises and the soothing voice of the Jainists nun brought peace to Kain's heart. He was growing to like the little nun, Rohini. She was so different from the self-proclaimed "Buddhist monk" hippies, that often roamed the beach side selling peace of mind, and LSD. Rohini was petite, with short hair, olive skin, brown eyes and a unibrow. She always spoke softly, while she covered her mouth with a handkerchief. She gave her knowledge freely to whoever sought her. When she preached, her voice was devoid of authoritarianism. She never made anyone feel ashamed for not believing what she believed.

"You know…this is actually quite pleasant," said Jack assuming the seated twist pose.

"If it wasn't for the blistering heat, I could almost call it enjoyable," said Kain changing to the seated forward fold.

"You should put on some suncream," said Jack reaching into his supply bag.

"Look at you being such a mommy," giggled Kain.

Jack sprayed a bit of sun lotion on Kain's face, and shoulders. The Yoga class came to an end. All participants felt rejuvenated in body, mind and spirit. The party got inside Eugenia's Hippie Van and they drove towards Islamorada. Instead of driving in silence, conversation resumed.

"Hey, you! Kain's dad. How old are you?" asked Alexia.

"I am 34," said Jack.

"Wait, so if you are 34 and Kain is 23…then that means," said Alexia doing the math.

"Please don't do the math," said Jack sighing wearily, "Things are already weird enough as it is."

"I am not one to judge, Mr. Jack," said Eugenia, "My mom had me when she was 41. She was a real old cougar. And my dad, he was 20 years her junior."

"Can we talk about something else," said Jack sighing with frustration, "Alexia are you seeing anyone?"

"Just the usual dregs," said Alexia sighing sadly, "When morning comes, I find an empty bed."

"Monogamy doesn't come naturally to your kind," said Jack.

"I would like to say that this is a stereotype, but it really isn't," said Alexia sadly.

"Dad. Be nice to Alexia," said Kain putting a stop to that conversation.

"What music do you want me to turn on?" asked Eugenia turning on the radio.

"Oh! Leave that song," said Bruno dropping his mask. He began to sing the lyrics in spite of himself, "…Ballerina…you must've seen her."

At the end of the song, Bruno's ears turned red when he realized what he had done. Carina giggling said, "I like this new side of your Bruno! So, you like Elton John. There is no need to be embarrassed about it."

"I like his music too," said Kain.

"I think Elton John is going on tour next year," said Alexia, "If we fly to Connecticut we can probably catch one of his concerts."

"Kain doesn't do well in planes," said Jack, "The first time he flew to one of my concerts, he spent the entire hour spewing his guts."

"I was three years old dad," said Kain smiling sadly, "My motion sickness got better with age."

"We will see," said Eugenia parking in Wahoo Bar and Grill, in Islamorada.

The party left the car and they boarded a 2000 Garlington Sportfish Motor Yacht. It was perfect sailing weather. The sea was calm, the water was warm, and it was slightly windy. Bruno turned on the yacht and he left the dock at a leisurely pace. He was testing the passenger's endurance. He drove the boat to a shallow bank to allow the passengers to swim if they felt like it.

Carina and Eugenia stripped down to their bikinis and they jumped into the water. Bruno brought out his fishing cane and he settled down to catch dinner. Jack was thankful to have brought his guitar along for the ride. This gave him something to do to pass the time. Alexia sat on the edge of the boat to dip his toes in the water. Kain after analyzing his options jumped into the water. He splashed around a bit with Carina and Eugenia. He then swam a few laps around the boat to get some exercise out of the way. When he finished tiring himself out, he sat beside Alexia to drink a soda. Alexia imbibed the sight of Kain's chiseled torso. Kain looked even more beautiful under the Florida sun, with his body still covered by saltwater droplets that glistened like tiny diamonds.

"Have you ever slept with a man?" asked Alexia before he could stop himself.

Eugenia and Carina started giggling. The maidens had noticed Alexia drooling over Kain ever since he sat beside him. Their mirth quadrupled when Jack said, "I did once. Wouldn't recommend it."

"I am sorry. It is just that your son is such a beautiful man… and…I am going to shut up now," said Alexia turning redder by the second.

"I am not really that beautiful. I just workout a lot," said Kain.

"Do not speak bad of yourself, for the warrior within hears your words and is lessened by then," said Bruno before casting his line again.

Carina jumped back into the boat, and she went to kiss the mouth that had delivered such a beautiful, piece of wisdom. Carina brought the camera and she took a selfie with Bruno. The boat wabbled a bit and the camera fell to the water. Eugenia swam after it and she brought it back to the boat. She sighed with relief when she noticed that it was waterproof. Eugenia returned to get her picture taken. She posed with the snapper Bruno had just caught. She also took a few photos with Jack's guitar. She handed the camera to Jack to have him take photos of herself with Kain. Jack assisted with this task with a dull expression on his face. This expression was hidden by his 1980s Polarized Sunglasses. His comically large sunhat added to Jack's charm. Eugenia had Kain carry her for one of the photos.

When she went to kiss him, Jack intervened by placing his hand over Kain's mouth. Jack said, "Do you like Eugenia?"

"I liked dancing with her. I enjoyed conversing with her," said Kain placing Eugenia down, "She is pleasant company when she is not pressuring me to sleep with her. She reminds me of my mother. She even laughs like her."

"Yes…I noticed too," said Jack dryly.

"I mean…Eugenia, you wouldn't sleep with a guy who resembles your dad, would you?" asked Kain coming over to stand behind his father.

"I guess I wouldn't," lied Eugenia. Eugenia frustrated passed her hand over her wet hair. She then asked, "So, let me get this straight, because of your mother, you are never going to be physically attracted to me?"

"You already experienced the answer to that question," said Kain alluding.

"You were pretty into Eugenia when you were drunk off your ass," commented Bruno.

"Hehehe…if I was, I don't remember," said Kain apologetically, "I am sorry, Eugenia. I have a lot of baggage. I don't know if I will be able to be the boyfriend you want me to be."

After saying his piece, Kain went to sit beside Bruno in order to fish. The two fished in silence, quite at peace with the world. Eugenia who was feeling physically starved jumped into the water to swim laps. Carina jumped back into the water in order to race Eugenia. Carina was starting to perceive Eugenia as a threat. As if sensing that Carina was starting to feel jealous, Bruno handed his fishing rod to Alexia before jumping into the water. While Carina and Bruno tainted the ocean water with their juices, Alexia attempted to have a normal conversation with Kain. This was easier said than done. Alexia was extremely distracted by Kain's beautiful suntanned body.

"You are starting to burn up," said Jack bringing from his supply bag the sunscreen.

Jack applied it to his son's back and face, while Kain did the front and legs. Kain noticed that Alexia was almost overcooked so he offered the suncream. Alexia blushing said, "Can you help me apply some lotion…on my back?"

Kain obliged without thinking. Alexia trembled at the touch of Kain's strong, masculine hands. This simple act alone was able to get a rise out of Alexia. Jack extremely angry pushed Alexia into the water in order to help the youth cool off. Alexia who didn't know how to swim started splashing and yelling in a panic. Bruno swam to Alexia and he held him up.

Bruno said dryly, "Alexia…the water isn't that deep."

Alexia feeling stupid said, "I am sorry I panicked there for a second. I don't know how to swim."

"Today is a good a time as any to learn," said Carina finding a new person to boss around.

"I tried to learn…but I panic whenever my head is submerged," said Alexia apologetically, "When I was small, my father threw me into the pool to force me to learn to swim…and I almost drowned."

"Most parents are lazy," said Bruno, "They expect their children to instantly master a skill, without the adults putting in the effort."

"Here is a life jacket," said Jack throwing a life jacket at Alexia,

"Just because you can't swim doesn't mean that you should never try to enjoy the ocean."

The hours rolled peacefully by. Jack after silently judging Kain's friends came to the conclusion that they were overall, well intentioned fools. The two he disliked the most where Eugenia and Alexia. He felt that the two were only there to sleep with Kain, and then toss him aside after they grew bored of him. Jack pondered how his father Raphael would handle this situation. After meditating things a little, Jack decided to put the cards on the table.

"I find Eugenia and Alexia's company disagreeable," said Jack folding his arms in mimicry of his father Raphael.

"In what way have we offended you?" asked Eugenia raising an eyebrow.

"We have been so polite," said Alexia.

"If I wasn't here, you two would probably be taking all sorts of liberties with my son," said Jack remembering the speech that his father Raphael gave to a bunch of groupies that showed up in his house uninvited, "The fact of the matter is that my son is someone who is vulnerable, and he is an easy prey to lust demons. Not that I am implying that you two lovely maidens are succubae. I am simply imploring you to exercise a bit of self-control."

"Wow…I got goosebumps," said Carina rubbing her shoulders.

"For a moment there, you sounded just like grandpa," said Kain resting his head against Jack's knee.

"Dad was not the type of man to mince words, when he felt that he was right," said Jack.

Eugenia had never been in a situation where she was the one accused of harassment. IF Kain was a woman, and she a man, her behavior would be considered borderline criminal. Eugenia feeling genuinely remorseful said, "From now on, I am going to ask you for permission."

"More than a girlfriend, what I really need is a friend who doesn't pressure me," said Kain.

Eugenia shook hands with Kain and she said, "Let's start over as friends then. Hello. My name is Eugenia."

"Please to meet you, Eugenia. My name is Kain," said Kain smiling warmly.

With that handshake, Eugenia and Kain laid the foundation of their friendship. Alexia mimicked Eugenia, in part to feel once again Kain's touch. Alexia decided to suppress the attraction he had for Kain. The alternative was to live without breathing the same air as the man he fancied.

CHAPTER 7

Wheel of Fortune

◆ ◆ ◆

When the sun started to set, the wind began to pick up. Over the horizon, Bruno was able to see that a storm was coming. He jumped back into the boat and he began to pack. By the time all were able to set sail, the storm was already there. The water became choppy, as the party was tossed left and right by the surf. With such turbulence, Kain became seasick. Kain proceeded to feed the fishes with his stomach content. Bruno noticing that one of the passengers was ill sped up in order to return to the dock. This strategy proved to make things worse, with Bruno hitting the waves at full speed. After twenty grueling minutes, Bruno finally arrived at the dock. As soon as they docked, the rain stopped and the sea grew calm. "WE should have just waited for the storm to pass," commented Carina narrowing her eyes.

"With Florida weather, you never know," said Bruno starting to clean up the boat, "I want you to give the catch to the cook of Wahoo's Bar and Grill. He will be able to process the fishes into a meal that we can all enjoy, at a discount price."

Carina delivered the fishes. She went to the bathroom and she changed out of her wet clothing. Swimming had left her rather weary. The Wahoo Bar was a wooden structure set on stilts. It gave a great view of the dock, the ships and the ocean. Carina found a chair in the closed balcony and she sat down to rest. She sent a group test to her party to tell them that she had found a chair. Meanwhile, Eugenia and Alexia were helping Jack with his son. Kain wobbled back to the car and he sighed with relief. Jack wrapped his son in a towel, and he got him changed into his dry clothing. Jack looked through Carina's supply backpack. He found inside heartburn medication.

"Are you certain you want to eat Kain?" asked Alexia, "You did throw up a lot."

"I am feeling a lot better now," said Kain rubbing his belly.

"Do you need help walking?" asked Alexia.

"I am fine. Really," said Kain standing up.

Back in the balcony, Carina was still waiting for her friends to arrive. She heard the chair beside her being pushed back. She turned her head to see who was sitting beside her. It was the thin, green eyed man from her dreams. Carina blinked incredulous. Her friends came to sit down beside her.

When Bruno came to sit beside, Carina said, "I...I...know this man...this seat is taken."

Bruno looked at the chair where the thin man was sitting. Bruno's mask dropped and his face showed genuine surprise and concern. Carina showed the menu to the thin man. The waitress came and she served water to all, but the thin man.

"I need one more glass of water," said Carina pointing to the thin man. Carina then said to Bruno, "This is the man I keep seeing in all my nightmares. Are you one of my father's patients?"

The thin man opened his mouth, and he spoke. For some reason, Carina wasn't able to hear what the man said. Carina turned to look at the menu, she said, "What am I going to have...what am I going to have...excuse me, waitress...there is something wrong with my menu."

The waitress came she asked, "What is the problem with it?"

"The letters are too blurry. I can't make out what is written there," said Carina, "Forget about it, I am just going to order the usual. And my companion here is going to have…"

"Water…water…" said the thin man in a hoarse voice. Carina pushed the water closer to the thin man. The Thin man said, "I… can't lift my arms…Ca…Cari..na…water…water…"

Carina lifted the glass and she brought it close to the thin man. The man drank his water and as he did, his hair began to grow back, and even his hollow cheekbones began to get filled up. Carina alarmed said, "Am I the only one who is seeing this? No. This can't be real…"

Bruno concerned placed his hand on Carina's shoulder, and she turned her head before screaming into his face. Her scream was echoed by Alexia and Jack, that were totally freaking out by Carina's sleepwalking episode. Jack alarmed called Unla and he described to her everything he had seen. Unla very calmy explained that Carina used to suffer from sleepwalking episodes when she was wee small. The food arrived and Carina frowned when she saw that she had ordered two meals for herself. She didn't remember falling asleep and of her sleepwalking episode the only thing she could recall was that the thin man was very thirsty.

"I keep telling you. This thin man is your father, Carina," said Bruno, "Due to his illness, it makes sense that he lost a lot of weight before passing on."

"It is a possibility," said Carina sadly, "Take this extra meal for instance, my father always ordered the snapper with yellow rice, instead rice and beans. And when I was small, I would only order chicken tenders and French fries…and sure enough, I ordered chicken tenders for myself."

Carina looked at her plate with the baby food. As an adult, she was completely bored of chicken nuggets. Though, when she tried it again, after not eating it for a long time, Carina found herself enjoying it. The extra fish dinner was shared among everyone in the table. With the weird moment in the past, the party attempted to recover their good mood. Those assembled talked about movies and books in order to ward away the silence.

At a certain point, Alexia remembered something funny that Jack had said. He asked the pertinent question, "Did you really sleep with a man, Mr. Sanson?"

"I was playing truth or dare with my bandmates. And I chose dare," said Jack.

"Whatever happened to the members of your band, daddy?" asked Kain.

"After we broke up, Salazar returned to school, and now he runs a small Bistro somewhere in Kentucky. Onyx tried to make it on his own, but he failed miserably, so he hung himself. Our lead singer Caravina crashed and burned spectacularly. So much so that he didn't survive his accident. And our drummer, who was also our songwriter, got killed by a Sicario," explained Jack, "Of our motley crew, Salazar is the only one who was able to return to the real world, and make something of himself. He sends me a postcard once a year."

"Why did your band break up?" asked Alexia.

"...you don't have to answer that father," said Kain, "Do not forget that Alexia is a reporter."

"I do not care what he writes about me," said Jack, "My band broke up because of money. Since my father was a better negotiator, I always got paid more than my peers. My so called friends didn't know, and even I didn't know because my father managed all my finances. Even in death, he is still controls what is left of my small fortune. Which is evenly split between me and all my siblings. On Christmas, we all get 500 bucks."

"Doesn't seem fair," said Alexia, "You worked really hard, and now others get to profit from it."

"Well…my brothers and sister took care of me when I fell ill, so they deserve their little Christmas bonus," said Jack.

Alexia continued with his interview, knit picking every aspect of Jack's life. Jack answered with the cool disdain of someone who isn't ashamed of the life he led. At a certain point, Alexia asked about Kain's mother Bela, whose name in Hebrew means devouring.

"All that Bela had to do was look after the baby. And most of the time she was relegating her responsibilities to my parents," said Jack pointing to his son Kain, "I didn't demand her fidelity. I didn't tell her what to do. I didn't force her to work, and I paid for her education. I even bought her the stupid castle she wanted. Nothing I ever did was enough for that monster!"

"But did you make her feel loved?" asked Carina.

"I didn't make her feel loved because I didn't love her. I didn't even like her as a friend. The wench knew this, and she still agreed to the sham marriage were her only responsibility was to love the baby. And she couldn't even do that one simple thing," protested Jack.

"Maybe she suffered from post-partum depression," said Carina playing devil's advocate.

"If she was unhappy, she hid it well," said Jack, "She was smiling when she was spending my money. She was happy when she would go out with her friends…but I grow weary of the topic."

"Did mom have any family?" asked Kain.

"She did…but I never cared to get to know them, and they never cared to get to know you, son. They shoved Bela at us as if it was our responsibility that she was now damaged goods," said Jack.

"Well…you did knock up the woman," commented Eugenia nibbling on her dessert.

"I was a virgin and she was 6 years my senior. So, who is the one truly responsible for bringing Kain into this world?" retorted Jack, "And we all know how women love to get knocked up in order to force the guys to marry them, so they never have to lift a finger…but enough about Bela. Let's talk about literally anything else."

Dinner came to an end. The group got inside the Eugenia's Hippie van and they drove back to Kendal. Eugenia insisted on driving. She didn't trust others to drive her party wagon. Jack settled down to sleep while resting his head on Kain's shoulder. Eugenia threw to the back seat a pillow she was sitting on in order to provide Kain some head support. Kain rested his head on that pillow and he too dozed off. One by one each of the friends began to fall asleep. Till eventually, only the driver was awake. Eugenia from time to time would slap her cheek in an attempt to stay awake. Eugenia reached into the glove compartment to get a quick pick me up. She opened a small little jar that had her cocaine. She thought of everything that Jack had said, and in the end, she chose to throw the metal jar out the window. Eugenia started falling asleep again. Before she knew it, her eyes were closed.

Just at the crucial moment the radio station switched to a heavy metal station. At full volume, the radio began to screech, "Wake up! Wake up! Grab a brush and put on a little make up!"

"I am awake! I am awake!" said Eugenia waking up.

"WE all are awake…sheesh!" said Carina, "Lower the volume on that music, you are going to wake up the babies."

"Gods! That song gave me a wicked headache!" said Alexia rubbing his temple. He added giggling, "Guys…look, Jack and Kain didn't wake up."

Jack feeling alluded to started snoring. Carina looked with a hint of envy at the two sleeping so soundly. She snuggled up against Bruno in order to continue sleeping. Bruno yawning said, "I am going to make the effort to stay awake Eugenia. If you start falling asleep, you can engage me in conversation. Or you can just let me drive."

"Yawn…or you can just let me continue driving," said Eugenia starting to fall sleep again, "Maybe we should just crash in my house. If we…try…to make it…to…"

With this plan, Eugenia drove to her mansion. When she entered the house sober, her father breathed in a sigh of relief. Eugenia wabbled left and right following the rhythm of the ocean. When her head touched her pillow, she immediately fell asleep. Eunice seeing the guests went to play hostess. She guided the visitors to the small, well-furnished guest house. The guest house was a two story, midcentury modern house. Bruno and Carina took the top floor master bedroom, Kain took the adjacent room with the view to the ocean, while Jack and Alexia slept in the bottom floor. Carina slept like a log, and she didn't have any nightmares. Though, she did wake up once when she heard a low moan. Before curiosity got the better of her, Bruno placed his arm around her waist to draw her deeper into his embrace. With Carina unable to leave the bed, she settled down to sleep. Carina set the timer in order to wake up early.

She needed to make it home to get changed into her scrubs. She started work this Monday. The morning came and everyone awoke to the smell of fresh bacon. The first person to wake up was Alexia. He found Unla in the kitchen making breakfast. Unla was already sporting her doctor uniform, and she had brought one for her daughter. Slowly, others awoke, until all the guests had rendezvous to eat breakfast. Carina informed her mother of everything that she did. Unla gave her daughter a dream journal. She wanted her daughter to record everything she did on the days when the nightmare manifested. Hopefully through these means, Unla would be able to pinpoint the trigger for her daughter's night terrors. Once everyone was fed, they crammed into Unla's car. First, Unla dropped off Kain and Jack to their home. Unla then drove to Bruno's apartment, from there they dropped off Alexia. With their driving duties concluded, Unla and Carina were finally able to make it to work on time.

Another Monday came, with it more of the usual. Eugenia changed up her Thesis in order to write about Kain's family instead. Her teacher approved of the change, since the Sansons sounded like a far amusing family to write about. Kain began to take photographs of his grandpa's collection, starting with the things Gent had in his office.

"Were my ancestors fond of pizza?" asked Kain holding up a torture device that resembled a pizza cutter.

"Don't play with dad's things Kain," said Gent taking the item away, "You are going to get Tetanus from these dangerous hunks of metal."

"Eugenia is writing a paper about our ancestors. And I am helping her by taking photos of dad's little toys," said Kain showing his camera.

"That's cute," said Gent giving a fake smile, "How are things going with Eugenia?"

"They are lukewarm," said Kain sadly, "I want to try to give her an honest chance, but she reminds me of my mother. Whenever I think of my mother, I completely lose my inspiration."

"Other than that stupid laughter, Eugenia is nothing like your mother," said Gent, "Yes. She is rough around the edges, but nothing that a weekend over at the Betty Ford Clinic won't fix."

Gent dug into the clutter of his desk till he found an old polaroid of Bela. The mere act of walking towards the table to get a better look at the photograph had Kain hyperventilating. Gent visibly grieved hid the polaroid from sight.

"Sigh…Kain…what am are we going to do with you?" said Gent hugging his nephew, "It's alright son. It is not your fault."

When his nephew returned to his workstation, Gent called up Unla. Gent reported the latest malfunction of his nephew. The two talked about the real possibility of putting Kain on medication.

At the end of the conversation, Unla said, "I only prescribe medication as a last resort. For now, I suggest he stops drinking caffeine. I also recommend that he does relaxation breathing exercises once every two hours. And do not let him stay past his bedtime. As for his phobia of his mother's visage, I have this idea. Leave it in random places, but do not tell him that this is the photograph of his mother. Once, he becomes desensitized to it, tell him that the woman in the photo is Bela."

Gent immediately got on that task. The first thing he did was photoshop Bella's photo into a missing person's poster. He mixed it among a bunch of other posters. He then gave Kain the pointless task of distributing those posters. At first Kain limited himself to placing those posters in the same block that housed the police station. Today, he was feeling particularly cowardly. So, much so, that he didn't want to cross the street. He noticed an old lady in a similar predicament. The two cross the street together, both quite thankful for each other's company. Detective Farley, one of the few persons who did any real work in that station, frowned when he saw Gent's nephew engaging in pointless busywork. Farley was in his late 40s, he was overweight, and already bald. Farley had been transferred over to Gent's department because nobody could put up with him. Farley spent of most of his time either critiquing or investigating his coworkers. The current target of his espionage/bullying was Kain, Gent's little errand boy. Farley crossed the street and he attempted to strike a conversation with his colleague.

"IF you want to know what I do…take it up with uncle Gent," said Kain seeing Farley approaching.

"That is not what I wanted to talk about…" said Farley.

"Every new face always complains about me," said Kain, "If you tell me what sweets you like, I can make them for you once a week."

"Is that your idea of a bride?" asked Farley laughing.

"You said it, not me," retorted Kain, "Instead of investigating a fellow officer, I suggest you go do some real work."

"I like you Kain," said Farley, "You seem like a real honest chap."

Kain reached into his pocket and he turned on his headsets. Instead of listening to heavy metal, he listened to Abba. Unla had suggested that Kain change up his music to something relaxing, in order to reduce his stress levels. When Farley attempted to take Kain's headsets, Kain ran away from his coworker. Farley tried to give chase, but he got short winded easily. Farley that day had read the article that Alexia had written about Kain. Based on the article, Farley felt that his coworker wasn't mentally stable to continue his duties. Farley went to speak to his coworkers about Kain. They all had nice things to say about Gent's errand boy.

The workday came to an end. Eugenia picked up Kain in order to visit a Raphael's storage unit. Following close behind was Farley. Kain opened the lock, and he turned on the lights. The dusty storage unit was covered with boxes and furniture protected with a sheet of cloth. A roach scurry by and Eugenia jumped on top of Kain.

"I...I...haven't been here since Grandpa passed away," said Kain with a degree of trembling in his voice.

"Do you feel guilty about what happened to him?" asked Eugenia.

"A little...a lot, actually," said Kain, "Rationally, I know that it wasn't my fault, but I can't help feel guilty sometimes. I try to imagine what my life would be like had I followed the path that my grandpa had laid down before me."

"What did your grandpa want you to do? Exactly? Did he want you to join the army?" asked Eugenia holding up a photograph featuring Raphael in his army uniform, "You look a lot like your grandpa when he was young."

"Yeah...they tell me that a lot," said Kain petting the old

photograph lovingly, "My grandpa, he wanted me to be a doctor or a lawyer. He wanted me to be a somebody…"

Kain removed the cloth that was on top of the largest object. It was the breaking wheel, also known as the wheel of fortune. Depending on the clumsiness of the executioner, death could take hours or even days. After the execution, the bodies were propped up on the wheel to allow for the birds to peck at the remains.

Eugenia passed her index finger around the breaking wheel, "It looks like a broken wagon wheel to me."

"I said the same thing," said Kain, "But grandpa was convinced that this was a genuine breaking wheel. The priest who sold it to him claimed that this wheel had been used to execute St. Catherine. When the saint touched it, the wheel broke into many pieces."

"I heard from my detective that your grandpa used to torture enemy spies in Guantanamo Bay," said Eugenia.

"Most of the things they say about my grandpa are things that nobody can prove," retorted Kain before showcasing the rest of his grandpa's collection.

Kain showed Eugenia the smaller items that included the pear of anguish, the Spanish tickler, the crocodile shears, and the heretic's fork. Eugenia overcome with morbid fascination photographed all these tools, and she jotted down everything Kain said about the subject.

"The things people used to do before the invention of television," said Eugenia with a sinister smile painted on her face.

Kain looked at the time and he said, "It is getting late. And I have to go home and make dinner for my dad and my grandma. Did you get everything you needed?"

"I still haven't photographed Gabriel's Noose," said Eugenia.

"That's right! I forgot to show you the hangman's noose," said

Kain before opening the floor safe. There perfectly preserved was the infamous Hangman's Noose. Eugenia noticed that this noose had 13 loops instead of the typical noose 8 loops, "Depending on how the noose is placed around your neck was how quickly you kicked the bucket. For a quick death, place the noose ahead of the ears. If you want to see the poor bastard suffer, place the noose behind the ears."

The two left the storage unit after locking up the place. Farley broke the lock and he entered the place in order to quench his curiosity. He wasn't able to look around much. The lock in the storage unit had a special chip that called the police if it was broken, instead of opened with a key. The cops came and arrested Farley for breaking an entry. Gent left Farley rotting in the holding cell overnight. The following morning Gent took Farley into Raphael's storage room to have him investigate till his heart's content.

"I feel that we got off with the wrong foot," said Gent smiling benevolently, "The time you are spending investigating my nephew is time that you could be spending doing some actual police work. I know that your pa got ate by a crooked cop, but if you look for corruption everywhere, corruption is the only thing you are going to find."

"I can't argue with that logic," said Farley extremely deflated, "Though, what you are doing with your nephew is something that I do not approve of. The kid is clearly crazy. He shouldn't be allowed to carry a weapon. He could hurt someone or himself."

"You are not a doctor! You don't have the authority of decide who is crazy and who isn't!" hissed Gent.

Farley shrank even deeper into himself. Farley returned home after officially antagonizing his boss. Farley's wife advised him to play nice with his coworkers. He only had a few years left till his retirement. Gent called up Unla to ask how things were progressing with Kain. Unla said that Rome wasn't built in a day.

"The boy is at least communicative. Once I finish my

preliminary observations, I will provide you with a list of triggers to avoid," said Unla, "Are you familiar with the spoon theory? I read an interesting essay about it. I think it can help you understand your nephew's chronic condition."

The word "chronic" didn't inspire Gent much confidence. Gent read the Spoon Theory Essay. The theory described how people with chronic illnesses start the day with a set amount of energy, symbolized by spoons. Certain actions consume spoons. Once, a person was down to a single spoon a person had to consider each action wisely. If a person didn't have enough time to recuperate at home, they would then start the next day with fewer spoons. She also sent Gent a few articles about Ego Depletion in order to add to his confusion. With Farley no longer being a bother, Kain's workdays progressed at a leisurely pace. He had managed to drive the patrol car past a green light without suffering a panic attack. Two lights was a tall order, but he was making "progress".

Carina's first day of work was extremely busy. She treated her first patients, and she did her first couple of basic procedures. While eating lunch, Carina saw one of her coworkers reading the horoscope. Carina almost recommended Irina, but she chose not to. Carina was still blaming the woman, for all her terrible decisions. The following day Irina showed up at Carina's clinic. Irina was with her youngest ward Marlene. Marlene had caught an ear infection from swimming so much in the public pool.

"You are not going to offer me a psychic reading?" asked Carina.

"I know when I have lost a costumer," said Irina. She added, "More the pity. I did warn you against the actions you were about to take."

"I would be been more inclined to listen to your warning had you explained to me the consequences of my actions," protested Carina.

"You ask too much of a humble psychic...You ask too much of everyone unfortunate enough to cross paths with you, Carina," said Irina, "Now, if you are not going to treat my granddaughter's earache, I will go take my business elsewhere."

"My apologies," said Carina switching to work mode.

Carina examined the little girl's ear canal. The ear was inflamed, so much so that Marlene was practically deaf, and in extreme pain. Carina realized that there were limits to Irina's powers. If she was so much of a psychic, why wasn't she able to protect Marlene from getting an ear infection. Carina applied the first dosage of the medication to Marlene's ear. While the two waited for it to take effect, Carina attempted small talk.

"My aunty Barbara dabbles a bit in the craft," said Carina.

"Fooling around with a Ouija Board doesn't count as dabbling in the craft. There is a reason why Hasbro sells those boards as kids toys," said Irina, "Like any profession, my craft requires study and practice to even master the basics. I do not belittle your job, so, do not patronize mine."

There was an awkward silence between the two. During that time, Marlene was busy playing her Gameboy. Marlene said, "I never got around to thanking your friend for saving me."

"So you where the stupid kid that almost drowned in the pool," said Carina smiling warmly. She added, "After you almost drowned, weren't you afraid of getting back into the pool?"

"Yes…it was scary at first, but I wasn't about to let fear stop me from doing something I enjoy," said Marlene.

"The floaties also helps," corrected Irina, "It allows Marlene to have fun in the pool, while completely removing the possibility of drowning from the equation."

"You should try the bumper cars," suggested Marlene, "Your friend can pretend to drive, while you remove completely from the equation the possibility that he might crash and burn, again."

"Have they found the driver that crashed into your friend?"

asked Irina.

"Uncle Gent was looking for that person for a while, but Kain told him not to waste any more resources on that pointless endeavor," said Carina, "Can you tell me who was the person that crashed into Kain?"

Irina brought out her deck of cards. She shuffled the cards while she focused on that particular question. She drew the top card from her deck. It was the Wheel of Fortune. This card always manifested whenever she was trying to scry Kain's future. Irina shuffled the cards again. This time she drew the card from the middle of the deck. Surprise, surprise, it was the Wheel of Fortune again. This time in reverse. The card that followed it was the Hangman. The final card was going to reveal the identity of the culprit. The card showcased a 7 of Pentacles.

"Since the 7 pentacles is in reverse, I can tell you that the person who crashed into Kain is currently stagnant in his career. He works really hard, but rarely sees results," said Irina focusing her eyes deep into the Pentacle card. She could almost make out what the person looked like, "When he is in the wrong, he refuses to take responsibility for his actions."

"Do you see him grandma?" asked Marlene looking at the Pentacle card.

"Just his soul. The shape of his body is harder to make out," said Irina pressing the Pentacle card closer to her face, "It is like trying to make out the face of a person who is underwater. Or like trying to guess what a person looks like based on the shape of his shadow. He wears something shiny, just over his breast pocket. It is kinda oval shape, with a little star in the center."

Carina handed Irina the prescription for Marlene's ear medication. Carina wrote down in her prescription pad everything that Irina had said about the man that had crashed into Kain's car. Carina called Uncle Gent and she repeated to him everything that the psychic had said. Gent looked at his badge, that was oval shaped, with a star. The psychic's theory was plausible. Police officers always felt underappreciated, and they often covered up their own indiscretions.

Gent opened up the case file again. The vehicle that had crashed into Kain was a Green "Christine", possibly a 1958 Plymouth Fury, or maybe a Savoy or a Belvedere. While Kain's car was completely totaled, the car that crashed into him drove away without so much of a scratch.

Gent said to himself, "They don't make vehicles like they used to…"

"Let it be, uncle Gent," said Kain noticing what Gent was looking at, "It was an accident. Accidents happen. Capturing the man who crashed into me is not going to change anything."

"I don't know Kain…if criminals don't get punished, or even caught. It will inspire others to engage in criminal activities. Did you even managed to get a good look at the guy?" asked Gent.

"His car had tinted windows," said Kain.

"Uh…that narrows it down," said Gent giving a sly smile, "Plymouth Furies don't normally come with tinted window."

Kain took the file from his uncle in order to personally archive it. He didn't want to hear any more talk about this accident. Kain returned to his desk to catch up on his paperwork. When he got bored of that task, he felt like going on patrol. It was then when he noticed Zidanta returning to the station with a drunk tourist he had arrested for disorderly conduct. Kain came up to Zidanta and he asked to go on patrol with him. Zidanta sat on the passenger side.

"Where are we headed?" asked Kain nervous about a patrol car.

"To Hialeah's Westland Mall," said Zidanta.

"Are you going to do a little shopping?" asked Kain.

"Unlike you, I do not fool around," said Zidanta, "Now, drive!"

"Ok…" said Kain regretting all of his life decisions.

Kain drove just fine as long as all the lights were green. When he got the Palmetto Express way, he breathed in a sigh of relief. So, far he had managed to avoid the trigger for his panic attack. When he got off the Express way, he reached his first red light. When the light turned green, Kain began to feel heart palpitation. These were the initial symptoms of his panic attack. Kain closed his eyes and he did his breathing exercises. The time that it took him to calm down was enough for the light to turn red again. Zidanta left passenger seat to trade places with Kain. With Zidanta driving, the two were able to make it to the mall. Zidanta parked his car and he started circling around Chili's to scope of all the entry points. Kain bored and curious, tagged along to see what was the problem.

"I want you to enter the restaurant," instructed Zidanta, "I want you to keep an eye on a waiter by the name of Jeremy. Observe and report everything that you see."

"It won't be much a stealth mission with me in this uniform," commented Kain.

Zidanta dug from the trunk of the car a hoodie. Kain removed his work uniform shirt and he changed into the hoodie. Kain entered the restaurant to keep an eye on Jeremy. The so called Jeremy was a lanky youth that almost resembled a teenager. His face was awfully pretty, too pretty for a man. Often times, Jeremy would be mistaken for a woman. His expressive black eyes had a feral quality to them. Almost as if he was expecting to get ambushed at any moment. Jeremy was up picking up the dirty dishes and washing them. On the first day of the stakeout, nothing happened.

The two repeated the stakeout the following day. On a particular busy Wednesday, Jeremy dropped a plate and broke it. The manage in a fury went to yell his ear off. He yanked Jeremy by the elbow before taking him out of sight, and out of mind of the costumers. Since this blatant bullying didn't sit right with Kain, he left his seat in order to enter the kitchen.

"Do you mind explaining to me what you are doing to that man," said Kain entering the kitchen. Kain had walked in time to see the manager about to smash Jeremy with a plate.

"Mind your own business," said hissed the manager.

"What you are doing is my business," said Kain taking out his police badge from his pocket, "You are under arrest for assault with a deadly weapon."

"Officer. Come on! It is just a plate! You can't kill a person with a plate," said the manager giggling, "Let me buy you a meal, so, we can put this all behind us."

"Drop the plate dirtbag!" said Zidanta entering from the backroom. Zidanta had his gun in his hand, while he waited for an excuse to pop a casket on the manager who was assaulting his employee.

The manager lowered the plate, and he accepted the handcuffs that Kain was offering. Kain collected the plate and he placed it inside a paper bag. He took photos of the crime scene and he took the testimony of the victim. Kain also photographed Jeremy's arm. The two returned to the station with the perp refusing to use his right to remain silent.

"I arrested someone today," said Kain reporting his activities to his uncle.

"I don't think a plate counts as a deadly weapon. Though, based on the evidence, we might be able to pin him for aggravated assault," said Gent after listening to the entire story, "Tell…one thing, Kain, how did you end up witnessing this crime."

"Zidanta told me to keep an eye on Jeremy. He was suspecting that the manager was bullying his little brother, and today, we caught him in the act. You should have been there uncle. The guy went mental just because the kid broke a plate," explained Kain.

"People with short fuses shouldn't be in charge of anything," retorted Gent.

The following day came. When Gent entered his office, he found a strange animal on top of his desk. Gent reached for his gun with the intention of shooting the giant rat. Before he did, the giant rat meowed.

Gent rubbing his temple commented, "That is the ugliest cat I have ever seen."

"Tybalt…Tybalt," said a voice passing by the office.

Gent approached the sphynx cat cautiously. The cat hissed as a warning. Despite the hissing, the cat allowed Gent to pick it up. Gent looked at the collard of the cat. It had a peculiar looking oval tag. Instead of a name, it had a picture of an eagle, with a cubic zirconia star in the background. On the other side of the tag, the name "Tybalt" was written.

"I take it this is your cat," said Gent handing Jeremy his cat, "This isn't a place for children to be roaming about."

"What about those children?" pointed Jeremy to a group of High Schoolers roaming about the police department.

"They are on a field trip," retorted Gent, "You should return to the group, you do not want to be left behind."

"I am not with them. I am not a child," protested Jeremy. Jeremy reached into his pocket to showcase his driver's license.

"I have seen better fake IDs before," said Gent, "I am keeping it."

"I wish you wouldn't," said Jeremy petting his cat nervously, "I need it to get around."

Before the situation got more complicated, Zidanta entered the Station and he cleared up the misunderstanding. Gent noticed that Zidanta and Jeremy had the same last name. So, Gent assumed that the two where brothers. The way Zidanta had been so overprotective of his "little brother" Jeremy, spoke to Gent on a personal level.

"Every once in a while, me and some of my coworkers get together to go Hunting. You are welcome to join us," said Gent.

"What are we hunting?" asked Zidanta.

"Pythons. They are ruining the Everglades, and the scientists pay big bucks for us to make a dent in their ever increasing population," said Gent, "The Hunting season for those critters is starting this August 15. Do you have a hunting license?"

"I do, but not Jeremy," said Zidanta, "He is a bit clumsy with guns, but if you give him a knife he can easily gut you like a pig."

"That's good. He can help process our kills," said Gent slapping Jeremy's shoulder in a friendly fashion.

"Ow…" protested Jeremy.

"Sorry. My bad," giggled Gent, "I need to remember that your little brother is fragile."

"I am not fragile…it is just that this was the arm my manager yanked too hard," said Jeremy removing part of his jacket to show the damage.

Gent saw the large purple bruise just over the elbow and he frowned. Gent thought of his little brother Jack. Jack was always a being bullied in school. This was a big reason why he jumped at the first opportunity to leave school, to become a big rock star.

Gent completely consumed in sad thoughts asked Jeremy, "How is work going?"

"I left it," said Jeremy.

"Too many bad memories?" asked Gent sadly.

"No. My boss was granted Bond and he was let out of prison. He is being allowed to continue with his life while he waits to be put on trial," explained Jeremy, "The way things are going, he is probably going to be found innocent of assault."

"Sigh…this country…" said Gent rubbing his temple, "What are you going to do about a job?"

"I don't know," said Jeremy cuddling with the cat.

Parallel to these events, Bruno was telling Carina about his newest client. He was representing a man who was wrongfully accused of assault with a deadly weapon. The two were having lunch in a Starbucks that was near the hospital that was employing Carina.

"Can you believe it Carina? A plate a deadly weapon?" scoffed Bruno.

"I am going to have to be careful the next time I pick up a plate," said Carina laughing.

"It is amassing the stupid reasons why people get sent to jail these days," commented Bruno with a sly smile painted on his face.

"How long do you think it is going to take for you to close the deal?" asked Carina.

"I demanded a speedy trial," said Bruno, "With such a simple case, I can have everything wrapped up in less than 10 days. Maybe even sooner. I am currently negotiating for a plea bargain. If everything goes as plan, my client will get charged for disorderly conduct, instead of assault with a deadly weapon."

With this idea in mind, Bruno persuaded his client to agree to a plea bargain. His client admitted to "shoving" his employee. The way Bruno sold the story was that the manager was frustrated by the clumsiness of his employee, who couldn't even handle the simple task of carrying a plate to the sink. Bruno's client after feigning remorse was able to avoid going to jail. Instead, he had to pay a 1000 bucks fine, and he was instructed to do 30 hours of community service.

CHAPTER 8

Cups

◆ ◆ ◆

The weekend came and those who wanted to take part in the Python Hunting expedition gathered in Gent's house. The ones in attendance where Gent, Jack, Kyle, Kain, Bruno, Jeremy, Zidanta, Farley and a couple of other men from the Police station. More than hunting Pythons, they were going to drink, and engage in male bonding. While the boys where playing in the woods, Carina, Eugenia, Unla, Stacie and girls where visiting the Lapis Spa at the Fountain Blue Hotel. Esther was babysitting Stacie's children, in order to give the woman a chance to decompress.

This was the first time Eugenia interacted with Stacie. Stacie was a blonde, chubby maiden, with expressive green eyes and a body covered in freckles. Whenever she was meeting new people, she would become quiet as a mouse. Stacie felt a little stressed about allowing Eugenia to pay for her spa day. Once, the Masseuse got started with the Harmonizing Massage, all the stress of the stay at home mother quickly dissipated.

After the massage, the girls went to get a Triple Cleanse Facial, followed by a Hair Nourishing Scalp Ritual. The next part of the journey of relaxation started in the Essence Mineral Pool. While the girls were roosting there, Stacie couldn't help but laugh while thinking of her husband trotting about the disgusting Everglades.

Gent's car arrived to the Everglade's Flamingo Camping Ground. Kain, Bruno, Alexia and Jack carpooled with uncle Gent. They were sitting comfortably in Gent's minivan. Jeremy and Zidanta showed up on a 1970s Chopper Harley Motorcycle. And then the others arrived. The guys got a good kick out of Zidanta's motorcycle. Some even took photos while pretending to ride the Chopper.

"Are we really going to hunt Pythons, Kain?" asked Alexia worried.

"What's the matter? Are you afraid of a little snake?" asked Gent laughing.

"Pythons can grow 15 feet long," said Alexia spewing all the information he had researched, "They have been known to eat entire crocodiles. And we are going to hunt that? Seriously!"

"Look sissy boy," said Farley, "If you aren't man enough to play with the big boys, you could have just gone to the Spa Day with the rest of the women."

"Farley…you are walking on thin ice," warned Gent.

"You have to forgive me, Gent. But I am the type of man that likes to tell it how it is," said Farley.

"And I am the type of man that punishes those who insult others!" said Gent getting into his boxing stance.

"It's a free country! I can say whatever I want!" retorted Farley gearing up to fight with Gent.

"Actually. You can't say whatever you want," said Bruno, "Freedom of speech only protects you from government censorship."

"But Gent and Farley are police officers. So, technically, they cannot sensor each other's words," retorted Alexia.

Alexia and Bruno began to debate on the strengths and limits of the First Amendment. Their legalism ramblings helped defuse the situation. The men unpacked the tent, the guns, and the picnic supplies. They went to the camp ground they had rented. Following behind Farley was his 14 year old son, Oswald. Oswald was blonde with angelic blue eyes. He was a little on the portly side, which was part of the reason why Farley had dragged his son to the middle of the woods. Oswald had no friends. Due to his job, Farley had uprooted his family 5 times. Farley hoped Oswald could make friends with Kyle, Gent's son. Kyle had inherited the same icy temper of his mother. He had black hair and emerald green eyes. Since Gent kept his son active, Kyle was fit, though he appeared weak due to his short stature. Kyle was a late bloomer, with a face that still retained all its childish charms.

"I finished the lyrics that you wanted uncle Jack," said Kyle handing his homework.

"That's a lot of curse words," said Jack raising an eyebrow, "Are the kids bothering you again, Kyle?"

"School doesn't start for another week," retorted Kyle.

"So…soon…they keep making school years longer and longer," commented Jack.

"I do not even know why," said Kyle, "It is not as if I am learning anything useful."

The party chit-chatted till they reached the camping ground. When they arrived, Gent said, "We are going to divide into teams. Each team will be in charge of carrying out a specific task. Once they are done, we will rendezvous at basecamp at 13:00 hours. Kyle I want you to go with the new kids to scout ahead. See, if you can find a Python for us to shoot at. And while you are at it, bring back some firewood."

Kyle went into to the woods with a very nervous Oswald and an extremely bored Jeremy. Oswald relaxed when he noticed that there was an adult tagging along. Kain was the designated chaperone of the children. Jeremy was carrying a backpack. Oswald giggled when he noticed that Jeremy was lugging about his pet cat.

"Aren't you worried that a Python is going to eat your cat?" asked Oswald.

"Tybalt is a fierce predator," said Jeremy stating a fact, "I once saw him take on a Pitbull to protect a toddler."

"Wow! That's very gutsy," said Kyle coming over to look into the backpack.

Jeremy brought out his cat from within the backpack. He place a leach on his cat, and he began to walk Tybalt as if he was a dog. While the younglings were assumed in the pointless task of gathering firewood, the adults were pitching the tents, and they were doing the final inspection of the rifles. Bruno and Farley went scouting the shore in search of a good fishing spot, while other fellows where getting a small fishing boat into the water. Jack was busy fastidiously cleaning the individual pieces of the rifle, before assembling them. The only person not doing much of anything was Alexia, though he was taking photographs of what everyone else was doing.

"Can you take a photo of me holding a rifle?" asked Alexia holding up a Marlin 1895 Rifle.

"I was under the impression that you were a Democrat," said Jack looking up from his work.

"I may be a Democrat, but I believe in the Second Amendment," said Alexia, "Responsible gun owners, shouldn't be punished because a couple of bad parents, who weren't able to keep their guns away from their children."

"In Japan, all guns are outlaw, and it hasn't done much to keep the murder rate from dropping," said Zidanta, "Though now, instead of getting killed by a gun, you get stabbed to death by a katana wielding Yakuza."

"Gang members prefer to use a knife, instead of a gun when killing people they find disagreeable," said Jack contributing to the conversation.

"Why is that?" asked Alexia.

"Because knife wounds are more painful," said Jack.

"Bunch of savages," said Zidanta, "We aren't really hunting for Pythons, are we?"

"That is just something my brother tells the newbies," said Jack, "This camp might be safe, but we have seen Pythons at least once before."

Kain's party finished gathering firewood. On their way back to camp, Tybalt stopped, and he began to emit a low pitch meow. Jeremy pushed the children back and he brought out the knife he carried in his person, everywhere he went. Kain brought out his revolver, and he looked in the direction that the cat was hyper focused on. The cat stopped meowing and he got into his hunting stance. From bushes, emerged a Florida Panther.

Oswald's first instinct was to run away. Kyle coiled his arms around the youth to keep him from running away. As Kyle explained, "If you turn your back on the Panther, you are going to trigger his predator instinct. It is safer to stand your ground, and show him that you are not afraid."

"But I am afraid, Kyle," said Oswald cowering behind the much smaller child.

Tybalt charged at the Panther. The sudden sprint of the cat startled the Panther so much that it ran away. With the panther gone, all breathed a sigh of relief. Tybalt returned to Jeremy's side and he began to rub up against his leg. Jeremy picked up his cat, and he placed Tybalt back inside his comfortable backpack.

"Wow! That was crazy!" said Kyle jumping with excitement.

"Can you believe it?" said Oswald also impressed by the cat's pluckiness.

The two brats proceeded to interrogate Jeremy about Tybalt. When the party returned, Gent and Farley were happy to note what quick friends the children had become. Oswald ran to his dad, and he told him everything that had happened. The tale was far too farfetched that none of the adults believed it, even with Kain providing eyewitness testimony. Once, they delivered the firewood, Jeremy settled down to drink a soda. He also brought out a bowl to pour spring water for his cat. Jeremy handed a cat wand for Oswald to play with Tybalt. Oswald sat on the floor and together with Kyle they played with the cat for about half an hour.

"I wasn't too certain about bringing the cat along, but it serves as a good distraction for the kids," said Gent.

"Do you have any K9 units in the police force?" asked Oswald.

"Our K9 had to be retired," said Gent.

"He was put down?" asked Oswald sadly.

"By retired, I mean retired," said Gent, "Marmalade lives at home with me. He keeps the girls company when I am not at home. I have been meaning to train his replacement, but I haven't gotten the chance to get around to it. Things keep coming up."

Oswald giggled hearing the name Marmalade. Kyle picked up two fishing rods. He then said to Oswald, "Time to fish for Pythons."

"Isn't that dangerous?" asked Oswald.

"That's the point, isn't it?" retorted Kyle teasing Oswald.

Oswald had never fished before, but he was enjoying the company. Since Kyle was short, Oswald didn't feel intimidated. Kain gathered some twigs, and the rubbed them together till he formed a small fire. He blew into it, until it started to grow. He slowly added more kindling, and soon they had a respectable cooking fire. Tybalt turned to stare at the fire, as if hypnotized by it. His tail wagged to illustrate his amusement. The hours rolled at a leisurely pace, all caught up in the relaxing August atmosphere. Some of the men including Kain went to hunt. Kain saw a delicious looking marsh rabbit. He took aim, and then he fire. It was clean kill: A bullet right through the skull of the poor, sweet, delicious little bunny.

"Perfect shot as always Kain!" said Gent proudly.

"Grandpa taught me well," said Kain shyly.

"Look! There goes a chicken! Shoot it Kain!" said Gent pointing at a new target.

"We can eat chicken at home, uncle," protested Kain lowering the riffle.

"Aw…You are no fun," said Gent.

Zidanta took aim at the chicken, and he missed. The chicken extremely frightened by the noise fled in terror. Kain picked up his dead bunny, and he placed inside his satchel. It was then when he noticed a bush covered in muscadine grapes. The hunting party was only able to kill three unfortunate bunnies. They had better luck collecting wild berries. Bruno fished five basses, and a couple of mullets. While the food was getting cooked, the men began to gossip about their romantic conquests or they complained about their wives.

"So tell me, little Jeremy, are you seeing anyone?" asked Gent.

"It is hard to see anyone when you spend all your time working in the kitchen," retorted Jeremy.

"What skills do you have as a worker?" asked Gent.

"Is this a job interview?" asked Jeremy.

"It could if you wanted to," said Gent.

"I suppose a job would give me something to do while Zidanta is at work," said Jeremy, "Originally, we were both going to be cops, but I failed to pass the physical. And like Zidanta already said, my marksmanship is all over the place."

"Maybe you need glasses," said Gent.

"Or a better gun," said Kain, "Police officers normally use Glocks, but I prefer my Grandpa's Revolver."

Kain handed Jeremy his Colt Python. Kain had inherited this gun from his grandpa. It was the first gun Kain had ever fired. This Colt Python had been modified by the original owner. It was 8 ounces lighter, than the Average Colt Python. Gent placed some empty beer bottles to act as targets. Kain handed the gun to Jeremy, and he instructed him to shoot. Jeremy took aim and he missed again, and again. Kyle borrowed Kain's gun and he shot all targets without missing once. Kyle handed the gun to Oswald. In order to fit in, Oswald participated in the target practice. The last person to shoot was Alexia. Much to everyone's surprise, he was a perfect marksman. Alexia giggling opened his purse to show the boys the type of heat he was packing.

All happy campers rendezvoused around the campfire. With the setting sun, the mosquitoes began to awake in search of blood. Parallel to these events, the maidens had ended their spa day. Just when Stacie was the most relaxed, she began to wonder if her son Kyle had taken his EpiPen. Stacie called up her husband, but his cellphone didn't have a signal.

"I am…I am…going to check out early," said Stacie.

"The girls are fine," said Unla.

"I am worried about my son!" hissed Stacie, "He always forgets his EpiPen."

"If your husband knows that, maybe he took the EpiPen with him," said Unla trying to comfort Stacie.

"Yes…maybe…probably. Hahaha…I am just worrying myself over nothing," said Stacie laughing nervously, "Were to know? What is the plan?"

The maidens cramped themselves inside Eugenia's party wagon. Eugenia had prepared a special surprise for Stacie's birthday. Before they arrived to the venue, Carina insisted that Stacie be blindfolded. Those who could see had to hold in their mirth. The maidens pushed Stacie up a flight of stairs, they took a left, a right, they bumped into a couple, and they sat the maiden on a chair. When the blindfold was removed, all assembled yelled: "Surprise!"

And boy, was Stacie surprised by what she saw!!

Back in Camp Flamingo, the guys were telling stories around the campfire. The boys on the meantime where burning marshmallows. At a certain point, the men began to ask Bruno for legal advice. In order to brag, Bruno mentioned his most recent case. When he concluded his tirade, he noticed that the officers surrounding him looked extremely hostile.

"But that man was guilty," hissed Zidanta, "I was there! He attacked Jeremy!"

"A lawyer only knows what his client tells him," retorted Bruno, "Even without my intervention, the prosecutor's case was held together by circumstantial evidence brought forth by the brother of the victim…and Jeremy's coworkers threw him under the bus because they need that job."

Zidanta furious began to scream Bruno's ear off. Jeremy growing wearing of Zidanta screeching like a peacock said, "Enough, Zidanta. This is all your fault for pressuring me into getting a job that I didn't want."

"I can't carry the house bills all by myself, Jeremy," protested Zidanta.

"It is your fault for buying a house you can't afford! I was fine living in an efficiency," said Jeremy.

The two began to bicker about money like an old married couple. Jeremy tired of arguing left in a huff to wander about in the Everglades in the middle of the night. Zidanta embarrassed entered his tent in order to sulk. He had made a scene in front of his new friends, so now, he didn't want to be seen. Bruno entered Zidanta's tent. He found Zidanta hiding inside his sleeping bag.

"I am sorry…this is all my fault," said Bruno apologetically.

Bruno added handing his card, "If you are ever in any legal trouble, I would be happy to give you a freebie."

"It's fine…don't worry about it," said Zidanta not bothering to come out of his hiding spot, "Jeremy was probably going to quit sooner or later. He doesn't do well with people."

"It is hard to do well with others, when you are a magnet for bullies," said Kain contributing to the conversation, "I am going to go look for Jeremy. Do you want to come with me?"

"Nah, don't bother…Jeremy can take care of himself," said Zidanta hiding deeper into his sleeping bag, "Unlike me, he has a great sense of direction."

"Your brother doesn't know these woods. He could get lost," insisted Kain.

"I can't face him when he is this angry!" said Zidanta, "I was hoping that his stupid cat would mellow him out, but Tybalt just made things worse."

"Moving to a new house always creates tension," said Gent mentoring his underling.

"I think it would help if you would stop calling Tybalt "his stupid cat"," said Farley offering his own unsolicited advice.

"But Tybalt is Jeremy's cat!" said Zidanta peeping out of his hiding spot, "Tybalt hisses every time I try to touch him. At night, Tybalt always falls asleep on top of my face. And you see this scar on top of my nose, that was the stupid cat! I can't walk five steps without the stupid cat ambushing my feet. The cat hates me! And I hate it because it hates me!"

Tybalt passed by the tent and it rubbed up against Kain's back. The cat was such an ugly cupcake that Kain had a hard time believing Zidanta's story. Kain picked up the cat and he went to look for Jeremy. In order to keep his nephew from getting lost, Gent tied a lifeline around Kain's waist. Even with the flashlight, Kain was barely able to see five steps in front of him. Tybalt began to shift uncomfortably in Kain's arms. In spite of his best effort, the stupid cat ran away. At moments like this, Kain was regretting all of his life's choices.

"Here...kitty, kitty! Psp! Psp! Come back! Tybalt," said Kain shifting around on the floor looking for the stupid cat.

Kain heard a low meow. He crawled through the darkness, looking for the source of the meowing. He found the source inside a hole underneath a tree. He dug his hand into the hole. Instead of Tybalt, Kain had pulled out a Panther kitten. The moment he picked up the Panther Kitten, Kain heard the Panther mother growling. Kain placed the kitten down and with a trembling hand he held up his gun. With the flashlight, he tried to find the Panther mother, but he just couldn't see her. The bushes began to rustle behind him. Kain turning around attempted to shoot towards the bushes he saw moving. The gun didn't fire because he forgot to remove the safety. In his panicked state, Kain imagined that the gun was malfunctioning. Kain ran away from the unknown creature that was pursuing him. He bumped into Jeremy, and he yelled thinking that he had gotten attacked by the Panther.

"Grandpa! Help!!" yelled Kain covering his face.

"Kain! Why are you yelling?" asked Jeremy placing his thin hand on Kain's shoulder.

"Jeremy! We gotta run! The Panther is after me!" said Kain taking in deep breaths. Kain felt the lifeline around his waist becoming heavier.

"But you told us not to run away from the panther," said Jeremy.

"I know what I said, Jeremy," said Kain with a hysteric pitch to his voice, "But I pissed off the panther! And now, she wants to kill me! Grandpa! I want my Grandpa!!"

Before Kain could say more, he was overcome by a crying fit. He was coiled up in a fetus position waiting for his grandpa or the panther to come for him. Jeremy took the gun and he coolly faced the darkness. There was something indeed stalking Kain, but it wasn't a panther. Jeremy narrowed his eyes, he removed the safety, he took aim, and then he shot something only his eyes were able to see. The noise stopped as soon as he fired the gun. At the sound of the gun, Gent left his seat. He took his flashlight, and he began to follow the lifeline. He found Jeremy walking back with Kain. Kain had his face buried in his hand, while he sobbed uncontrollably. His arms and knees where covered in scratches, caused by his mad dash.

"The panther got to him," explained Jeremy, "I shot something in the darkness. I do not know what it was, but it stopped chasing us."

"We will deal with it in the morning," said Gent guiding the two young men back to camp.

"I am sorry I caused so much trouble," said Jeremy apologetically.

"Don't worry about it," said Gent petting Jeremy's thin shoulder, "Though next time you get in a fight with your brother, please don't wonder off."

Gent brought out from his knapsack a first aid kit. He threated Kain's wounds. Jeremy apologized to the campers for all the trouble he caused. Jeremy then began to look for his cat. Kain didn't have the heart to tell him that he had lost Tybalt. Jeremy reached into his backpack and he brought out Tybalt's favorite food, anchovy. Jeremy took the can and he began to fan it in all directions in order to lure the cat back to camp. When that didn't work, Jeremy just left the can open, and he sat down to wait for the cat to return on his own accord.

"He always comes back," said Jeremy, "I have his favorite meal. He won't be able to resist temptation forever."

"Your cat's expensive food is another reason why you have to get a day job," retorted Zidanta coming out of his hiding spot.

"Let's not start again!" hissed Jeremy.

Zidanta went to sit down beside Jeremy. Jeremy brought out his pocket knife as a threat display. Zidanta taking the hint went to sit for away from Jeremy. The bad moment eventually passed, thought it was a pity that the cat was still missing. To kill some time, the men began to share spooky stories. The kids where already inside their tents, for it was past their bedtime. Kyle slept like a log, while Oswald kept waking up at the slightest sound. Oswald was eventually able to consolidate his sleep, when his father Farley got inside the tent. Farley petted his son's back till the lad finally fell into a deep slumber.

Parallel to these events, Stacie was looking upon the big surprise. Right in front of her face, was the biggest member she had ever laid eyes upon. The speedo didn't do much to mask it. Rather, it perfectly delineated its flaccid features. The music roared, and the performer began to dance seductively around the birthday girl. Stacie laughed nervously, and she covered her face wishing for the Earth to swallow her whole. Her face turned as red as a tomato, while her terrible friends kept taking pictures of this embarrassing moment. When it was finally over, Stacie breathed in a sigh of relief.

"Wasn't that fun?" asked Eugenia giggling.

"If you embarrass me like that again, I will kill you," whispered Stacie dropping her mask.

"What? I can't hear you?" said Eugenia coming closer.

"That was a little too wild for my taste," lied Stacie forcing a fake smile.

"Do you want another lap dance?" asked Eugenia, "My treat!"

"God! No! No. No. No. No. No!" said Stacie laughing nervously.

The awkward moment passed. The men began to flock around the younger maidens like Carina, Eugenia and Dorothy, who was finally old enough to party with her big sister. Keeping an eye on Dorothy was her mother Eunice. This wasn't her type of venue, still, she had found it amusing to see Stacie extremely embarrassed. Eunice was suddenly distracted from her maternal duties by Eugenia who asked her step-mother to dance.

"Why didn't dad go to the camping trip with the boys?" asked Eugenia.

"Your father doesn't like to socialize with people he hasn't fully investigate," guessed Eunice.

"He is so paranoid!" said Eugenia laughing.

"He has his reasons," said Eunice, "Since he was born poor, he knows how the proletarians think. Speaking of peasants, how is your new boyfriend working for you? I see you spending a lot of time with him."

"Calling Kain my boyfriend is a bit of a stretch mom," said Eugenia. Eunice smiled happily. It wasn't often that Eugenia called her mom, "I tried to sleep with him when he was sober, and regardless of my best efforts wasn't remotely inspired, if you catch my drift."

"Men cannot fake it like women do. If they are not into you, nothing you do will be able to get a rise out of them," said Eunice who was more experienced, "Though in your case, I think the problem was that you tried to seduce him while he was in mourning. That was very insensitive of you Eugenia, and I am surprised that you two are still in speaking terms considering all the trouble you have caused him. Other than his body, what else do you like about Kain?"

"I like the way he cooks. I like dancing with him. I like that he isn't constantly pressuring me for sex, but I also kinda despise him for it," said Eugenia frowning.

"So, he respects you and he threats you like a person. Why don't you like that, Eugenia?" asked Eunice putting things in perspective for her step-daughter.

Mother and daughter spent the rest of the night overanalyzing Kain, like he was a product. Back in the Everglades, the adults were starting to go to bed. Kain was by now extremely mellowed out. He was taking comfort in the brain massage that his father was giving him, with his cold, long, delicate fingers.

At a certain point, Kain asked, "Daddy…did you ever get around to looking inside that box I gave you?"

"I didn't want to open it without you," lied Jack. The truth that he had completely forgotten all about it.

"What box? Now, I am curious," said Gent.

"Kain had a little time capsule buried in the backyard of our original house," said Jack, "We should all get together and look inside."

"Ok…" said Kain yawning, "I think I fed the mosquitoes enough. Goodnight dad."

The last person to go to bed was Gent. He was keeping vigil over everyone's dreams. Farley who had the bladder the size of a walnut awoke close to midnight. He relieved Gent of his nightwatchman duties. Just when Farley was starting to fall asleep, he saw Tybalt returning to camp. Tybalt had something in his mouth. The cat flung that long object at Farley. Farley screamed when he noticed that the cat had thrown him a live snake. It was thankfully a nonvenomous baby python. Tybalt ate his food before getting inside his carrying bag. Farley took that chance to close the bag, to keep the cat from running away again. Farley took the bag with the cat and he placed it over his lap. He figured that if there was any danger, the cat was probably going to hiss or something. He dug his hand into the bag in order to pet Tybalt a little. The soothing purring of the cat eventually lulled Farley to sleep. With everyone finally asleep, Alexia took the chance to make his move.

He first visited Jeremy's tent. He poked the lad till Jeremy awoke. Alexia whispered, "Jeremy… Your face is identical to that of a woman. Where you born that way? Or did you get plastic surgery?"

"I was born this way," said Jeremy, "Zidanta says that I resemble Queen Nefertiti."

"Have you ever slept with a man?" asked Alexia.

"No. And you can't prove that I sleep with the same man more than five times a week," said Jeremy being evasive.

"Oh! You have a boyfriend. I am sorry, for coming on to you. Why didn't you bring him over?" asked Alexia lying down beside Jeremy.

"I couldn't get him to come out of the closet. He practically lives there," retorted Jeremy. Jeremy yawned and he turned his back to Alexia. Jeremy immediately fell asleep again.

Alexia entered Zidanta's tent. Zidanta extremely hostile kicked Alexia out of his tent, as soon as he showed his face. For his final stop, Alexia tried his luck with Kain.

"Is sleeping with you a requirement to be your friend?" asked Kain after hearing Alexia's indecent proposal.

"Yes! If you don't sleep with me, I won't hang out with you anymore," said Alexia's lust demon.

"You sound just like Carina," said Kain narrowing his eyes, "She too began to require that I sleep with her in order to maintain our friendship. Whenever a man broke up with her, it fell on me to lick her wounds. She always left me as soon as a new guy picked her interest."

"You are such a beautiful man. Why do you put up with that?" asked Alexia shocked.

"Because Carina always comes back. And even when she is with another, she is always there for me," protested Kain, "Every other woman I have ever dated always leaves me. But Carina… she cares about me. She is always trying to help me. And even when she hurts me, she does so, with my best interest in mind."

"You sound just like my mother," said Alexia, "My mom was always making excuses for my drunken and abusive father. Kain! You need to break free of that abusive relationship."

"Are you insane Alexia? The stupid things you say. Carina is neither a drunkard, nor an abuser," said Kain laughing. He added turning more serious, "Whenever people attack me, Carina is always there to defend me. When I get hurt, Carina heals me. When I am sad, she plays with me, to help me forget my woes. Carina is always trying to include me in her activities. Carina … Carina stayed! While the rest of you left, just because I didn't go to college."

Alexia gave a sly smile. He took Kain's hand and he said, "I promise to stay with you forever, if you become mine and mine alone."

"You are as shallow as all the women who came before. If I wasn't beautiful, you wouldn't even be bothering to talk to me," said Kain leaving his sleeping bag.

Kain left his tent, and he went to sleep beside his father Jack. Jack opened up his sleeping bag to allow for his son to roost there beside him. Jack was rather happy to not be sleeping alone anymore. Jack petted the lovely strands of hair off his son's face. Jack was surprised that someone so beautiful had come out of an ugly duckling, like himself.

"If I had your face and body, I would fuck every chick that brushed up against me," said Jack resting his head against Kain's strong shoulder.

"Eugenia is going to leave me soon. I wasn't able to rise to the challenge because I was in a foul mood. She has probably been telling the 4 winds that I am a Closet Case," said Kain, "Dad…I tell these people that I am hurting; their first instinct is to seduce me."

"Well… Kain. It is common for men and women your age to use sex as a coping mechanism. When you say, I am sad. What they hear is: Make love to me," explained Jack.

"Sex has never cured me of my woes," said Kain yawning.

"Your girlfriends must not be doing it right, son," said Jack giggling.

"Yawn…probably," said Kain falling asleep.

The following morning Kain awoke to the smell of bacon and eggs. When he left his tent, he was surprised to see the men taking photos with a large dead Python. On its forehead, it had the bullet that Jeremy had fired in almost absolute darkness. Even if it was a so called "lucky shot", it was still an impressive accomplishment. With the Python photoshoot out of the way, Gent went with the boys and the young men to an airboat tour of the Mangroves. The party saw gators, a herb of dugongs, and they visited the fishing grounds of baby bull sharks. For the next activity, Farley suggested that they go biking. Kain stayed behind with Jeremy. Nobody had ever bothered to teach Kain how to ride a bicycle.

"That explains why he only goes jogging," said Gent while lazily ridding his bike at the same speed as Jack.

"Has Kain always been like this?" asked Jack.

"Has he always been like what, Jackie?" asked Gent.

"I don't know. Something about him is not normal," said Jack worried.

"Define normal," said Gent.

"Touché, brother," said Jack agreeing with Gent.

Back in camp, Jeremy was showing Kain his sweet motorcycle. Kain sat on it, and he imagined what it would be like to ride on it. To remove the guessing work, Jeremy allowed Kain to sit on the side car. Jeremy drove around the parking lot a bit, to give Kain a general feel of what it was like to ride a motorcycle. Other bored men that had stayed behind also asked to ride on the sidecar. Bruno on the other hand insisted on driving the genuine article.

"If you crash it, you are paying for it," said Jeremy.

"Fair enough," said Bruno sitting on the bike.

Bruno got a feel for the control. After accelerating once, the bike left him behind. Jeremy said dryly, "You scratched the paint.

That will be 500 dollars."

"That much for a little scratch?" asked Bruno licking his index finger, before trying to remove the black scratches, "Surely, 80 bucks will be more than enough to fix it."

"It is a custom paint job, and you ruined it," said Jeremy dryly, "IF you don't have the money to pay for it, I am going to need your insurance information."

Despite Bruno's best efforts, he wasn't able to convince Jeremy to accept 80 bucks for a scratched paintjob. Bruno grudgingly forked over the 800 bucks for the costume paint job. He got charged an extra 300 dollars for being so immature about the accident. The camping trip came to an end without any incident. The first thing that Kain did when he returned to his home was open the Time Capsule with Jack, Gent and Esther. The Time Capsule was a tin lunch box featuring the Muppets. Kain never cared for the Muppets, but his mother only allowed him to see "educational" shows.

Inside the box, there were some water soaked letters. Based on the handwriting, the letters had been penned by Kain's mother Bela. The other letters had an unfamiliar handwriting. Jack looked through the envelopes in search of anything of value. He smiled when he found an envelope with 10,000 dollars. As for the correspondence, they were promptly thrown into the garbage. The final object of interest was Bela's Jewelry Box. The box was filled with all the expensive jewelry Bela had bought with Jack's credit card.

"So, you hid your mother's nest egg, and that is why she went ballistic," said Jack thoughtfully.

"Pretty much," said Kain, "Mother was going to run away with her lover, but she didn't want to start over without a penny to her name. So, I hid her nest egg, and I destroyed her favorite dress. Everything went according to plan…except for the part where she nearly killed me."

"If your mother was stealing from your father, you should have told us," said Gent.

"I did, but you didn't understand me, uncle Gent," said Kain, "At the end of our conversation, you bought me an Atari. I also told Grandpa that my mother hated me and about the Nyquil. I don't know what he understood, but the result of that conversation was that he gave my mother more spending money."

"The woman is dead Kain," hissed Jack rubbing his temple, "She no longer has the power to hurt you. Why do you keep bringing her up in practically every topic of conversation?"

"I don't always bring her up," said Kain meekly, "Before meeting Eugenia, I had never spoken about my mother. Eugenia reminds me of my mother, a lot."

"Kain…your mother left when you were four. There isn't a lot of your mother for you to remember," reasoned Esther, "Believe me when I say this, Eugenia is nothing like Bela. The two do not even look alike. If you do not believe me, take a better look at the photograph I left by your nightstand."

Kain went to his bedroom and he got a good look at the photo. After seeing that face so often in random places, he had grown desensitized to Bela's face. Esther suggested, "Tell your mother how you feel, Kain."

"What's the point? She is already dead," protested Kain.

"She can still hear you in the afterlife," reasoned Jack, "IF anything, this pointless task might be therapeutic."

Kain stared at the portrait of his mother. The black and white photograph showcased a medium built woman, with a perky bosom, raven hair and grey eyes, just like the ones of her son Kain. Kain awkwardly stared at the photograph, wishing to get away from this situation.

Jack took his son's hand, and he said, "Here is what I would like to say to your mother: Bela! You monster! How could you do that to the baby! There is a place in hell for demons like you! There. You see that Kain. I gave that woman a piece of my mind, and I feel all the better for it."

Kain after thinking his lines said, "Mother…if you didn't have the intention of loving me, I wish you would have left as soon as I was born."

Kain then buried his face into his palm to cry. Jack took Bela's photograph and he threw her in the garbage were she belonged. Since this time capsule belonged to Kain, it fell on him to decide how to divide up the money. He gave his father 4000 dollars. The other 6000 was divided among the other three siblings. As for the Jewelry, Esther was going to slowly pawn it off. The workday came and Kain fell back into his new happy routine. At the crack of dawn, he would go jogging. After his morning workout, he would shower and then make breakfast. His father would drive Kain to work, and Esther to the Senior Center. Kain would process evidence till he was bored to tears. He would then assist Zidanta in his patrols. In the middle of the day, he would be sent to Unla to do his Exposure Therapy for one hour, before being shipped back to his office. Once, he clocked out, Kain would spend two hours helping Eugenia with her Thesis. At night, he would watch TV with his father, or he would play video games while his father practiced the guitar. Kain was finally at peace with his father's presence.

Jack on the other hand was still iffy about the entire situation. When he started living with Kain, Jack imagined that the two would just be roomies. He had underestimated just how emotionally needy his son truly was. Jack had imagined that his son had grown up happy without him. It was convenient for Jack to think that way. One night, Jack was awake while staring at the unfamiliar roof. Sleeping beside him was his son Kain. When Kain was a toddler, he would always leave the crib to sleep beside his father. After the first few times of doing that, Jack would place the baby beside him, in order to save the infant the trip.

Jack kept thinking about his early life with Kain. He was trying to decipher what about his parenting style had inspired so much love and devotion, on a child he rarely saw. When the two where together, Jack was always playing with his son, and he would buy him many things to overcompensate. Jack was always quite complimentary of every little thing Kain did, even when he made mistakes. Jack would engage Kain in conversation, often asking his son to repeat himself, in order to be able to understand his babbling. Jack was also physically affectionate.

"Maybe he remembers me fondly because I was probably the only person who hugged him," said Jack more to himself. As if to confirm this fact, Kain snuggled closer to his father.

The following morning Jack used his lunch break to go speak with Unla about his big baby. When he entered her office, she was in the middle of giving her sister Barbara a treatment. Jack watched with curiosity the liquid being pumped into Barbara's veins. Once, it was over Barbara sighed with relief.

"Give me some of that," said Jack happily.

"It is just a B-12 supplement," said Unla, "And the other injection is Steroids. My sister suffers from Psoriasis, and the steroids help clear up her condition…you wanted to check up on Kain's progress."

"Or regression," said Jack, "He has been a little clingy these past few days."

"I can only imagine why," said Unla dryly. Unla opened her cabinet and she dug up a few articles about Touch Starvation. She photocopied those articles in order to give Jack a bit of literature to help him understand his son's latest malfunction.

"So…the days he gets extra clingy is because he is under a lot of stress," commented Jack. Changing the subject, Jack said, "How is your daughter doing?"

"She is pretty busy with her new work, and her new boyfriend," said Unla, "Now that she has a full time job, she has completed her transition into adulthood."

"When Kain is with you, what does he talk about?" asked Jack.

"Doctor patient confidentiality," said Unla, "I can't give you the specifics, but mostly your son feels guilty for not living up to his grandpa's expectations. He also doesn't like his job, but he likes the financial security and he enjoys spending time with his uncle. He is currently conflicted with the Eugenia situation. He likes her, but he doesn't want to develop an emotional attachment to someone who is incapable of loving him."

"Why does he think that Eugenia won't fall in love with him?" asked Jack.

"What I got from his tirade was that Eugenia will leave him, because not even his own mother was able to love him," Unla added, "All the woman who have dated him leave. Carina is also guilty in this department."

"Nobody is perfect," said Jack trying to be conciliatory, "If I was Kain, I would just enjoy Eugenia's body without forming an emotional bond. Not every affair needs to be important or meaningful."

Jack returned to his work with this thought in mind. He debated this topic with his boss Arjuna. Arjuna gifted his underling a copy of the Bhagavat Gita, to gift to Kain. This Hindu book gave Kain a lot of food for thought. He decided to date Eugenia, without stressing about the real possibility that she was going to leave him, as soon as she was bored of him.

CHAPTER 9

The Fool

It was a cloudy September afternoon in Eugenia's beachfront property. With her Thesis completed, she was pondering what to do with her newfound free time. There was an unexpected knocking at the door. Dorothy was the one to answer it. She giggled when she saw Kain clutching a Tupperware filled with home baked goodies. Dorothy took the goodies and she went to the kitchen to munch down on the elegantly decorated cupcakes. Michael was at home for a change. He wasn't in a working type of mood. He was sitting in the couch with his wife Eunice. The two were watching MythBusters. Michael frowned when he saw Kain's cheap tribute. After trying the cupcake, Michael had to admit that Kain was an excellent pastry chef.

"Do you know any other recipes?" asked Michael.

"I do...but, most of the cooking I do is purely utilitarian," explained Kain. He was about to rant about his sad pathetic, lonely childhood, but he chose not to, "Though, when I get bored of eating the same thing over and over, I attempt to learn new recipes. I recently learned how to make a Cuban flan. Unla taught me how to make it..."

"Why are you here?" asked Michael interrupting Kain's baking rant.

"I came to hang out with Eugenia," said Kain.

"Her thesis is already done," said Michael. He reached into his pocket and he handed Kain 500 bucks, "For your troubles."

"Are you paying me to go away?" asked Kain becoming offended.

"Take this payment for what it is," said Michael placing his arm around Kain's shoulder, "You provided a service, and now you are receiving renumeration for all your hard work."

"Thanks…I guess," said Kain grudgingly accepting the money.

Kain went to Eugenia's room. After helping Eugenia with her schoolwork, he had become familiar with her bedroom. The balcony windows were littered with orchids that Eugenia watered religiously. There was the library filled with her coursework. Her writing table and expensive Apple computer. Her walk in closet was overstuffed with dresses, shoes, handbags and just about everything she needed to shine. Her flavor for craftsman furniture made of reclaimed wood contrasted greatly, with the Midcentury Modern décor of the rest of the house.

Eugenia was roosting on top of her bed, while she watched an episode of Blind Date. She had not bothered to change out of her pajamas. Kain sat down on the bed and he offered Eugenia a cupcake. Eugenia took the cupcake absentmindedly. She waited ten minutes and then she sighed with disappointment. She turned her head and then she saw that it was Kain who was sitting beside her.

"You didn't like the cupcake?" asked Kain.

"It was fine. It was great even," said Eugenia not desiring to elaborate, "What are you doing here Kain?"

"I came to…never mind. See you around, Eugenia," said Kain leaving the bedroom.

"Bye, Kain," said Eugenia still zoning out. Kain made his way downstairs.

Eunice commented, "Leaving so soon…Can't say that I blame you."

"I wasn't leaving," lied Kain, "Eugenia simply wanted me to bring her a glass of water."

Kain made his way towards the kitchen. Michael watched with mild amusement the lad struggling to find the refrigerator. The fridge seamlessly blended with the cabinets. Eunice playing hostess left her seat and she opened the fridge for Kain. She dug from within a sparkly water and she handed it to Kain. The young man returned to sit beside Eugenia. Kain placed the cold water within Eugenia's grasp. The maiden opened it absentmindedly, without bothering to look at the man sitting beside her. There was an awkward silence. Kain fiddled with the wad of cash he had received from Michael. Since he didn't feel right about taking this money, he left it beside Eugenia's nightstand. During the commercials, Kain tried to talk to Eugenia.

"How are you doing today, Eugenia?" asked Kain.

"I am fine, and you. Do you need anything from me?" asked Eugenia.

"I didn't come here to take anything from you, Eugenia," said Kain.

"Then, why are you here?" insisted Eugenia.

"I came to hang out," said Kain.

"Oh!" exclaimed Eugenia surprised, "I am not in the mood to go out with you. I am feeling a little cozy."

"That's fine. We do not need to be doing exciting things to enjoy each other's company," reasoned Kain.

"Right…" said Eugenia dryly, "If you say so."

The commercials ended so Eugenia returned to focusing on the

Blind Date episode. When the episode finally ended, she looked at the clock, before stretching her elegant limbs. She turned to look for Kain, but he was gone. Kain drove under the rain to Carina's house. He knocked on her door. The person who answered was Bruno.

"If it isn't my favorite third wheel," said Bruno giving an exaggerated fake smile, "Come in! Come in! Make yourself at home."

Bruno returned to the couch to sit beside Carina. The couple were watching a telenovela called "Besame, Tonto" (Kiss me, Fool!). In the episode, the heroine was running away with her beloved. Kain sat down on the floor beside Carina. He rested his head against her knee. Bruno narrowed his eyes, but he knew that it was a moot point to protest. Carina began to absentmindedly pet Kain's hair.

At a certain point, Kain said, "Carina...would you still have hooked up with Bruno had I accepted your marriage proposal?"

Carina laughed nervously. Bruno pondered how to respond to this scenario. In the end, he said, "Well, answer him Carina. We have a right to know."

"I am going to level with you Kain," said Carina, "As much as we like to joke about the topic of getting married, you and I have unreconcilable differences. I want children. You don't want children. I am ambitions, while you are content to live in complete stagnation. I like to experience new things, while you are afraid of what the world has to offer. More than anything, my main problem with you Kain is that you are too immature..."

Kain sat there like a stone while he listened to Carina's long list of criticisms. Bruno interrupted Carina at a certain point, "Be that as it may, the problems that you find in your friend, may not be perceived as defects by another. You need to find a woman that goes with your lifestyle. The whole opposites attracts thing is a myth, because people are not magnets."

"I don't quite agree with you Bruno," said Carina, "My parents were opposites, who ended up becoming inseparable. My mother is serious, but my father he was lighthearted and playful. My father he was passionate about his work, while mother only gets emotionally attached to patients she personally knows...and..."

"Those are superficial differences. It was our core similarities that laid the foundation of our marriage," said Unla entering the room with snacks for her guests, "So, tell me Kain, why are you here? You didn't just come here to watch telenovelas?"

"If you want me to leave as well, just say so," said Kain wrapping his arms around Carina's leg.

"Did Eugenia dumped you already?" asked Unla guessing the problem.

"Yeah...we used to spend a lot of time together while we were working on her Thesis, but as soon as she finished her homework she stopped calling me. I sent her a text message two days ago, and she hasn't even looked at it," said Kain pouting while looking at his cellphone.

"Are you certain you sent it to the right number?" asked Carina taking the phone.

"Yeah...that's her number," said Kain frowning.

"Maybe she is doing a powerplay," suggested Carina.

"What a bother...I hate it when women get into that powerplay mentality," protested Kain, "Why is it so important for her to be the one in charge? Why can't we be equal partners?"

"You are making a baseless assumption based on her failure to respond one text message," said Unla.

"With women, I find it more efficient to take a direct approach," said Bruno, "I want you to go to the store and buy the cheapest flowers you can find. Put on a nice outfit, and invite her to a date...thought there is a possibility that during the time you were hesitating she found herself another."

"That is something that I hadn't considered," said Kain, "Though, I suppose it was bound to happen sooner or later. A beautiful rich heiress probably has hundreds of suiters."

"Let's find out then," said Carina calling up Eugenia. The two maidens chatted like parrots for a bit. Carina eventually brought up the question, "So, are you and Kain a couple? I see the two of you hanging out, often."

"Me and Kain…we are…Is he listening? Did he put you up to this?" asked Eugenia sitting up. There was a sly smile painted on her face. The powerplay that her stepmother had suggested had actually worked.

Bruno took the phone from Carina. He then said to Eugenia, "Eugenia, Kain wanted us to ask you to go on a date. Just the two of you, without any other chaperone. Do you accept?"

Eugenia pretended to carefully consider her options. She eventually said yes. As part of her powerplay, she insisted that Kain pick the venue for their date. Kain began to think of possible date ideas, but everything that popped into his head sounded boring.

"The venue is not important," said Bruno offering unsolicited advice, "As long as the two of you are enjoy each other's company, it won't matter where you take Eugenia."

"Then again…if Eugenia is doing a powerplay there is a good chance that she is going to hate everywhere you take her," said Carina thoughtfully, "So, regardless of what you pick, you are going to choose wrong. So, there is no pressure Kain."

"I have a suggestion," said Unla bringing a cap and some paper strips, "We are each going to write date ideas, and then you are going to draw from a hat. The first set of suggestions are going to be possible restaurants. You can't have a date without eating out."

Carina and Bruno amused began to write possible restaurants. Bruno wrote down his favorite junk food restaurants, while

Carina wrote down her favorite sushi places. Unla also threw inside there a few suggestion of her own. Kain closed his eyes and he drew from the hat Cici's Pizza Buffet. Bruno laughed sinisterly seeing that they had chosen his favorite Buffet. The entertainment venue Kain randomly picked called Boomers.

"What is Boomers?" asked Carina looking at the suggestion.

"It…it is a park I went to once with my Grandpa. It has minigolf, go-karts, arcade games and a laser tag arena," said Kain shyly.

"Sounds like a lot of fun," said Carina giggling. As soon as Kain left, Carina said to Bruno, "That sounds like the perfect date for two teenagers."

"Seems about right for those two immature brats," said Bruno dryly.

 Kain drove back to Eugenia's house. He had managed to drive without suffering any panic attacks. It was a good day, even if it was rainy day. Eugenia saw through the lens the type of outfit Kain was sporting. She frowned when she realized that they were not going anywhere fancy. She went into her walk in closet and she dressed herself with the cheapest thing she could find, some ripped jean shorts, and a Within Temptation T-shirt. Kain drove for an hour till he arrived at the Boomers Amusement Park. Eugenia raised an eyebrow extremely perplexed by the situation. She was starting to regret not accepting Kain's original offer of staying in the bedroom, doing nothing. Kain opened the door for Eugenia. The two got completely drenched as they ran towards the entrance of the park. The interior had an arcade. The two went to the coin machine and they got 100 bucks in Quarters.

The first game Kain insisted they try was the arcade port of Guitar Hero. This was the first time Eugenia had ever attempted to play a video game. Her mother had been more doll oriented. The two butchered a couple of songs together, till they got a game over thanks to Eugenia. The two then went to shoot hoops. When Kain finally ran out of quarters, Eugenia breathed in a sigh of relief. She no longer needed to pretend to be having fun. With the rain pausing, Kain took Eugenia out to play a bit of mini-golf. Eugenia played regular golf with her father. It was one of the few activities that the two still did together. The first straight course was simple enough for Eugenia to perform. There was a tricky one with a pyramid in the center. Eugenia got on all fours in order to calculate the proper angle of entry. Some of the teens took that chance to snap a few pictures of Eugenia's sublime caboose, as seen through her shorts. Another course that gave Eugenia a headache was themed after Tetrix. The blocks were at odd angles. Regardless of how much Eugenia tried, she couldn't get the ball into the hole.

"The trick is a bit counter intuitive," said Kain hitting his golf ball backwards, at a right angle. The ball bounced around, and through a miracle it made it past the obstacle of Tetrix blocks. Giggling he said, "You have no idea how many hours it took for my Grandpa to figure this gimmick."

"I take it you visited this place a lot with your grandpa," said Eugenia.

"Yeah…it was a good way to kill a few hours under the blistering sun," said Kain.

"So we finally have something in common," said Eugenia, "Have you ever played real golf?"

"I did a couple of times, but grandpa became frustrated that I wasn't any good at it," said Kain, "So, we went back to playing minigolf."

"Minigolf may not be considered a serious sport, but it does offer its own unique trills," said Eugenia trying out the beer pong minigolf course, "So, tell me Kain, other than golf and video games, what else is your idea of fun?"

"We…could try lazer tag," suggested Kain.

"I feel that you would have an unfair advantage in that game," protested Eugenia.

"We don't have to playing against each other," said Kain, "We can be buddy cops."

The two went to the lazer tag arena. They were playing against a bunch of brats, a couple of teenagers and their parents. As soon as the game began, Kain ducked for cover and he dragged Eugenia down with him. He kept close to the walls, he looked over the corner, and then he delivered a merciless barrage of lasers against a little kid. Once the brat was out of the game, Kain continue to make his way through the maze, while keeping Eugenia behind him. When a man entered through Kain's blind spot, Eugenia began to fire blindly. The noise she was making alerted Kain of to the presence of the enemy. He turned around to finish overkilling the man that had tried to sneak up on Eugenia. At the end of the game, Eugenia and Kain were the sole survivors. The first half of the date concluded successfully. The two then went to eat at Cici's Pizza Buffet. Eugenia didn't know if Kain was dirt poor, or if this was a powerplay from a miser.

Kain coughed nervously before saying, "IF you do not want to eat here, we can go somewhere else."

"Fuck it! I am starving," said Eugenia getting in line.

Eugenia got some rotini and a few cheese pizza slices. The pizza was good, and so was the pasta. Eugenia figured that making terrible pasta was something easier said, than done. With some food in the pit of her empty stomach, her mood improve. Kain got for himself a slice of every pizza. It was his first time at this restaurant and he wanted to try everything. The main show stopper was the cinnamon rolls. Even Eugenia, with her fancy paladar, was forced to admit that they were delicious. The fact that everything was freshly backed also added to its yummy factor. Eugenia looked at the time and she saw that there was at least four more hours till midnight. Eugenia could only consolidate her sleep past midnight.

"Do you want to go to the Movie Theater?" asked Kain saying the first thing that came to his mind.

"Movie Theaters are not really my thing," said Eugenia, "I have my own Home Theater. You can come to my house, and we can watch a flick."

On the drive back to Eugenia's house, Kain would sneeze from time to time. Eugenia had suggested that they shower to avoid catching a cold. Eugenia also wanted an excuse to ogle the merchandise. Kain undressed and he got inside the standing shower. Instead of curtains, the shower had a clear glass sheet that kept the water out. Eugenia stood there while she examined Kain's nude body. When he turned around, she saw what type of package he was carrying. It wasn't the biggest she had ever seen, but it was certainly very pretty.

Kain saw Eugenia starring at him, so he began to pass the soap over his body in a slow, seductive manner. The sexy show that always worked on Carina, had a similar effect on Eugenia. Kain figured that he might as well sleep with Eugenia, since he was in a good mood, for a change. He imagined that the reason why Eugenia had become distant was because he had yet to sleep with her. Even in the heat of passion, Kain remembered to reach into his wallet to get some protection. After building up Eugenia's expectations, she was disappointed to discover that lovemaking wasn't Kain's strongpoint.

After an hour, Eugenia got bored of the exercise in futility. She did her best mimicry of a woman who was satisfied, before leaving the shower. She pressed a button and a movie screen lowered itself. She made a quick stop to the living room to fetch a Blue-Ray. Her sister Dorothy regularly rented Blue-Rays and DVDs. After looking at the new films over the top, Eugenia decided to watch How to Lose a Guy in 10 Days. Kain left the bathroom wrapped in a towel. He was completely oblivious to the fact that he had not matched Eugenia's high expectations. Eugenia's first instinct was to critique Kain's technique or lack thereof, but when she saw his childish smile she chose not to. Kain laid down beside Eugenia and he drew her closer to have her rest her lovely head on top of his chest. With his free hand, he started to absentmindedly pet Eugenia's hair. The two began to watch the romantic comedy film, while they snuggled. Eugenia had to admit that her new boyfriend was good in the snuggling department, and his conversation was pleasant. At the end of the movie, the two went for another round, with similar.

Kain was the first to fall asleep. Eugenia looked at her boyfriend, while she meditated on all her life choices. It was a pity that such a beautiful man didn't know how to make use of his assets. While Eugenia was extremely unsatisfied, in another part of Miami, there was Bruno rocking Carina's world. As a man with high ambitions, he wanted to be the best at everything he ever attempted. Before choosing Carina, Bruno had plowed through hundreds of maidens in his search for his First Lady. He would immediately break up with any woman that he perceived was just there to fool around. Carina was the first maiden he had ever ran into that wanted to have a serious relationship. Her little jealousy outbursts were a minor defect, but it was a problem that flattered Bruno's ego.

At the end of their first play session, Carina received a photo from Eugenia. Carina giggling showed the photo to Bruno. The photograph was a selfie of Kain and Eugenia in bed together.

"So, they finally did it. Good for them," said Bruno.

"I hope he used protection," said Carina worried, "Eugenia is a confirmed party animal. Who knows what sorts of cooties she carries."

"You can be experienced and disease free. It is all a matter of being careful, and paying attention to the signs," said Bruno, "As soon as I hear a maiden complaining while she pees, that is my cue to scram."

"So, tell me Bruno," said Carina, "You certain know how to gyrate. How many others came before me?"

"I can only give you an estimate," said Bruno after kissing Carina on the nose.

Carina gave Bruno a playful slap. She then added giggling, "Well. I can't judge. I am also far more experienced than I care to admit."

"Have you ever slept with a woman?" asked Bruno teasing Carina.

"No. Do you want me to?" asked Carina.

"Yes. It would amuse me," lied Bruno teasing Carina.

"Who do you have in mind?" asked Carina.

"Eugenia is a good option. I feel that the two of you have a lot of chemistry," lied Bruno.

"What would you have me do to Eugenia?" asked Carina narrowing her eyes. Bruno falling for the trap went on a rant about all the perverted things he would like Carina to do to Eugenia. At the end of the of his tirade, Carina screeched, "If you like Eugenia so much, why are we even dating!?"

"It was a joke," said Bruno giggling nervously, "If you felt uncomfortable about the topic, you could have politely asked to talk about literally anything else."

"I am not stupid Bruno! You like Eugenia! Admit it!" screeched Carina.

"Calm down Carina! You are going to wake up your mother," said Bruno.

"You are not talking yourself out of this mess, mister!" hissed Carina jumping out of the bed. She began to pace the bedroom in mimicry of Bruno, during his court proceedings, "Oh! How could I have been so blind! Why didn't I see the signs! All the time, I wasted on you…"

Bruno left the bed and he started getting dressed. The pause created by his sudden spring out of the bed, allowed him to mentally write up a rebuttal.

"Carina…You are right. There are things that I like about Eugenia," said Bruno coldly, "Eugenia doesn't write letters to distant family members to force painful reunions. She doesn't hex her lovers whenever they act contrary to her wishes. She doesn't throw tantrums whenever she imagines that her boyfriend is cheating on her. I love you Carina, but I can't stand living like this, anymore! I am sorry I am not perfect! But neither are you woman! I can't spend every waking moment watching what I say or do. If you do not change, you are going to spend the rest of your life miserable, and alone!"

Bruno left the house and he drove back to his apartment. He sat down on his couch to face his chessboard. This retreat was a dangerous move, but he was so close to checkmate. He fell asleep while facing the chessboard. As soon as Bruno left her house, Carina threw herself on top of the bed to kick and scream up a storm. Her mother who had heard everything entered her daughter's room in order to do damage control. Unla wanted her daughter to reconcile with her boyfriend, instead of crawling back to Kain. Carina barely slept after her first big argument with Bruno. When she drove to her day job, she fell asleep while driving. She realized that she was asleep because she saw her father's emaciated ghost in the passenger's seat.

The presence woke her up before she smashed against tree. Carina decided to err on the side of caution. She parked her car and she went down her contact list to see who could give her a ride. Bruno happened to be driving by when he saw Carina looking visibly distressed. Bruno entered the parking lot and he left his car to see what was wrong with his girlfriend.

"Are you stalking me now?" asked Carina with a hostile tone in her voice.

"I was driving to work when I noticed you had car problems," explained Bruno, "We may not be getting along for the moment, but that doesn't mean that I am going to turn a blind eye when you are in need of aid, Carina."

"I don't need your help!" protested Carina.

"Stop being a brat!" yelled Unla over the phone.

Carina looked at the time. Since she was late for work, she reluctantly accepted Bruno's help. Bruno drove slowly through the Miami traffic. Carina rested her head against her fist, and she began to doze off again. Bruno too yawned in spite of himself. When Carina snapped out of her power nap, she was right at her work. She walked out of the car with a weary step. As soon as she entered the front door, the manager began to give her an earful. Bruno seeing Carina getting yelled at went inside to bully, the bully. At the end of the shouting match, the manager yielded to Bruno's reasoning. There were going to be days that regardless of how early you awoke, the Miami Traffic was going to conspire to make you late for work. To further reinforce this idea, the owner of the establishment arrived a few minutes after Carina. The boss happened to have played Football with Bruno. With the power dynamics shifting, the manager decided to leave Carina alone, for the time being. Carina worked half asleep, without much enthusiasm. Her manager had yelled at her for being a few minutes late.

After work, Carina was picked up by her mother. She showered and she went to sleep. She slept four hours straight. She awoke around 9 p.m. She thought of Kain, and her old habits compelled her to visit her Best Friend. She knocked on his door. The one to answer was Jack.

"I know why you are here Carina," said Jack narrowing his eyes, "And I am not going to allow you to misuse my son."

"Your son! Your son! You two wouldn't have reconciled if it wasn't for my intervention!" protested Carina stomping the floor in anger.

"And you have my eternal gratitude, Carina. Now Scram! Shoo! Shoo!" said Jack.

"It's fine dad," said Kain coming to the door, "Let her come inside."

Jack stepped aside to allow Carina to enter within. The same ritual played out as before. Carina cried and vented about Bruno for hours. Kain hugged his friend, and he offered her a sympathetic ear. When Carina kissed Kain, her friend did not kiss her back. This time things played out differently. Carina attempted to make love to her friend.

Kain moved away from her and he said nervously, "I am still with Eugenia. She…she…hasn't broken up with me yet, so I, in good conscious, cannot be with you Carina."

"I was here first!" protested Carina.

"And you left me for Bruno! You always leave me Carina," said Kain with a trembling in his voice, "And frankly, I am tired. Aren't you tired too? Carina?"

"So, that's how you want to play it? Alright Kain! It was nice knowing you," said Carina picking up her purse to leave in a huff.

Carina had expected for Kain to try to detain her, but her power move failed. She slammed the door, and she began to fumble with her keys.

Before she moved away from the door, she heard Kain's voice say, "You are not the only who is suffering, Carina. While you were busy being angry at Bruno, do you know what your man did? He came to me and he begged me not to sleep with you. Carina… Never mind. Just do whatever you want! It is not as if you ever bother to listen to what anyone else says."

As soon as Carina drove away, Jack said to his son, "I am proud of you son. You don't need that alley cat. You can do better. You can do so much better."

"I hope Carina works things out with Bruno," said Kain lying down on the couch to sulk, "The guy really likes her. Of all Carina's boyfriends, he is the first to beg me for help."

Carina began to drive around Miami with no clear direction or purpose. She was still angry at Bruno, and she wanted to cheat on him. With Kain finally growing a spine, she was forced to go on the prowl. She drove to the Blue Martini, a bar with a lake view near Kendall. She roosted by the bar for a few hours till she caught a fish. Her catch of the night was a brutish, extremely inebriated man. The two went to the bathroom, and after the man burped his cigar breath into her face, Carina decided felt like going home. The man who was still in the heat of passion didn't allow for Carina to leave. When Carina started struggling, the man infuriated punched her in the face. Carina screamed like a wounded animal. Her scream attracted the attention of Bruno who had been stalking Carina for hours. He jumped into the bathroom to save her. He punched the man who had attacked Carina with much fury. Bruno even went as far as smashing the guy with the tank lid. Bruno drove Carina home. Carina was meek and silent.

Bruno after thinking of a good line broke the silence, "I think you need to go to anger management classes. You go from zero to one hundred very easily, over the stupidest of reasons. Not only are you hurting yourself, but you are making miserable those around you."

"I am sorry Bruno…I don't know what got over me," said Carina.

"I am the one who needs to apologize," said Bruno speaking truthfully, "I should have intervened sooner, but, I wanted to see how far your fury was going to take you."

Carina sighed, and she said, "If you don't want to be my boyfriend anymore, I won't hold it against you."

"It is only our first bump in the road. It is way too early to call it quits, don't you think?" reasoned Bruno.

"You really, really want to put up with me?" asked Carina smiling sadly, "After you caught me cheating on you?"

"All I saw was a drunkard forcing himself on my girl. I would have to be a petty, mean spirited individual to consider that an infidelity," said Bruno taking Carina's hand to kiss it.

"I changed my mind at the very end. That is why I screamed," said Carina, "I am sorry I am no longer First Lady material."

Meh…you are good enough, thought Bruno. Instead, he said, "There is no such thing as a perfect First Lady. As long as you are not a drug addict or a drunkard, I am quite happy to put up with your little abuses, Carina."

"Wow…you really set the bar low for me, didn't you," said Carina.

"I am inflexible with regards to unhealthy vices," said Bruno, "Everything else is negotiable."

The two arrived to Unla's home. The moment Unla saw her daughter returning home with a swollen cheek, the woman pitched a fit. When Unla was calmer, Carina explained to her mother how she had gotten punched in the face by a drunk guy she had picked up. Bruno spent the night licking Carina's wounds. Close to midnight, Carina managed to consolidate sleep. She dreamed of her father Juan Carlos again. He was looking more skeletal than ever. Her father was in his blue scrubs and he was rocking a cradle at an unnatural speed. Carina came to stand before her father. Bloody tears were rolling down his emaciated cheeks.

"I wanted to keep the baby…but your mother wouldn't let me," said Juan Carlos.

Carina looked into the crib and she saw inside the crib was her plushie Nana. Carina opened her mouth to speak, but her words came out as gibberish.

"A sick man cannot take care of a baby. He cannot take care of a plushie. He cannot even take care of himself," said Juan Carlos rocking the cradle with even more feverish energy.

It took much willpower, but Carina managed open her eyes. She had escaped her nightmare for the time being. She left the bed and she petted her bunny Nana nervously. She looked with envy at Bruno sleeping with his big mouth open. How she envied the fact that he could so easily fall asleep. Carina opened her drawer and she took a Tylenol to help her fall asleep. The next day she had Bruno to take her to work. At the end of her shift, she visited Irina to get a psychic reading. Carina described her most recent dream.

"When you see a crib in your dream, it represents protection. You might also be pregnant, or somebody you know is going to have a baby," explained Irina, "The crib also represents your desire to be a mother. What was the color of the crib? What was it made of?"

"I think it was blue, and it was made of wood," said Carina straining her memory.

"If it is blue, it means someone is going to have a baby boy. The wooden crib represents family unity," explained Irina, "Dreaming about stuffed animals is common, especially among those who grew up playing with plushies. When they manifest in your dreams, they represent a longing for much simpler times. As a small child, you had all your needs met, and you didn't need to worry about the wellbeing of others. What was the size of the stuffed animal?"

"He was a little bunny plushie?" said Carina bringing out from her purse her little Nana Plushie.

Irina touched the little plushie, and she spaced out for a bit. She blinked twice, and then she said to Carina, "Tiny plushies remind us of the fragility of life. Also, those who start new relationships tend to dream about white rabbits."

"In the dream he was kinda gray," said Carina.

"Then it means that someone is manipulating you," said Irina.

"And my father?" asked Carina, "Why has he been haunting my dreams?"

"In the dream world, your father is not your father. Rather, he is a manifestation of you assert yourself in your relationships," said Irina.

Carina thought of her father's frantic way of rocking the cradle, how it echoed the hysterical way she approached all her relationships. Carina paid Irina for the psychic reading. Carina then went to her mother for advice. Carina told her mother her most recent dream. Unla began to digest the information from a clinical standpoint.

"When was the first time you dreamt of your father?" asked Unla.

"I think it was the night I met Bruno," said Carina rubbing her temple, "Both have the same green eyes."

"You have dated men with green eyes before, and you never had nightmares," said Unla dryly, "What happened before you met Bruno."

"I was with Kain. He threw up all over the floor of the bathroom, and I cleaned it up," explained Carina looking at the floor.

"I would do that for your father, whenever he didn't make it to the bathroom," said Unla, "That incident must have reminded you of him. I do not think that you ever truly processed his death. Do you want to talk more about your father, with me Carina?"

"If you think it will help," said Carina shrugging her shoulders.

The two ranted about Juan Carlos for hours. When it came time to sleep, the nightmares did not return. The following morning Carina got a text message from Alexia. Alexia had been invited to an office party at his boss's penthouse, and he wanted Kain to be his plus one.

Carina texted back, "Why don't you just ask Kain out on a date?"

"He has been a bit distant ever since we came back from the camping trip," texted Alexia.

"That's funny. Kain tells me that you are the one who is staying away," texted Carina, "He thinks that you do not want to be his friend, because he refused to sleep with you."

"He tells you everything, doesn't he?" texted Alexia before adding a frowny face.

"We are best friends," texted Carina.

Carina texted Kain, "Alexia needs you to be his plus one. He doesn't want to be the one single loser at the office party. Are you willing to help him?"

Kain read the message. He called up Eugenia to see if she wanted to hang out. Eugenia said that she was going to be spending time with her little sister. Kain then called his father to see what he was up to. Jack was having a jam session with Arjuna, so, he was also busy. Kain asked Zidanta to hang out, but his coworker said it was date night. Destiny had ordained that Kain was to be Alexia's plus one. The alternative was for Kain to spend the night alone, in an empty house. Kain opened his closet and he wore the blue tuxedo that Bruno had gifted him. Alexia drove up to Kain's house to pick him up. Alexia opened the door for Kain. Kain rubbed his temple, and his face contorted into a grimace. Alexia feeling sheepish went back to the driver's seat to allow his friend to sit down without his help.

The two did not speak to one another for an hour. Alexia arrived to Brickle. He parked near his boss's penthouse apartment. The two left the car and they started to walk towards the skyscraper.

"I miss being a child," said Kain sighing, "Back then, we could just be friends, without the pressure of having that friendship evolve into something else."

"Hehehe…yes, things were much simpler back then," said Alexia laughing nervously.

"I missed the old Alexia," retorted Kain, "We were able to hang out, without you flirting with me every 5 seconds."

"The old me was a coward, too afraid to come out of the closet," retorted Alexia.

They arrived at the entrance and Alexia showed his invitation. They got inside the clear glass elevator, and Alexia pressed down the number 58. They got a good view of Brickle on their ride up to the penthouse.

"If I was a woman, would you still reject me Kain?" asked Alexia.

"Yes. I don't like pushy women," said Kain, "I only tolerate Carina, because she is the only true friend I have left in the entire world, but with other women, as soon as they start barking orders, I run for the hills, or I pretend to listen to them, only to do the complete opposite. That's quickest way to get them to break up with you."

"Have you ever been in love?" asked Alexia.

The elevator door opened and the sappy conversation came to an end. All the guests hyper focused on Alexia and his plus one. Alexia switching to work mode began to gossip with all his coworkers. As for Kain, he began to roam about the penthouse while examining the decoration. His eyes gravitated towards the balcony pool. A servant passed by with some champagne, so Kain took a glass in order to relax. In the balcony, he found a chair and a table in a dark, unlight corner. He sat down and he brought out his Gameboy Advance from within his coat pocket. With his headsets on, he was able to immerse himself in the game. He was struggling to memorize the pattern of Phoenix Magnion. Just when he had the boss almost beat, Alexia gingerly took the Gameboy away.

"You couldn't wait five seconds for me to finish!" yelled Kain slamming his palms against the stable.

"Aw…that's too bad…was that your last life," giggled Alexia looking at the game over screen, "Stop being a wallflower, and come mingle."

"I don't know anyone here," protested Kain getting back his game. He turned it off and he placed it back into his coat pocket.

"I miss the old Kain. There was a time when you were the life of the party," said Alexia pulling at Kain's arm.

Kain grudgingly allowed Alexia to guide him back to the living room. Alexia's coworkers began to interrogate Kain. They asked about his job, his sexual preference, his religion, how much money he made, his education level and his political affiliation. Kain responded with the mechanical politeness of a politician. He had heard all these questions before, and he rehearsed vanilla answers to all those inquiries. When he could no longer tolerate all those strangers nitpicking his life, Kain pulled at Alexia's arm to drag him to the dance floor. If he was dancing, Kain couldn't answer any more questions.

Alexia was sporting high heels, and after an hour of dancing nonstop, he was forced to sit down. A maiden began to brush up against Kain, so the young man turned around to dance with her. When she started to interrogate Kain, he went to dance with another. With this dancing strategy, Kain was able to avoid speaking to anyone for three hours. He was completely drenched in sweat. When his legs could no longer sustain him, he wabbled to the bar and he sat down to have a cold beer. He gulped it down since he was thirsty. He was immediately overcome by a fit of paranoia. The beer had come from an open container. The bartender could have easily drugged him, when his back was turned. Kain looked for the bathroom, and he threw up. He gulped down water from the sink in order to quench his thirst. Waiting for him outside was Alexia. He had seen Kain run to the bathroom, and he worried that his friend was drunk.

"I am fine. I only had that one glass of champagne, and a beer bottle," said Kain, "I think that caviar is rotten. It didn't sit right with me."

"Yeah…I agree. It wasn't all that good," said Alexia equanimous.

"Are you ready to go home, or do you need to bootlick a little longer?" asked Kain.

"I had more than enough bootlicking for one day," said Alexia, "I am going to need you to look tipsy, to use you as an excuse to leave this party early."

Kain rested his arm over Alexia's shoulder. He did the best

impression of a drunkard who was struggling to walk. Alexia apologized to his boss, and then with his permission, he was able to go home already. When the elevator door closed, Kain stopped malingering and he went to stand in the corner.

"I was thinking…Kain…why don't I give you a quick pick me up, and then you give me a helping hand," said Alexia coming to stand beside the moody Kain.

"I am with Eugenia," said Kain folding his arms.

"And pray do tell where is this Eugenia you speak off?" asked Alexia giggling, "Is she hiding in your pocket?"

Alexia placed his hand into Kain's pocket to look for Eugenia. Kain annoyed placed his hands on Alexia's shoulders to keep his horny friend at arm's length.

"Kaine! If you are with Eugenia, then why are you with me?" asked Alexia caressing Kain's strong muscular arms.

"I hate being in that house by myself. Since everyone was busy, I agreed to be your plus one," explained Kain.

Alexia extremely deflated went stand at the other side of the elevator. Alexia then said, "Aren't you afraid of being seen with someone like me? People will talk."

"People always talk. I know what I am, and what I like. It doesn't matter how I project myself to others, el Ladro siempre juzgara por su condicion," said Kain.

"I don't get it," said Alexia.

"You live in Miami and you don't speak Spanish? Get with the program, Alexia!" said Kain laughing.

"Haha. Very funny. IF I learn Spanish, will you sleep with me?" insisted Alexia chasing after Kain, "Suavemente! Besame! Kain! See, I Speaka Spanish my love."

The two ran around that enclosed space till they reached the first floor. Kain giggling said, "Sheesh! Enough already! Have some self-control. Alexia."

Alexia tried to give chase, but his high heels were slowing him down. The two ran out of the building, and into the walkway. Kain stopped running when he heard Alexia scream in pain. Alexia had stumbled and fallen due to the ridiculously high heels he kept insisting on wearing. Kain returned to Alexia's side and he gingerly picked up the skinny youth.

"My hero kiss!" said Alexia kissing Kain on the cheek. Alexia could walk just fine, but he was malingering for attention. His bruised knee did look pretty bad though.

"I can still drop. So, stop pushing your luck, Alexia," said Kain, "I know that you are lonely, and that sex is like your main coping mechanism or whatever, but try to have some self-control."

"Look at you. Mr. Sanson, using big words. Did you learn them from your shrink?" asked Alexia giggling.

"Yes," said Kain, "Maybe you should visit her…Unla has a way of shrinking your problems, to make them more manageable."

Kain began to walk towards the parking lot while carrying his friend. The conversation carried them as far as the car. Before they got inside, someone threw a rock at Kain. The rock missed and it struct the back window of the car. Kain placed Alexia down before turning around. Under the flickering streetlamp, the two were able to see a group of bald men walking towards them. Kain reached into his pocket and he brought out his revolver. This made the men pause. Alexia got inside the car quickly. Kain opened the passenger seat and he got inside the car while still aiming his gun. Alexia turned on the car and he drove out of the parking lot quickly. Once the two were in the express way, they breathed in a sigh of relief.

"Next time, we are paying for valet parking," said Kain.

"I am sorry…Kain," said Alexia apologetically.

"It's not your fault. Don't worry about it," said Kain reclining back.

After a half hour drive, Alexia arrived to Kain's home. He

lingered in front of the door, since he didn't have the desire to return to his empty apartment.

"Kain…It has been a while, and I…have needs that I want you to meet them. I am begging you, just for tonight," insisted Alexia taking Kain's hand.

"Everyone just takes, and takes…but no one is ever interested in giving me what I want," said Kain more to himself.

"If I give you what you want, will you become mine and mine alone," insisted Alexia.

"I want something you are incapable of giving me, Alexia. Respect!" hissed Kain, before closing the door in front of Alexia.

Kain looked about his house and he frowned when he noticed that was still empty. With no one in the house, the bad thoughts began to creep inside his head. He opened the door and he allowed his friend to sleep in the guestroom. The following morning Jack returned home. His jam session with his sponsor had not gone as planned. The two had gone to the Sand Bar at Islamorada to play live music. Their music had gotten a lukewarm response. Jack was depressed and he angry at Arjuna for pressuring him to play in front of a real audience.

"I should have never turned my hobby into a profession," said Jack more to himself.

Jack went into his bedroom and he got changed out of his stage attire. He looked at his scrawny reflection in the mirror. Nothing he wore ever looked good on him. He grabbed the guitar to smash his reflection, but then he remembered that he was living in Kain's home. The new target for his fit was his pillow. When he got tired of punching it, Jack screamed into it. Kain who was an early bird, like his grandpa, came into his father's room to see if he was home. He caught his father in the middle of his fit. Kain sat down beside his father, and he petted his hair lovingly.

When Jack was calmer, Kain asked, "How do you want me to make your pancakes today?"

"I am not hungry," said Jack refusing to get out of bed.

"If you are not planning to eat, can you at least come sit with me at the table," said Kain, "There is nothing more depressing than to eat alone."

"Tell me about it," said Jack getting out of his bed, "I am going to shower first."

Jack cried alone in the shower for half an hour. When he finally regained control of his emotions, he went to the breakfast table. The smell of bacon lured Alexia out of the guestroom. Jack narrowed his eyes when he saw Alexia coming into the room wearing one of Kain's pajamas.

"When I told you to live in the moment, this was not what I had in mind," said Jack pointing to Alexia.

"Nothing, happened between us. You can relax," said Alexia scratching his navel.

Before Alexia got a chance to settle down, Jack said, "That seat belongs to Kain."

"Can I sit in this one then?" asked Alexia changing places.

"That one also belongs to Kain," said Jack narrowing his eyes.

"Alexia. Pay him no mind. Dad is just a little moody because he is hungry," said Kain coming over with Jack's plate, "You can sit wherever you like. You are my guest."

Jack stabbed at his food without much enthusiasm. The smell of fresh bacon eventually awoke his hunger, and he started to eat. Alexia was the next person to be fed, followed by Kain. There was an awkward silence reigning over the breakfast table.

In order to break the ice, Kain asked Alexia, "Do you still play with Pokemon cards?"

"Not really," asked Alexia raising an eyebrow, "I was never into that card game. I only played it because you seemed to be very into that stupid kid's game."

"I only played it because I thought you liked the game," lied Kain.

"Kain still to collects pokemon cards, though, he doesn't play the game with anyone," said Jack contradicting his son, "Every time he goes to Publix, he buys 1 Pokemon card worth 50 cents."

Alexia laughed in spite of himself. Kain narrowing his eyes said, "You don't see me laughing at you for wearing a dress and make up."

"I am sorry…" said Alexia apologetically. He added giving a fake smile, "I still have my old deck. I would be happy to play with you every one in a while, Kain."

"You shouldn't torture yourself for want of company Alexia," said Kain, "We like different things, and that is fine. We shouldn't let these minor differences get in the way of rekindling our friendship."

"I don't want to be your friend Kain!" complained Alexia, "I want to be your lover."

"In life, we don't always get what we want," said Kain in mimicry of his grandpa, "You can either accept the friendship that I am offering you, or we can go our separate ways. The choice is yours Alexia."

Alexia meditated his options. He tried the pancakes. In the end, his stomach decided for him. Alexia said without much enthusiasm, "Fine…we can be friends. Just friends."

"Can I be your friend too, son?" asked Jack meekly.

"We never stopped being friends, dad," lied Kain.

Hearing this white lie lifted Jack's spirits. He dug into his pancake with much enthusiasm. After breakfast, Alexia went home. He felt that he had abused Kain's hospitality enough. Kain picked up the dishes and he went to the sink to clean them up.

"How good is your singing voice, Kain?" asked Jack brainstorming an idea.

"I don't know. You tell me. Do. Re. Mi. Fa. So…" said Kain singing scales. Jack covered his ears when Kain hit the high note. His singing voice was just ghastly, "Just give it up dad. So, what if you never become a famous musician, or even a moderately successful one. As long as you have fun playing your music, who cares what the audience thinks."

"You sound just like Arjuna," said Jack resting his head on top of the table, "How do you do it Kain? How can you do that soul sucking job, you care nothing about?"

"Doing a job I don't like isn't as bad as you might thing," said Kain, "My coworkers are nice. I make a decent salary and I have health insurance. As long as I do what my uncle tells me, I can make it to retirement without getting shot at. What's not to love about being a cop?"

"Did you ever consider making a career out of being an artist? Your portraits are quite realistic. Have you tried painting?" asked Jack.

"I am color blind. Why do you think I only draw in black and white?" said Kain.

"I thought you were just being cheap," said Jack.

"Even if I wasn't color blind, I am a talentless hack that can only mimic nature," said Kain after he concluded the dishes.

When Kain returned to his work, something had changed. Jack had pitched to his brother the idea of having Kain work as a Forensic Artist. Kain was brought before the current artist. Officer Ricard was a failed painter. He had followed the artist's path from a young age, and he even had a Batchelor of Fine Arts. Kain entered the Station with his portfolio.

Ricard wanted to see the level of skill of his prospective student. Ricard was way past retirement age, and his wife was pressuring him to quit his day job already. Ricard was a short fellow, with a bald head, small suspecting black eyes, and olive skin. He looked through Kain's portfolio without much enthusiasm. As an draftsman, there was nothing special about Kain's drawings.

For the purposes of working as a Forensic Artist, he was good enough. All that mattered was that Kain could render realistic human faces. Ricard gave Kain a drawing test.

"I am going to give you a transcription of a victim's description of her attacker. This is a person that has already been caught. So, there won't be any pressure for you to get the details right. You have until the end of the day to deliver your finished sketch," said Ricard before departing.

Kain read the transcript. He spent the rest of the day doing that homework. He made three sketches based on the flimsy information he had to go by. Ricard passed by to see the final results.

"You get an E for effort Kain," said Ricard looking at the drawings over the top, "Though in the future, try not be so literal with your drawings, let's you create caricatures, instead of human beings."

"I drew exactly what the person described," protested Kain.

"Yes. And that is the problem," said Ricard, "People do not normally find themselves in a situation where they have to describe what a person looks like. And with child victims, things are much harder, due to their limited vocabulary. It is the role of a forensic sketch artist to sort through the muck, in order to bring the perpetrator to light…Your second sketch was the most accurate."

Ricard reached into his portfolio and he brought out the artist sketch he made. He then showed Kain the photograph of the assailant. Kain had gotten pretty close, the second time around. Ricard handed his apprentice some workbooks to have him practice drawing human faces. For homework, Kain had to write down a description of his father's face. This would give Kain a good idea of how difficult it is to convey with words, what a person looks like. Kain didn't show any opposition to this new role. He was getting free art lessons, free artbooks and he was getting paid to draw all day.

CHAPTER 10

The Empress

◆ ◆ ◆

It was a rainy September day in Carina's home. She awoke to the smell of burnt toast. She found beside her bed a grilled cheese sandwich, oatmeal and a bottle of mineral water. Bruno had attempted to make her breakfast in bed. He had left early for work. Carina tried the grill cheese sandwich. It was delicious, but a little too fatty for her slow metabolism. She had the oatmeal with the mineral water. She felt bad about throwing away sandwich, but she had to start watching her weight. As of lately, Bruno was spending all his free time with Carina.
He only ever bothered to go to his apartment in order to work on his cases. Carina pondered on this current state of affairs. With her boyfriend sleeping over practically every day, it almost felt as if they were living together. At the end of her breakfast, Carina went to work. Carina was finally used to her job. One could almost say that she was enjoying it.

Her coworkers were a different story. Most spent their time gossiping like parrots. There was one in particular that kept checking up on Carina. Carina didn't know what was the deal with that woman, but her constant interruptions were distracting. Her workday came to an end. She texted Bruno to see what he was up to. Bruno reported that he was buried under at mountain of paperwork. He sent a selfie of him surrounded by paperwork. Carina drove home to be with her mother. Unla took that chance to give a bit of therapy to her daughter. The topic of conversation was a new behavior that Bruno was exhibiting. When he thought he wasn't being watched, he would start pacing the room while mumbling to himself.

"Society has conditioned men to live lives of quiet desperation. Women only find out that there is a problem when their men explode," said Unla, "I found out your father was sick, when he started coughing up blood…And Bruno, the two of you only recently started dating. You do not know the type of baggage he is carrying, or what is his true "normal" behavior. So, when his mask starts dropping, do try to keep your temper in check. Otherwise, you are never going to know the true Bruno."

"Keeping my temper in check, is easier said than done mother," retorted Carina.

"You never know, until you try," said Unla, "Let us discuss your most recent jealousy outburst. What did your man do that made you feel insecure about your relationship?"

"Bruno has been working long hours with a coworker," said Carina, "Yesterday, I came to his office to bring him dinner. If I don't feed him, he just orders takeout, and I am worried about his cholesterol levels. The point is…that, I made a scene because he didn't told me that his coworker was a woman."

"It is irrational for you to expect Bruno to avoid working with other women," said Unla.

"I know mom! I know! It is just. She is very pretty. Almost as pretty as Eugenia," said Carina, "And the way she was leaning over Bruno…that slut was trying to seduce my man."

"Eureka!" said Unla giving a sly smile, "Every time you speak of other women, you bring up the name Eugenia. Your first major fight with Bruno was because of Eugenia. Tell me Carina, what is your problem with Eugenia, exactly?"

"I don't have a problem with Eugenia. My problem is that I find it difficult to sleep with Bruno, while he is thinking of another woman," said Carina rubbing her temple.

"The only person who can't stop thinking of Eugenia is you Carina," said Unla shaking her head sadly, "Let's put that problem on hold, for the time being. I let us discuss your first boyfriend, Malik. If I remember correctly, he left you for a girl that resembled Eugenia."

"I don't want to talk about Malik, momma," protested Carina.

"You are never going to have a healthy relationship, if you do not process the grief that this betrayal caused," insisted Unla putting her finger into her daughter's festering open wound.

Carina was saved from the situation by Bruno arriving to her home early. He was bringing a gift box for his girlfriend. When she opened the box, she found inside some furniture for her little dollhouse.

"I was rummaging through a yard sale, when I found these miniatures for your dollhouse," said Bruno.

"Thank you Bruno. That was a really thoughtful present," said Carina looking at the miniature chaise chair, "You are not angry anymore?"

"I wasn't angry at you Carina. Just exasperated. A man does get tired of getting yelled at every five seconds," protested Bruno.

"Perfect! Now that you are here, let's do some couple's therapy," said Unla changing gambits.

Carina and Bruno spent an hour talking about their feelings. While Carina laid her heart open, Bruno only said half-truths. It flattered his pride to know just how obsessed Carina was with him. With therapy out of the way, the two settled down to watch telenovelas. All was forgiven, all was forgotten. The two made love after dinner. After they finished, Carina got a new present from Bruno. By the looks of the box, Carina imagined that she was getting a wedding ring. When Bruno opened the box, inside was the keys to his apartment.

"You bought me a car?" asked Carina smiling happily, "Thank you."

"No. This is just the keys to my apartment," said Bruno yawning, "You can show up, unannounced, whenever you want to."

"Your apartment stinks Bruno. I never want to set foot in that pigsty ever again," said Carina frowning, "But thanks for the sentiment, thought."

"Your welcome," said Bruno not feeling offended by the truth. His apartment truly was a pigsty.

"Why do you even live like that?" asked Carina, "You clean up after yourself everywhere else. Why don't you clean your own home?"

"I work a lot. So, I rarely have the energy to clean up after myself," lied Bruno. Carina narrowed her eyes when she noticed that her man had lied straight to her face. She began to poke his belly to pressure him to tell her the truth. Bruno sighed with frustration, before telling Carina a different lie, "My apartment serves purely utilitarian purposes. I have no reason to clean it, because I spend so little time there."

"There! Was that little bit of honesty so hard to manage?" asked Carina resting her head on Bruno's shoulder.

"Yes. I even felt myself dying a little," lied Bruno.

"Go to sleep. You big goof," said Carina closing her eyes, "And try not to snore."

"I can't control what I do when I sleep," said Bruno.

"That is why I said try," said Carina pressing herself tighter against Bruno's bare flesh.

Bruno stayed awake starring at the roof. Carina was sleeping soundly beside him. The more time he spent with Carina, the easier it was for her to tell when he was lying. She was sharper than he gave her credit. It annoyed him to the very core to be forced to be honest with the woman. Bruno ran through his head all the times that Carina had noticed that he had been lying. He began to ponder what about the inflection of his voice or his mannerism had given away the truth. He needed to refine his act, in order to get the woman to trust everything he said. Perhaps, if he had a moment of brutal honesty with her, maybe it would make it easier for Carina to believe everything that he said from that point forward.

The morning came. Carina frowned when she noticed that Bruno had left already. He was such an early bird. It peeved her that he could awaken on time, even without the alarm. Instead of a fattening breakfast, she found egg whites omelet, with toast. Carina had to give her boyfriend an A for effort. Her lecture about cholesterol had created an immediate change. She opened the gift box that had Bruno's apartment key. She took the key and she added it to her own set of keys. Now, she could visit Bruno whenever she felt like it.

Carina went to work. During her lunch break, she decided to visit Bruno's apartment. It was only a short drive away from her workplace. Since she only had 20 minutes left, she limited herself to vacuuming the floor, and washing the dirty dishes. On her way out of the apartment, she bumped into a stranger.

"Pardon me. Do you live in the apartment 25B?" asked the green eyed woman.

"Yes. I live there with my husband," said Carina marking her territory.

"I see…I must have the wrong address," said the woman departing. The woman added internally, or maybe he moved without giving me the address.

"Yes. You definitely have the wrong address, bitch," whispered Carina being passive aggressive. She reached into her purse to bring out her bunny plushie. She said to her doll, "We best stay on our toes, Nana."

Carina drove back to her workplace. Her newest patient was a familiar face. After rattling her brain, Carina said, "You are Farley's kid…According to the charts, your name is Oswald. What happened to you? Did the bullies beat you up?"

"Is it that obvious?" said Oswald who had a swollen eye, and he was bruise from head to toe, "My father told me to fight back. That they will leave me alone if I show them that I am a man. Today, I tried doing things his way, and this is the final results. I even got expelled for defending myself."

"Maybe you should change schools," said Carina examining the swollen eye.

"To change schools we would have to move," protested Oswald.

"Maybe you could try homeschooling," suggested Carina.

"Both my parents work, and their jobs are far more important than their own son," said Oswald pointing towards the door.

Carina peeped outside, and she saw Farley talking on the phone to one of his coworkers. Carina finished threating all the booboos on Oswald's body. After reading Oswald's address, she pitched his father this idea, "How good are your son's grade?"

"I don't know," said Farley, "How much is all of this going to cost me?"

Carina wrote in her prescription pad, "If you bring the kid over to my mother's clinic, we will be able to give you a family discount."

Farley was about to thank Carina, but the girl raised her finger to her lips. Changing the subject, she said, "That is for the insurance to decide. I am only a cog in the system. I was looking at your son's charts, and I noticed that you live close to a really good Charter's School."

"We can't afford it," said Farley.

"You can't afford to have your son getting beaten up on a regular basis. I too went to public school. The bullies will be back Mr. Farley and in bigger numbers," said Carina.

Farley looked at his wimpy son, all beaten up. Even with Carina's medicine, the kid still looked like a mess. Farley was afraid to face his wife, with their baby looking like this. Carina gave Farley the address to the Charter school that Kyle attended. The school went by the fanciful name Omega Academy. Farley left with his son in order to check out the new school. Carina felt quite proud of her good deed for the day.

Her workday came to an end. When she arrived home, she smile when she saw Bruno already inside, waiting for her. In his hand, he had his Middle School yearbook. Carina giggling went to the attic to dig up her own yearbook. She fancied what it would have been like to go to school with Bruno. Carina sat down on the couch with her man. She looked through all the pages in search of a kid that resembled Bruno. When she couldn't find him, Bruno flipped to the page that had his name and face. Carina laughed when she saw just how fat Bruno was as a child.

 "I was an unsightly beast, wasn't I?" commented Bruno, "The type of beast that nobody gave a second glance to."

"At least you had green eyes," said Carina, "I always had a weakness for guys with green eyes. So, had we gone to school together, there is a good chance that I might have dated you."

"Did Malik have green eyes?" asked Bruno.

"Yes…" said Carina pouting.

"I brought this here to tell you a little bit about myself Carina. Like you, I had my heart broken at a very young age. I got so enamored with the girl, that I even gave her my grandma's wedding ring. One day, I caught the bitch cheating on me. When I asked her to return the wedding ring, she claimed to have pawn it…She told me that a disgusting, whale like myself should consider himself lucky to have the attentions of someone as pretty as herself," said Bruno.

"What a happened after you two broke up?" asked Carina.

"I started working out, till I became strong enough to join the football team. I was no longer the fat nerd, that nobody gave two shits about. Over the years, I reinventing myself till I became the person that I am today, but deep down, I am still the same loser, who is bitter and angry that his girlfriend broke up with him," said Bruno.

Carina began to vibe with Bruno. Bruno vented about his girlfriend Kathy, while Carina ranted about Malik. At a certain point, Carina said, "You know what will make us feel better?"

"What?" asked Bruno dryly.

"We should hex them. Let's go visit Irina to have her put a major curse on those bastards that cheated on us," said Carina laughing sinisterly.

"If you want to curse Malik, I won't stop you. What I really want is my grandma's wedding ring. My grandma gave me that ring before she passed away. She told me to give that ring to the person I loved the most. And I stupidly gave it away to a creature who was incapable of loving me," said Bruno bitterly while pacing the room. His masked had dropped while talking about the ring, "I gave that bastard my grandma's ring!!"

Bruno slummed over on top of the couch to sulk. This was the first time Carina had seen true human emotions from her boyfriend. Before going to bed, Carina went to her household shrine. Carina had been raised as a Roman Catholic by her parents. Though, she had stopped going to church due to a curious incident that occurred when she was four. The priest had asked her to come on stage. With her in front of the congregation, the priest went on a rant about her "slutty" outfit. The only person who had a problem with her dress was the perverted priest, who sought fit to publicly shame a four year old child. Her father furious got into a shouting match with the priest. From that moment on, Carina's family had stopped going to church. Even though her family had divorced themselves from the Catholic church, they didn't stop being Catholic.

Carina showed Bruno the little shrine that consisted of 3 Virgin Mary statues and a dozen saint statues. In the center, there was the little statue of St. Jude, the Patron Saint of Lost Causes. Carina lighted a candle for the saint, and she gave him a glass of water.

"I get the candle, but why the glass of water?" asked Bruno.

"Irina says that if you want the Saints to hear your prayers, you must leave them a glass of water," explained Carina, "It is a Cuban superstition."

"Does it work?" asked Bruno.

"Not with that attitude. You have to believe that it works!" insisted Carina.

"Let me rephrase my question, have your prayers ever been answered, Carina?" asked Bruno.

"Yes. Duh! But sometimes I don't like the answers that the saints give me," said Carina, "Let's go to bed now. Do you mind if I pray before going to sleep?"

"I take it you also want us to start going to church?" asked Bruno dryly.

"Heavens no! My family divorced themselves from the Catholic church decades ago," said Carina smiling happily.

"So, why pray?" asked Bruno.

"The Lord's Temple is inside of me. I do not need a judgmental priest as a mediator, I can talk to God directly," said Carina taking out her rosary.

Bruno decided to stop questioning Carina's belief system. She was entitled to her hobby. Carina prayed an entire Mercy Rosary. Bruno found it hypnotic to listen to Carina say over and over: Ten Misericordia de nosotros y del mundo entero. Bruno was so entranced that he fell asleep, while listening to Carina's soothing voice. The following morning he awoke late for work. Carina had seen him sleeping, and instead of waking him up, she had allowed him to oversleep. Bruno got dressed without showering, and he rode to his office.

He sent text message to Carina during a red light, "My job isn't as secure as you might think. Please. Don't ever let me oversleep!!!"

"Three exclamation points...he must really be angry," said Carina reading the text message, "What was I thinking? I hope Bruno doesn't get in trouble because of me."

Carina texted her cousin Rodrigo, "Rigo...Bruno was really tired, so I let him oversleep. Please don't be angry at him. Alright. It was my fault."

Rodrigo read the text and then he spoke to his boss. When Bruno showed up to work, nobody made a big deal about his tardiness. Bruno breathed in a sigh of relief, and then he got to work. Just when he was getting into the flow, he heard a knocking on his door that broke his concentration.

"What!! I am busy!" yelled Bruno with his mask momentarily dropping. He added in a calmer tone, "I am sorry for raising my voice. Please, come inside, and tell me what you need."

The secretary Darcy peeped into the room. Darcy was a paid-intern, whose job was to man the front desk. In her previous job, she would get yelled at on a regular basis. For that reason, poor Darcy was trembling from head to foot, when she entered Bruno's office.

Darcy managed to stutter, "There...there...is...some...some..."

"Text me what you what to say," said Bruno rubbing his temple.

The secretary said trembling, "I...don't...have...your cellphone."

Bruno jumped out of his desk and he shoved a notebook and pencil into the woman's face. She scribbled down this message, "Your sister wants to speak to you."

"I have a lot of exes that call themselves my sister. Please, send her away," said Bruno returning to his desk.

"She looks a lot like you Mr. Bruno. And she has your same last name…and…she has green eyes," said Darcy switching to gossiping mode.

Before she could say more, Bruno's oldest sister Rebecca pushed herself into his office. Rebecca was in her late 40s. She had the same skin color, and green eyes as her brother. She was obese like most of the women of Bruno's family.

"You don't write, you don't call. You stopped answering my calls. For a minute there, we were starting to worry that you might be dead," said Rebecca. She added smiling, "You grew a beard. It looks good on you."

"Thanks," said Bruno coming to sit behind his desk, "Why are you here Rebecca?"

"Look at the calendar Bruno. You missed Becky's birthday," said Rebecca pointing to the wall calendar. Becky was one of Bruno's nieces.

He was of the habit of making sporadic visits to Kansas, in order to spend time with Rebecca's daughters. On average, he would visit once per season. This year he had stopped visiting, under the excuse of being extremely busy with work. One day, he stopped calling his sister, and then just two months ago, he had stopped answering her calls. He had even gone as far as to mark Rebecca's phone number as spam.

"Oh…right. Once I get paid, I will send her a present," said Bruno, "If don't want anything else from me, please leave. I am busy! Unlike you, I have to work to earn my daily bread."

"If you are in need, you can always ask your big sister for money," retorted Rebecca.

"I rather die than ask you for anything, Rebecca," said Bruno, before pointing to the door, "Please, go home. And don't ever bother me again."

"What is your problem, Bruno? What did I say or do to make you become so distant?" asked Rebecca.

"You did the same thing you always do, sister," hissed Bruno.

"Just tell me what I did wrong so I can make it better," yelled Rebecca.

"You ruined my life Rebecca!!" yelled Bruno raising his voice. Outside his office, all his coworkers had their ears pinned to the door. Bruno was acting completely out of character and they wanted to know the reason, "All because grandma gave me the ring that you coveted!"

"I thought we got past that already," asked Rebecca, "Why are you still pinning after that woman?"

"You have never been in love, so, I don't expect you to understand," said Bruno passing his hand over the left side of his head. He brought out a sticky note, and he wrote down Carina's address, "I have a new girlfriend. Here is her address. You can interrogate her till your hearts content. She isn't poor so you won't be able to bribe her to go away."

"Oh...so, Tanya told you that I paid her to go away?" asked Rebecca shyly, "She was cheating on you, Bruno. Why do you always go for the sluts, Bruno? Why haven't you ever tried dating any of the girls I have introduced to you?"

"Rebecca, I don't have time to argue with you! Just because you have never worked a day in your life, doesn't give you the right to get me fired," said Bruno dryly.

"Motherhood is a job!" protested Rebecca.

"If Motherhood was a job, you would have been fired ages ago," said Bruno pointing towards the door, "Instead of meddling in my affairs, why don't you go home to take care of your daughters."

Rebecca opened the door to get out of Bruno's office. She giggled when she the audience that was piled behind the door. As soon as she left, Rodrigo began to interrogate his friend about Rebecca. Whenever Bruno flew home, all he said was that he was going to put flowers on his grandma's grave. Now, Rodrigo knew that his friend had a meddlesome older sister, and even nieces. The hours rolled with Bruno mentally preparing himself to endure his sister's visitation. He practiced his lines before a mirror to make certain he created the perfect mimicry of a person who was in a happy and in love.

Rodrigo warned Carina that Rebecca was going to visit her after work, in order to interrogate her. Carina was equally surprised and distraught by the fact that Bruno had never mentioned that he had a sister. Then again, if Bruno hated his sister enough to pretend that they didn't exist, he had to have his reasons. Carina decided not to question the state of affairs. She was going to take a page from Kain, and just go with the flow. The promised hour came. She felt tense about meeting the strange woman. She heard a knocking on the door. When she opened it, she saw Kain with his drawing supplies.

"I need help with my homework," said Kain with a whinny tone to his voice.

"Now is not a good time. I have a visit," said Carina agitated.

"Relax, Carina," said Unla giving her daughter a cold mineral water, "Today will be the same as any other day. Pretend that this stranger is just another patient."

Carina drank her cold water and she felt more at ease. She welcome Kain inside and she began to help him with his homework. Kain wanted Carina to describe someone, while he tried to draw the person based on her spoken words. Half an hour passed with the two occupied on this task. Kain finished his drawing.

Carina frowning said, "Close…but not quite there."

"Do you have a photograph of the person you were thinking of?" asked Kain.

"Don't need a photo. The woman I am thinking of is going to make an appearance real soon," said Carina.

Bruno entered the house next. He seemed like a completely

different person. He was pale, and he kept nervously fidgeting with his hand. While he waited for his sister to arrive, he paced up and down the living room. Whenever he passed near Carina, she was able to hear the man mumbling. Bruno heard a familiar knock, and his personality immediately changed. He opened the door for his sister, and he gave her a warm kiss on the cheek.

"Rebecca. This is my girlfriend Carina," said Bruno placing Carina in front of him, to have the petite woman serve as a physical barrier between himself and his sister.

"Pleased to meet you Carina," said Rebecca shaking hands with Carina.

Unla brought tea and biscuits for her guest. Bruno had warned Carina that his sister thought she was British. While sipping her tea, Rebecca started with her interrogation. The two gave Rebecca a fragmented account of their adventures, that only focused on the positives.

At a certain point, Rebecca asked, "How often do you two sleep together?"

"Rebecca!!" yelled Bruno visibly infuriated.

"Almost every night," said Carina weirded out. She petted Bruno's hand till the veins disappeared from his temple. Carina added, "I can give you all the sordid details, if you want to."

"That won't be necessary," said Rebecca laughing heartedly.

"How long are you going to be staying in Miami?" whispered Bruno.

"That all depends on you Bruno," said Rebecca turning serious.

"How irresponsible! Instead of meddling in my affairs, you should be taking care of your daughters," said Bruno.

"You have nieces! OMG! Can I see their pictures?" said Carina.

All with the except Bruno crowded around Rebecca's cellphone. Bruno standing up said, "I have to go to the can."

Bruno lingered in the bathroom for 20 minutes while he pretended to do his business. When he left the bathroom, his sister Rebecca was in the middle of saying, "...my brother is a pathological liar. So, take everything he says with a grain of salt."

"Thank you for telling this to my girlfriend. Now, Carina is never going to trust anything that I say," said Bruno dryly.

"I was telling your girlfriend stories from when you were little," said Rebecca blissfully unaware of the harm she had done, "Now that you are older, I have no doubt that you have become a truthful and honest individual."

"That's nice. That's nice. There is nothing I love more than for my sister to expose my dirty laundry to all who have ears to listen!" said Bruno coldly. He added raising his voice, "Why don't you tell Carina about my Bulimia while you are at it!?"

There was an awkward silence. Bruno could no longer tolerate breathing the same air as his sister Rebecca. He got his car keys and he drove away. Rebecca sighed sadly and she handed Carina a business card with her contact information.

"We didn't realize that Bruno had a problem till he collapsed. If you see him binge eating, but not gaining weight, he is probably throwing up when your back is turned," said Rebecca.

Rebecca picked up her purse and she left. Carina texted Bruno to tell him that Rebecca had left. She didn't get a reply. The following day Bruno didn't show up to work. Rodrigo went to Bruno's apartment to check up on him. He found Rebecca tidying up the place.

"Your brother didn't show up to work," said Rodrigo.

"That can't be good. Rain or shine, Bruno always goes to work," said Rebecca.

Rebecca tried to call Bruno, but he didn't answer. Rodrigo texted his friend, "I am worried Bruno. Are you alright?"

With no reply, Rodrigo started to worry. He called Kain to have him put out an APB on Bruno. Back in the station, Kain was gossiping with his uncle about Rebecca. Their conversation was interrupted by Rodrigo's call.

"Alright, I am on it," said Kain before hanging up. He then said to his uncle, "Bruno is missing."

"Missing how?" asked Gent completely unperturbed.

"He wasn't at his home. And he didn't show up to work," explained Kain, "Bruno never misses a day of work, or so Rodrigo claims."

"Bruno is a grown man, not a child. He is probably at a bar drinking away his woes," reasoned Gent, "He will come back on his own."

"I don't know…uncle," said Kain worried.

"When you were fixing Bruno's cellphone, did you put the thing?" asked Gent.

"Ah! Yes. The thing!" said Kain remembering the tracker he had placed in Bruno's cellphone.

Kain went to his desk and he came back with his computer. He texted Bruno in order to trigger the pinback. According to the pinback, Bruno was in the Domino Park in Little Habana. Cubans regularly played Chess and Domino in that park. Kain texted the address to Rodrigo. Rodrigo drove with Rebecca to the Domino Park. They parked beside Bruno's car. Rodrigo opened the hood, and he removed a core component to keep the car from turning on.

The two found Bruno playing chess by himself. At the moment, his black King was cornered. Regardless of what move he made, it was going to end in checkmate. All the other pieces in the chessboard where white. They were Totems of how Bruno perceived his relationship with others.

The two sat before Bruno. Rodrigo was the first to break the silence. He looked at the chessboard and he asked, "Are you winning?"

"Does it look like I am winning?" said Bruno pointing to the black king, "At this point in the game, all I can do is avoid checkmate."

"I have the ring Bruno," said Rebecca taking out of her pocket her grandmother's ring, "You can give it to Carina when you are ready to marry her."

"Keep it," said Bruno putting away the chess pieces, "Give it to someone you love, Rebecca."

"Were are you going?" asked Rebecca.

"Were you can't follow," said Bruno. Bruno went to his car and he turned on the ignition key. As much as he tried, the car just wouldn't start. He sighed wearily and he started to walk aimlessly.

"Please Bruno. Don't shut me out," insisted Rebecca pulling at her brother's arm.

"Everything was perfect until you showed up," said Bruno flinching away from Rebecca's touch, "Why couldn't you just let me be happy? Why did you have to come to ruin my life, Rebecca?"

"You can't pretend that I don't exist Bruno. I am going to be a part of your life, whether you want to or not," said Rebecca.

"I HATE you Rebecca! Leave me ALONE!" yelled Bruno.

"Let's go home Bruno," said Rodrigo mediating, "You sister is not going to be able to stay in Florida forever."

Rodrigo placed his arm around Bruno's shoulder to keep his friend from escaping. Bruno wearily stopped showing resistance. After meditating things, Rodrigo decided to take Bruno to Carina's house. While Bruno showered, Rodrigo conversed with Rebecca.

"Every time you called, Bruno would tell me that you were a psychotic ex-lover," said Rodrigo laughing.

"Bruno can hate me as much as he wants. He can wound me with his words as much as he wants. I am never going to stop taking care of him," said Rebecca.

"What did he tell you about his life in Florida?" asked Rodrigo.

"He just limited himself to Status updates. Though he did mention you by name, often," said Rebecca.

"What did he say about me?" asked Rodrigo curious.

"He would say something like I am helping Rodrigo with his homework. We are going to football practice. Or we are going to a party. I am visiting the strip club, with Rodrigo. Rodrigo got me a job in his law firm. I am working on a case with Rodrigo," said Rebecca.

"I see," said Rodrigo sitting down on the bed, "It is funny how you can interact with a person for so long, and not truly know anything about him. I once asked him about his family, and he told me that he was found in a garbage can."

"My father told that to Bruno as a joke, and it scarred him for life. My dad...he isn't the type of man to mince words. If he doesn't like you, he will let you know," explained Rebecca.

"He sounds like an asshole," commented Rodrigo, "But is your brother adopted?"

"I was at his birth," said Rebecca, "Trust me. He isn't adopted."

"Why should I trust you? We just met," commented Rodrigo suspicious of the stranger that called herself Bruno's sister.

The conversation was interrupted when Bruno left the bathroom wrapped up in a towel. He jumped into his side of Carina's bed, and he closed his eyes to pretend to be asleep. The hours ebbed away while he tried to regain control of his emotions. Carina arrived after finishing her shift. She had spent the day digesting all the recent developments. From time to time, she would get status updates from her cousin Rodrigo. She was peeved that Bruno had never spoken about his family, but in his defense, Carina had never asked about them. Carina also didn't like the childish overreaction Bruno had to his sister Rebecca calling him a pathological liar. Then again, Carina didn't have the moral authority to judge Bruno for having a moment of childishness.

"This is just another bump in the road," said Carina while driving home, "It doesn't make sense for Bruno to open up to a woman he has only known for a couple of months. The fact that he still lies to me, just means that he doesn't trust me yet. And why should he? It is not as if I have given him a reason to trust me."

Carina arrived at her house. She dug into her purse and she brought out her keys. The first one she tried didn't open the door. When she looked at it, she recognized it as Bruno's apartment key.

"He was starting to open up. He told me about his first love, and his grandma's ring. Given enough time, Bruno would have told me everything else," said Carina starring at Bruno's key, "Rationally speaking, there is no reason to be angry at him."

Carina took a deep breath and then she entered her house. The moment she came inside the conversations stopped abruptly. Unla was in the middle of getting interrogated by Rebecca. Unla responded to every question with the cool disdain of a trained health care physician. While Rebecca was judging Unla, Unla was diagnosing Rebecca. Unla was certain that Rebecca had diabetes. Her puffy face also told Unla that Rebecca had hypothyroidism. Unla wanted to ask Rebecca about her overall health, but Unla didn't care much for the intruder that had shattered the fragile peace they were enjoying.

"Mom. I am home," said Carina.

"Welcome home honey," said Unla completely switching gambits.

She removed her daughter's coat, and she took her bag. Carina went to her bedroom to take her shower. While she undressed, she noticed Bruno's green eyes staring at her from within the safety of her bedsheets. Bruno closed his eyes and he turned his back to continue pretending to be asleep. Carina showered quickly. She came out of her bathroom in her pajamas. She sat down beside Bruno and she petted his back till he turned around. He drew Carina into his embrace. He said nothing, while he continued to sulk.

"You shouldn't have left just because your sister called you a lair," said Carina breaking the silence. When Bruno didn't answer, she added, "Still. I get while you were so on edge. She ruined your first relationship, so you were afraid that she was going to spoil everything again."

"Why couldn't she just let me be happy?" protested Bruno.

"Look Bruno, it makes sense that she would freak out after not hearing from you for months," said Carina, "It wouldn't have killed you to give her a call every once in a while."

"I didn't want to fly to Kansas to prove to you that I was talking to my sister," lied Bruno.

"You are not as good a liar as you might think, Bruno," said Carina petting her man's black curls. He really did have quite the pretty mane of hair.

"I don't want my sister in my life. I hate her!" said Bruno, "Everything was going perfect for us, till she showed up. Since her marriage sucks, she spends all her free time thinking of different ways of making me miserable. She just can't stand seeing me happy. She only ever tells bad things about me, Carina, and Rebecca still wonders why I despise her so."

"The only bad thing she said about you was that you were a chronic liar," said Carina.

"A woman can forgive an infidelity, but never a lie," reasoned Bruno, "For as long as we stay together, you are always going to be doubting everything I say."

"And you Bruno, do you believe every word I say?" asked Carina.

"Yes," lied Bruno. Bruno reached under the pillow and he brought out a gift box. When Carina opened it, she saw the infamous ring that Bruno had been bitching about, "Here is my grandma's ring. Rebecca had been keeping it safe from my poor judgement. She wanted you to have it, since she deems you worthy of being my wife. That little prayer you made to your Saint worked, a little too well."

Carina tried on the ring, and she smiled. She said giggling, "Does this mean what I think it means?"

"No. No, it doesn't," said Bruno, "This isn't a marriage proposal. Think of that ring as a goodbye present. I want you to give that ring to someone you truly love, Carina."

"You are breaking up with me because your sister approves of our relationship!?" asked Carina.

"Yes," said Bruno speaking truthfully, "If you want to be angry at someone, be angry at my sister. She ruined everything!"

"Stop being a big baby, Bruno!" said Rebecca entering the room, "You are the one who is ruining everything, this time around. Why are you breaking up with your girlfriend, just because of something thoughtless I said?"

"That has always been your problem sister. You never think before you speak," hissed Bruno, "For as long as I can remember, you have been poking fun at my weight. Every time I sat down to eat ice cream, every time I ate a slice of pizza, every time I tried to eat a little cookie, you would criticize me. And now you wonder why I have an eating disorder? You did this to me Rebecca! You did! All because grandma gave me the ring you coveted."

Rebecca wasn't able to contradict that statement. Her silence told those assemble that Bruno was speaking the truth. Now, Carina understood why Bruno had moved halfway across the US. He was trying to get away from the bullies that called themselves his family. Carina took Bruno's hand and she returned the wedding ring.

"Here you go Bruno. If this ring means so much to you, keep it," said Carina petting Bruno's hand lovingly, "Now, stop bellyaching and get out of bed. You can't expect me to play host to your sister all by myself."

Bruno hid under the bedsheets. He finally had his Grandmother's Wedding Ring. He petted it lovingly, while his mind began to be invaded by all the happy memories he had of his Grandmother. Bruno putted on the ring, and he sprung out of the bed with a chipper step. Unla prepared dinner for her family and her two guests. After dinner, Bruno went with his sister to get his car. The two spent the night in his depressing apartment.

Rebecca commented, "This place hasn't changed one bit. Would it kill you to buy a single decoration?"

"I haven't a need for decorations," commented Bruno, "Unlike you, I am not a hoarder."

"Then what do you do with your money?" asked Rebecca.

"I eat out. I go watch movies. I go to the Strip Club with Rodrigo. I take Carina out to eat in fancy restaurants. While you hoard objects, I enrich myself with experiences," said Bruno.

"Bruno. If you want your girlfriend to take you seriously, you need to fix up this apartment," said Rebecca.

"Carina was taking me seriously, until you showed up," said Bruno, "But it is fine. I am already used to you ruining my relationships. Thanks to you, Carina no longer respects or loves me. The only feelings I now inspire in her are pity. I give our her about a week before she dumps me."

"If she leaves you because of me, then she isn't the one," said Rebecca, "A loyal woman is supposed to weather the storm, not leave when things become slightly difficult."

"Good night, Rebecca," said Bruno going to bed.

The following morning Bruno went to work. It was the only thing he felt he had left. He poured his body and soul into his defense. Despite his best effort, his client was found guilty. At first he blamed his sister for his failure. Bruno felt his grandmother's ring in his pocket. He sighed and he became convinced that he was to blame for everything. Regardless of Bruno's perceived failure, he had done a good job defending his client. Instead of rotting for a decade, the client was only going to be in prison for less than a year. Since Bruno was still looking grumpy, Rodrigo suggested that all go out for happy hour. Bruno texted his plans to Rebecca, who self-invited to the party in order to interrogate Bruno's coworkers and boss. He figured why delay the inevitable. He found her presence so life draining that he couldn't even summon the energy to pretend to be having fun.

Around midnight, Bruno went home with his sister in order to allow his coworkers the freedom to have fun without him. Bruno looked at his clean, organized apartment without much enthusiasm. He removed his shoes, jacket and tie. On his way up to his bedroom, he stepped on something unfamiliar. When he turned on the light of the stairs, he saw that the trail of rose petals. Waiting for him, inside his bedroom was his girlfriend Carina.

www.ingramcontent.com/pod-product-compliance
Lightning Source LLC
Chambersburg PA
CBHW071310140726
47996CB00005B/1703